Jim's fist clenched into a tight ball. "You son o' a bitch," he nearly shouted into the phone, the bartender blinking as the man's accent became almost too thick to translate, "Let 'em go or I'm gonna--"

"I am sorry, James Lowery," Voodoo countered coldly, "but I cannot allow that. Doctor Versailles has decided you are a threat, and you need to be eliminated. By the way, I would suggest you duck."

The warning was unnecessary, and the machine probably knew it. Even before Voodoo offered his addendum, Jim heard the men pull up in their van, outside. He'd heard it open, heard the bolts of their rifles get pulled back, and heard their six pairs of boots stomp toward the door in what they'd hoped would be silence. They clearly hadn't been briefed on their target's capabilities as a killer, but his state of furious distraction - *almost* fear, for his ladies' sake - gave them an edge they didn't recognize they'd had.

Physics Reincarnate

A Novel,
A Sequel to Physics Incarnate

Jesse Pohlman

Pohlman Press   Freeport, NY

This novel is by Jesse Pohlman, copyright 2013; Pohlman Press. Cover art by Lawrence Shvartsberg

ISBN-13: 978-0615848310 (Pohlman Press)
ISBN-10: 0615848311

Thank you for your purchase! Other novels by Jesse Pohlman include...

Physics Incarnate, the predecessor to this novel;
Protostar: Memoirs of The Messenger, available on Kindle;
...And much more! Visit www.jessepohlman.com for updates!

This book is dedicated to my father, Thomas Pohlman.
It's probably not your style, but it's real!

Chapter One
Malcolm's Alley Pub

New York City played host to more than one authentic Irish Pub, for reasons that were far from surprising. Rooted deeply in the "Melting Pot" mentality, and followed up by eras like "Boss Tweed's" Tammany Hall period, the trade in orthodox Celtic fare was quite common! They had common traits: They were smoky; the scent of beer and whiskey was so strong one could taste it on the air; all while hints of corned beef, cabbage, and soda bread added some spice, as well as something to soak up the liquor. There were more stereotypical, cookie-cutter pubs in the Big Apple than a hypothetical counter would have fingers for. On this particularly warm March evening, however, there was only *one* on the mind of a particularly blonde Irishman: Malcolm's Alley Pub.

Located at street level along one of Manhattan's least active sidewalks, tonight the Alley Pub was as spacious as it was empty. It could fit impossibly intoxicated crowds on Saint Patrick's Day, but on a quiet night like this one in early March, only the local college roughs were out and about, mainly searching for a bar that didn't check proof-of-age as well as it should. Fortunately for the delinquents, Malcolm's was "carding at the bar" tonight. In other, less legal terms; if you looked and acted like an adult, you were treated like one. However, tonight's visitor wasn't searching for quick thrills and illegally-acquired booze. As the blonde man stepped in, his world-wary blue eyes sharply scrutinizing every last crack in the wood planking over the concrete floor, he took note of a few scattered pockets of modern-day pre-alcoholic "twenty-one years old" patrons.

He smirked, ridiculing them as them amateurs in the back of his mind.

Fearless of the risk of being rudely escorted from the bar, let alone being subjected to the dreaded "carding," the blonde man sporting a five-o'clock-shadow slid right on to the seat nearest the cash register. He was the only one seated *at* the bar, and he was convinced that it was because the young men and women in the room feared being identified as underage if, say, they slipped and gave out their real age to a prospective mate. He didn't even need to *look* at the patrons; he could tell just by the precisely-measured strain in their whispered voices who had enough years on earth (or, at least, life experience) to belong, and who didn't. If only they knew.

"What c'n I – Oh!" began the bartender in a curt Celtic tone, brushing a strand of dark hair from before his brown eyes. "S'You. Ain't seen y'in a year, it feels! How's Downtown?"

A soft chuckle escaped the blonde male's lips. "I got a new gig from 'ol Miguel on my mind; but this week's a bitch fer other reasons. Y'know what I'm askin' for, yeah?"

The liquor supplier didn't seem all too amused; though he did remember working with the Mexican-American in question. Nevertheless, he reached under the bar and produced a tall glass occupied by a small amount of ice. "As you'd put it, yer voice's tellin' me you want Vodka'n help." He reached behind himself and studied his liquor cabinet for a second. "But you're always better'n me a'tha' kind o' trick."

The two grinned, and for a moment they were looking at one another through mental photographs; age three, six, eight, twelve, to present. The dark-haired one licked his lips. "An' y'know th' rules. Yer startin' on the blood o' *our* people, in *my* pub," he insisted, grabbing a bottle of the strongest whiskey he hadn't locked up for a special occasion and pouring it nearly to the top. A second glass, a shot-glass, was produced and filled.

"Yep! I'm havin' a helluva day, Malcolm," the blonde resigned, lifting the larger chalice and raising it. "For 'ol Erin, then," he declared warmly. "May 'er warmth forever shine on 'er sons an' daughters."

Malcolm met the benediction, and met the blonde's glass with his own. "Aye, for Erin - an' may she even shine on us poor sinners, Malcolm Smith an' Jimmy Lowery!"

The two tilted their heads back and drank; Malcolm was done first, which only made sense given the disproportionate doses of the drug the duo downed. In spite of this, Jim chugged the whiskey as if he had a chance of winning a race the proprietor of the pub couldn't quite remember entering. Watching his childhood friend pickle his liver with an unusual ferocity, the goatee-sporting bartender raised an eyebrow. He exchanged the glass of whiskey for one containing vodka alongside of a lemon-lime concoction that would hopefully disguise just how little liquor he'd put in. He knew this to be a futile effort. "Lord save ya, Jimmy, I ain't seen y'drink like that since y'came back from Africa!"

Grasping and sampling the new flavor, James licked his lips and exhaled softly. He didn't mind having the edge dulled on this second cut, since the first had been so great in volume. "Well, me'an the ol' ladies had a bit'o a fight."

"Aye, aye, ladies." A half-concerned laugh escaped Mal's lips. "James Lowery, th'only drunk Irishman who can have not one, but two bonny lasses - as they like t'say! Yer vergin' on a fookin' mess, Jimmy, an' you don't come by here anymore, 'cept when yer a mess." Malcolm grew more stern in his expression of concern. "What's really buggin' ya?"

James once more laughed, and the blonde brushed his short back over his head, as if concerned about an imaginary bald spot. He stared down at his glass and pulled another quick swig from it, then his left hand carelessly messed up all the straightening he'd done atop his head. "I'm sorry, Mally, I jus' needed some air, an' this's th' one place I can come'n feel at home."

"Aye, Jimmy," Malcolm replied, nodding his head in understanding. Another shot was poured and downed, and he offered his friend a weak smile. "Tha's why I made it look like Brian's," the owner explained, "but without all th'madness of our former Republican colleagues."

James leaned back in his chair and his blue eyes measured Malcolm's dark ones. He could hear Mally's heartbeat, could feel the ambient body heat radiating off of the man. It was natural paranoia, and it was what had kept the two alive for the last thirty years. He didn't need long to be sure that there was no game at play, today. "Brian was a fuckin' nutjob." A harsh condemnation. "Raisin' kids into the Real IRA like Joe Kony, only wi' red hair." He nearly spat at the man's mental image; it always towered over him, for some Freudian reason. "Good fuckin' riddance, I say."

"Tha's th' whiskey talkin', Jimmy," came a quick chiding from his childhood colleague. "Hate 'im all ya want, we left because of th'murder, an' not th'family 'e gave us."

Lowery glowered for a moment, tapping his fingertips on Malcolm's bar as if contemplating whether the moral rebuke was warranted and - regardless - whether or not he planned to stick around any longer. He decided to lean in and nod, a rare instant of humility striking him in the nose. "Yeah, I went too far," he acknowledged despite the burning in his gut. "An' I don't wanna pretend tha' if it wasn't for 'im, we'd never'ave met. That we'd never 'ave *lived*," Jim grumbled softly.

"We wasn't more'n a couple of dirt-poor kids outta Donegal. 'E gave us food an' family, an' all 'e asked was for us t'join th' family business. Got a lot've blood on'r hands, workin' for 'im, but we'd never've discovered good from evil if we 'adn't seen it on both sides." The Irishman scowled. "We wouldn't'ave had this life. But I also ain't gonna let *you* preten' tha' we didn' tell the SAS where t'plant th'bomb, or tha' we didn't have a reason t'stop 'im when 'e went too far."

The two stared at their glasses for a moment before Malcolm filled them up. As new patrons entered the bar to a set of chimes hanging from the doorway, the waitress - the only waitress in the Pub, or so it seemed - immediately went over toward them to escort them to a table. She took their orders and went about filling them wholly independent of the establishment's owner. "Ain't cuttin' yer business, am I?" James asked his friend sincerely.

"No more'n you give me t'keep this place open, brother,"

Malcolm replied with a droll chuckle. "I still don' get it. I could make bankroll easy, but y'make sure t'feed me hundreds a month."

James glanced over his shoulder, his eyes taking note of each and every vacillation of the light. "You give me a place't get away, Mally. S'all a man like me c'n ask fer. It's quiet - not like half'a the joints claimin' to be from Erin in this city - an' its got th'only bartender I c'n trust in town..." A quick peek over to the entryway ended his sentence prematurely.

Malcolm's eyes focused on the doorway as the chime on the door rang again. A grin touched the man's lips as two women walked into his pub wearing unusually professional attire. The first was a tall brunette, toppling six feet tall with ease, and practically radiating a Russian heritage - complete with eyes which has most certainly seen their share of violence. The second was fair-skinned for the winter, sported red hair, and while she was shorter and had a quieter demeanor, she was simmering with a strange degree of irritation; emotions kept tight to the chest.

"Oi! Trust, remember?" James was grinning, but something seemed off about him; even to his old friend, this James Lowery was unusually strung out. "Oh, why th"ell'd they come by?"

Meeting nothing more than a shrug from Jim's friend, the waitress, seemingly unaware of her latest pair of guests' importance, politely sat them and took their drink orders. Both pointedly requested a vodka with sprite, and diverged from their path to take a certain memory-invoking seat, silently. Jim smiled inwardly. He was kept from any reverie by another set of arriving patrons. All male, each with an audibly over-muscled and un-aged bodies, Lowery didn't even look over his shoulder to acknowledge them. He relied solely on his hearing to assess them.

It was a decision he wouldn't really regret.

Before long, the silence was broken by two of the muscular figures. They were nothing short of stereotypes, wearing over-tight T-Shirts from one of New York's many city-governed colleges. The first one had a nearly-shaved head and might have at some point tried out to be in the military. His eyes, however, lacked the certainty and experience of a disciplined soldier. The second had black hair which had seen its fair share of gel in its young life, and was spiked upward like a porcupine's. It seemed like he lived in a tanning booth, and was asking for an early death via melanoma.

"I didn't know there were pretty ladies on the two-for-one specials!" declared the first man, the baldy.

The second man merely folded his arms over one another and grinned wolfishly. "Damn girl," he remarked as he stared the brunette over. "Where're ya from?"

The Russian accent quickly betrayed the dark-haired one, who hardly paid the men any attention as she sipped a drink. All she replied was a soft quip, "The Soviet Union, Mother Russia."

Spikey-head raised an eyebrow slowly, "Oh!" Clearly he thought himself the front-man. We got a foreigner up in this place! And you, Red? Did you spend a lil' time in the gulags, too?"

The Irishwoman slowly rotated her entire body around to face the man, looking him up and down without a hint of intimidation or fear. "We aren't interested in y', boys. Go away."

"Woahhh!" the first non-gentleman answered with a soft laugh. "Hold on, you don't even know us! I'm Barry, this's Mark, and we're from--"

The brunette pointed at herself stoically, offering a cold introduction. "Katrina." She next pointed at the red-head, who seemed to grow suddenly amused. "Lark." Finally, tilting her head to the side slightly, she actually smiled, cracking her icy demeanor. "And Jim."

As the two men sat there puzzled, the owner's voice echoed across the room. "Jimmy! What're ya thinkin?" shouted Malcolm warily, who was already walking his way around the bar and toward the blonde Irishman now ominously standing behind Barry and Mark. They quickly spun around and stared angrily at the one before them.

"Evenin' gentlemen," James' voice was concice; although he was clearly shorter than the one with short hair, and definitely less muscular than both of them, he seemed unimpressed by their physical stature. He had no reason to be. "I think me'ladies told y' t' leave 'em alone."

Spikey Mark looked the blonde over from head to toe before chuckling. "Who th'fuck do you think you are, shrimp? *Your* ladies?"

"Absolutely, friend," Jim replied reflexively. "Katrina an' Lark are *mine*." Strangely enough, the two ladies swooned. He gazed around the two men forming an ad-hoc wall near him, his eyes moving from one woman's to the others'. "Oh," he relented, "I'm so sorreh, ladies, I didn't mean t'get upset at'ya. I understand what yer sayin', I'm jus'--."

Their conversation was interrupted before either party could explain exactly *why* the two were mad at him. "Hey, shrimp, I'm talkin' to--"

James' sharp eyes stared up at the speaker; spike-head, again. Clearly the ring-leader. "That's nice, dear, run a--" He didn't have much of a chance to finish his sentence, because Mark's friend moved with a nearly unexpected quickness. A lesser man would have found himself on the ground with a broken jaw, but Jim? He was a fetish icon for the underdog crowd.

As Barry wound up, he could hear the man's muscles and bones creaking; he could smell the assailant's increased sweat production, including a new set of pheromones, and he could even hear the brute's heart pumping fresh adrenaline into his system. For the Irishman, there was no difficulty judging exactly where the blow was going to fall. He leaned out of the way of the punch's angle of acceleration. While it grazed him in the face, and it *felt* like a solid connection to the attacker, he was still standing. It was like he hit by a pillow.

He looked up at Barry, his face turned to the side dramatically. "Nancy," he spat, "you don't wanna do that again." Jim's confidence remained strong, a fact which *should* have changed once six other bar patrons stood up and started flocking to the attacker's back.

"Jimmy! You alright? How bad'd he get ya?" shouted Malcolm, sounded half surprised at the scene - and that half was just stunned his friend had been hit in the *first* place.

Mark cracked his knuckles, but Jim just grinned to himself. In fact, he held a hand up to Malcolm, a hand which the goateed establishment owner respected all too readily. "Odds ain't even fair t'th' nancies." He glared upward at the knuckle-cracking muscle-head defiantly. "Do i'again, an' y' go t'th' hospital, get me?" This taunt was far too much for the muscle-bound man to bear, but it was his friend who again took a swing at the Irishman.

Once more, Jim could hear the almost imperceptible movements of bone and muscle that propelled his attackers' fist forward. Evasion was easy enough, even though the man displayed a competent, combat-trained form. A simple change of his positioning, performed much faster than Barry could hope to keep up with, arranged James to the big man's side with his entire ribcage exposed. It was a tantalizing target, but Jim knew that one blow couldn't finish this. He decided his initial judgment was wrong; the bald one had probably gotten kicked out of basic training, maybe due to an over-abundance of aggression? He'd investigate another day.

He had other problems. He could tell within a split second that even if he put Barry down, Mark would be too close for comfort. The one contest he couldn't dance through with these dolts would be a wrestling match, and that was precisely what the reality-TV show reject was hoping for. He could almost taste the man's aggression approaching, and judging from Mark's build, well, Jim did *not* want to get grappled. Once he couldn't keep his distance, his advantage was diminished.

So, he just ignored the boot-camp reject's open stature and, shifting his weight sideways, lifted his left elbow square into the charging Mark's nose before he could bring his arms down around the smaller Irishman. This allowed Barry take another swing at Jim; but the Irish scrapper chose to swing his own fist upward and

connect with a particularly loud, brittle section of forearm bone –
something only James could know existed in the first place. A
crack echoed through the room as the weakened calcium gave
way to a compound fracture, and Barry found himself on the
ground, screaming in agony.

Of course, this meant that James now had six more
attackers to get through. He could hear Malcolm's footsteps as
his friend advanced to aid him. "No weapons? No help!" roared
the blonde, already anticipating the next series of attacks he'd
have to answer. A quick glance captured the position of each of
his enemies; their stance, their momentum, their physical
characteristics. He contemplated for an instant whether or not to
reach down to his boot and pull his bowie knife out.

But *that* wouldn't be fun - and Jim needed some punching
bags.

No, he contented himself with raising both of his arms in
an X-like fashion just before his first foe's fist struck him. He
stepped *in* toward his rival, his wrists turning inward and grasping
the attacker's wrist while his hip turned and pushed into the guy's
leg. He bent at the waist, and his arms served as a pulley while
his waist served as a wedge to jerk the attacker through the air
and square onto his back, on the ground.

His eyes lost their focus for just a moment; he heard the
whistling of a clothesline - a forearm strike - inbound toward the
back of his head. A peek to the floor and he could see the next
attackers' feet to his left. James dropped to a knee, then leaned
his weight to his right and used his arms to launch himself up to
deliver a brutal, inverted kick directly into this name-unworthy
assailant's jaw.

It was about now that the next of his foes shouted, "What
the fuck, is this guy a fuckin' ballet dancer?!" It was
accompanied by a fierce front-kick, one that James only escaped
by immediately shifting his weight once more, rolling to his side.
As momentum spun him, he extended his lower leg first -
contacting, but hardly damaging the kicker's ankle. With a swift
hook he brought his upper leg around and slammed his heel into

the back of the brawler's knee. This incapacitated James' foe rather quickly, and so far he'd taken five down in the span of about ten seconds.

Rolling backwards to his feet, he spread his legs shoulder-width apart, crouched slightly, and - as unorthodox as it seemed - waited. It was a *Kibo-Dachi*, or "horse-stance," one of the very earliest teachings of Shoto-Ryu, more widely known as Karate. It was anything *but* a defensive stance, since it put the entirety of one's body forward; ordinarily, defense came from presenting as little a target as possible! So it came as no surprise when yet another of Mark-and-Barry's gang ran toward him and threw a rather surprisingly well-executed jump kick.

Too bad that all Jim had to do was shift his weight, grasp the leg, and turn. "Not bad!" James commented mockingly, even as his attackers' own momentum carried him through the air and into a table.

"Oi! Jimmy! Less damage t'tha pub, please?!" Malcolm roared, seemingly unimpressed by the relative ease with which his old buddy was taking the attackers apart; on the contrary, he almost seemed to want to jump into the melee just for the hell of it. In the back of his mind, he registered the alcohol's influence on his desire to box.

James had just enough time to nod apologetically before pulling his head back and avoiding another fist. This was followed by a second movement of the same limb, and it almost connected with his face! Making like it was limbo night, James leaned backwards as the swing skimmed over the space previously occupied by his nose, and he followed his own momentum into a vicious round-house kick which smashed into the fist-flinger's face and sent him flying to the floor.

"What the fuck are you!?" cried the last of Mark and Barry's posse as he flicked his wrist and readied a switch-blade knife. Jim could hear the weapon start to slide from its concealment, and he identified the very make and model of the stiletto just from that.

Snarling, he almost effortlessly regained his balance and

threw a kick into the air to meet the thrust from his attacker. It *should* have split his leg wide open, leaving a laceration. Instead, it bounced off of Jim's sheathed bowie knife. "Wrong fuckin' move, sugar," Jim declared, swatting the assailant's fist and sending the knife landing with superhuman precision - tip-first into the Alley Pub's dart board. "Fer that ya get two!" The first punch James threw broke a rib; the second was aimed right at the sub-acromial joint of his left shoulder, tempered just enough that it didn't fully sever the man's tendons - the pain would only hit an eight out of ten.

It was only then that soft clapping emerged from behind him. It was Malcolm, who seemed entirely unfazed by the brutality his friend displayed. "Well! Y'ain't lost yer touch since ya last stopped in to Donegal, 'ave ya? That's the good news, matey. Th'bad?"

"I'm pretty sure I heard someone callin' 911, didn't I?" James remarked with a grin, his head jerking to one of the other populated tables. "An' somehow I don' think they'll buy self-defense so quickly." His eyes immediately shifted to Lark and Katrina. "Oh, loves, I'm so sorry."

They moved over toward him and wrapped their arms around him, hugging 'their man' until the red and blue lights started bouncing in through the Alley Pub's windows and New York's Finest came to pick up the new neighborhood bully - and, of course, to call for a few more ambulances than originally planned.

*****

He despised the rapport of the assault-rifle in his hands; unlike the smaller, gentler sub-machine guns he'd used in Ireland, the M-16 tucked into his shoulder fired a larger and louder round, and it had a more significant recoil. Two years after he and Malcolm tipped the SAS off on their former boss Brian's position, they'd been employed together by the CIA. They were "civilian contractors," experts trained and re-trained in the field of counter-terrorism, since they had already served on the "villain" side of that equation.

It wasn't so much that the gun deafened him, or that the kick was enough to knock his accuracy out of whack. He knew he was the best shot on Earth, already! Nevertheless, he hated that feeling of a burdensome, heavy weapon which would only slow him down in an actual firefight. He moved not with panic, but grace. He preferred stealth to brute force, but was quite good at both, when necessary.

In spite of it all, with each and every shot, he could tell, by the precise volume of the exploding gunpowder, just how much force had been exerted; and from the vibrations in the barrel he could feel precisely which direction the gun was going to kick. He could compensate instantly, re-aligning his sights on the target and firing at full-auto as if he was taking thirty seconds between each shot.

The clip emptied within seconds. He disassembled the weapon and retrieved his paper target close. A perfect line, from the target's oval-shaped, human-reminiscent 'head' straight down the chest. If it were a person who fell down following the first impact, he would have put bullets into the victim's brain with virtually every shot. He stepped away from the firing range, heading for another part of the facility.

"Lowery! How the hell'd you pull that off?" A deep voice barked from behind the concrete wall. "I saw the first shot clip the head, and you walked the gun down *instead'a up!" The range chief rose up from his seat and offered James a hand. The Irishman shook it, looking thoroughly unfazed.*

"In'nit a pro'llem fer me," he responded casually, "S'jus' in th'fine motor skills."

The man laughed softly, clearly impressed. "Bullshit, there's no way you can adjust on the fly to an M-16 pouring out a couple hundred rounds a minute. What's the secret?"

He was about to scramble for an explanation when a miracle (oh, how little he knew) happened. A soft, female voice echoed from behind the gunnery chief, now; it belonged to a blonde-headed woman who had soft, delicate features yet the most piercing blue eyes he'd ever seen. It made his heart stop. She didn't belong in a military facility like this one, but despite her lack of army-instilled poise she had a look about her that spelled trouble.

"James Lowery!" she announced with a smirk brushing over her lips. She held up a hand to the range chief; it palmed a business card with absolutely nothing printed on it, yet the man saluted out of respect. "My name is Erica Hall. I'm afraid I need a minute of your time. I promise, it'll be quick."

The Irishman stared the slender woman down, flashed a hint of a smile, and listened - to her heartbeat. It was perfectly calm, thoroughly in control, and - shockingly enough - in a nearly perfect synchronization with his own. Oh, the range officer had already lost his focus, seeming to forget about the stunning accuracy Jim had just displayed; a woman this pretty, with whatever that card signified, was just too good for the Irishman. "What can I do fer ya, lil' lassie?" James asked with the most sly of smiles on his lips; it was a confidence that had gotten him through the IRA, through the SAS, and into this "civilian contractor" facility.

"Let's put it this way, James," the woman remarked with a cagey, yet friendly smile. "I'm sure you're listening. My heart is beating at the same rate as yours because I want it to, just like you can hear it over the sound of gunfire because you want to." The Irishman's pride fell, surprise striking his eyes as he found himself completely unable to predict what this woman was thinking. Every time he tried to read her body, it only showed what he subconsciously expected it to show. "Don't worry," she reassured him, "we aren't alone, not in the sense of our uniqueness. Come on, I'll show you!"

Shrugging with irritability, he allowed her to lead him off of the firing range, the heavy steel door closing behind the both of them and that particular page of their history.

*****

The loud clanging of the prison door's opening and closing was met with a gruff, "Alright, Mr. Lowery, your bail's been posted," uttered by a rough-spoken police officer whose gentleness was betrayed by the soft hand on his shoulder. Being printed and processed had been annoying, but at least nobody in the holding cell dared to talk to him after they received an initial warning amounting to, 'he's in for beating up a half-dozen grown men without getting a scratch on him.' Had he needed to shower, he'd bear no fear of dropping the soap.

"Great," Jim muttered as he was guided through the exit process.

He came upon a desk where his personal items were waiting. His knife was taken into his hand and re-affixed to his ankle. His wallet, change, and car keys were handed to him. He signed a notice making clear that he'd received everything he possessed when he was arrested, and another notifying him that he was to appear in court on a date that he was fairly certain would never come - Katrina and Lark, if he knew the two, were already working on convincing a judge to throw the charges of assault out, and to expunge it from his record. Even if they failed, the charges wouldn't stick: Considering that the CIA would have his prints flagged as "theirs" in the first place, chances were that the worst punishment he'd receive would be a phone call's worth of annoyance from an old contact.

No, it was the face which greeted him outside of the final checkpoint, and outside of the police building, that actually caused him to frown.

"Y'know," James mumbled self-consciously, "A'least if i'was Geddy, I'd only get a bit 'o a mean poke an' a warnin' not t' be an idiot again."

That face was adorned with a pair of glasses, and rested upon a head nestled atop the shoulders of a man who, all in all, was 5'11". He had black hair which, as he approached forty years old, one painstakingly long day at a time, was inexorably getting replaced by gray strands. His eyes were a dark obsidian, and his outfit? The same style as it had been on the day he met the man almost two decades ago - brown jacket, brown pants, and brown leather gloves on his hands.

"You're the deceiver here, James," Emmett Eisenberg remarked with a hint of a sad smile on his face. "You said that precisely because it'd convince me to say what I'm saying now. That's just what you do, and its what you've always done, so I'm still gonna berate you. Sound fair?"

Stepping away from the precinct and delivering a soft punch to the taller man's ribs, he grinned weakly. "Fuck off, Physics-Boy."

Emmett shook his head as the two started heading down the streets of New York City. He just *had* to become serious. "Jim, look, I don't care about you beating up a bunch of punks. You picked the week we're all in the same town to do it! You're James Lowery, you don't *ever* leave people with a choice over their own actions, do you?" An eyebrow raised slowly. "You could've conned them into walking away. Why con them into swinging first?"

"Look, Em, I needed to blow off some steam. Lark and Katrina, they got in on me for somethin', an..."

The physicist - for that's precisely what Dr. Emmett Eisenberg was, in both the strictest and most conventional meanings of the word - gazed at his friend. "What, exactly, did you three fight about?"

A sheepish look came over the Irishman's face. He was clearly embarrassed. That, or he was about to tell the worst lie he'd ever uttered. "We were talkin' about *Lost*. Tha' show on th'island? Magical boojums an' whatnot?"

Emmett raised an eyebrow cautiously. "Okay, and what has this got to do with anything?"

"They hated th'ending," Jim heresied, "I loved it."

A gloved hand found the bridge of Emmett's glasses and pushed them securely against his face; just the moment before his hand covered it up against the painful light of Jim's logic. "Oh, you've gotta be kidding me."

The blonde glared up at his friend as they stepped into a crosswalk. "No! It was fuckin' excellent!"

Emmett laughed weakly, a chuckle which turned into a sigh of exhaustion. "James, you went out to a bar, got drunk, started a brawl - and drew attention to *us* - all because of a damned TV show? And one that ended, what, six-something years ago? I mean, come on!" He held his hands out in exasperation. "Our meeting is tomorrow, Jim. You don't fuck up like this, you *know* better."

James shrugged callously. "Lissen, I was jus' fed up wi"things. It's gonna be one 'elluva meetin' "morrow." He paused. "I know I usually go first, but I ain't this time."

Emmett nodded slowly. He came to the door of a small hybrid car, one without any particular brand associated with it - mainly because it was a prototype. "Yeah, yeah. Listen, you're catching a cab, right? I'm going back to Sonia. We'll be meeting in the usual place, tomorrow?"

"Of course," James remarked with a grin. "Lowery Security Services' Executive Loft. 1:40 PM, jus' after lunch. See ya then!"

Chapter Two
The New Consortium of Trust

Jethro Marx was *always* the second man to arrive at these meetings. He was a short man who was now thoroughly bald, his face adorned with a black and gray mustache and his stomach having grown ever so slightly rounder as the muscle from his youth seemed all too willing to grow squishy. His only saving graces were a final hint of squareness in his jaw, one that reflected a heritage in boxing, and arms which were still fairly developed, in terms of bicep mass that wasn't cellulite. His wife had been hitting the gym with him, as of late, and it had certainly worked wonders!

But she *wasn't* with him, precisely because she had caught a cold from the sweaty men at the gym.

"I always wondered why yer feet don't make a sound," Jim mused as he turned over his shoulder. He had been seated in one of the many spinning, rolling, leather-bound executive chairs which adorned this office and watching the busy bees of New York City. "Its like y'always 're already standin'. First thing I'm hearin is yer heartbeat. No pops, no poofs, no taps; 'cept when I ride wi'ya."

Jethro's dark eyes lit up with a smile. "Jimmy boy, can't you figger it out? I ain't exactly a bottle'a mysteries."

Of all of the people meeting today, Jethro was by far the oldest. Approaching middle age as far back as when they first gathered almost fifteen years ago in Africa, under rather dubious grounds, the man nicknamed 'Geddy' had never kept many things under his ever-expanding belt. Still, they were all mysteries in one sense or another. The Irishman ventured an answer. "If I'm correct, s'cause yer standin' when you move. Yer trick accounts fer grav'ty, an' Earth's movin', so it's..." he couldn't quite find the proper words, so he improvised. "It's 'cause yer already there."

The dark-skinned one laughed loudly, a laugh that came

from a joyful soul. "Tha's the ticket, Jimmy. It's just what I *move* tha' moves." This particular accent was from America's southern regions, with Jim's best guess being a Louisianan one. There was a certain melding to it that implied a migratory lifestyle, however; bits of cajun spliced with 'southern gentleman.'

"Well, tha' makes an' interestin' trick indeed. Y'mind goin' first t'night?" The Irishman looked at his friend.

Geddy, however, looked concerned. "Don't we always do *counter*-intelligence first? Especially with tha' bitch still on tha' loose?"

*****

Two-by-two, perfect lockstep. Even if he tried to vary up his cadence, she'd match it and make him think it was his idea. In a way, they both did the same thing: The difference was that Jim could work out his mark's emotional state through subtle physical cues, then manipulate it; she could set that emotional state directly, and then some.

They approached the construction site in question without clearance or ID. They didn't need it - they had access to anything, anywhere, any time, so long as it was run by people. That's how they'd come upon a story of a man in his late-thirties who ran a small construction company that had extraordinarily low material-shipping costs. Too low. They'd observed the muscular Black man for quite a while, waiting for him to make a mistake. He did, because he had no way of knowing he was being watched! And that's when they visited him.

"Jethro Marx," Jim stated in a polite voice, laying eyes upon his mark for the first time. It should have halted the entire work site, but Erica's willpower saw to it that they were all entirely wrapped up in their menial tasks; far too caught up in 'the routine' to get involved in their boss' doings.

For his part, Jethro merely lowered the hunk of wood he was carrying and stared at the Irishman and his companion. "Yeah, that's me. Do I know ya'll?" The man was big, alright;

clearly a well-trained builder from the Southern United States, an heir to the brutal legacy of slavery. The man they'd later call Geddy was - at this point, anyway - merely a man on the middle road.

"Not yet, but I'm Jim. Jimmy Lowery. This's Erica Hall, and we're with--"

Geddy laughed. It was evident that the big man was used to far more intimidating interrogation tactics than the boy-girl team were presenting. Judging from his face, the man had expected a badge. When one didn't manifest itself, the situation devolved into a bad joke. "What's all this about then? Cut to that chase," he commanded.

James shrugged, leaning in to whisper ever so softly into the larger man's ear. "Y'ain't normal, are ya?" The suddenly-stunned look that the large man gave him told him everything he needed to know - those 'Consortium' *people were damned good at their work; and while he understood what he and Erica did, what this man could do? He knew full well that if the wheels in Jethro's head turned the wrong way, he'd end up back in Ireland – or worse! "S'alright, Mister Marx. Miss Erica 'ere and I? We're like y'are. We wanna pay ya. Triple yer salary! We need y'thelp us build somethin', an' when its done y'll be free t'go - or t'stay on. S'up t'you."*

Now, Jethro seemed more intrigued than worried. He glanced down at the hunk of wood he was carrying then cracked a smile. "Whadda ya have in mind?"

"Simple 'nuff," Jim answered bluntly; Erica jumped in to finish his sentence. It was as if they'd rehearsed it.

"We're going to save the world," she pronounced quietly, yet boldly. If it were anyone besides Erica and Jim, it would be a baseless - downright crazy! - statement. But belief was easy to inspire in someone when you could control their emotions. Of course, it was sometimes easier to use what was already there. "And I know just how much you've wanted to hear you aren't *alone."*

The prospect intrigued Jethro, alright. It wouldn't be long

before the group was in Africa on a one-way trip towards their
fate, and toward memories James didn't care to recall.

*****

"Please?" the dim blue eyes of the blonde implored, "It's
kind o'complicated, otherwise I wouldn't ask."

Jethro folded his arms and nodded his head, finding a seat
near James' rolling chair and looking at the door. Jim sighed and
gazed out of the window once more, striking up a conversation -
or, at least, addressing another concern. "S'a beautiful city, really.
Ain't much've a reason t'think somethin' special happens here.
Speakin' of..." James trailed off slowly, putting on a rather grim
tone. "Before anyone gets here, where do you'n Alejandro stand,
these days?"

Geddy responded almost predictably to the forlorn tones.
The Black man sighed and also looked down toward the street.
Height was something the older fellow was quite familiar with. "I
took his 'ol man up to the roof of a building and *dropped* his ass.
He's *always* gonn' hate me, even after he saw all tha' old records
you showed 'im. We're okay, but he *damn* sure ain't my best
friend."

The Irishman licked his lips and gazed out of the window
for a moment. "Can't say't don't surprise me, can't say't don't
make Sari's job easier. Guessin' by th' footsteps tha's 'er."

No sooner did Jim reveal what he was hearing than the
doorway to the executive meeting room opened and a - to Geddy's
surprise - a *pair* of women stepped in. The first was all but
unfamiliar to him, but not entirely alien. She was pale, had red
hair, and she stood taller than James did. Her arm, most
surprisingly, was wrapped around the waist of someone he knew
quite well.

Wearing a golden robe and with a golden *Tilaka* (a variant
of the Indian "dot") covering the tanned skin above her forehead,
Sari was indeed the most incredible sight Jethro had laid eyes on
in some time. The woman was a Brahmin, a Hindu Priestess, and

moreover she was just like Jim and himself; special. She was a decade Jim's junior, and they all regarded her like a very impressive step-child. She was together with...

"Molly, eh?" Jim remarked, grinning a touch. "Lark's sister finally finds a friend! Always kinda thought you'd end up wi'Alejandro, t'be honest."

Molly gazed to Sari, then laughed. Very un-like Lark, she had by-and-large been raised in America, as she was a good six years younger than her more 'foreign' sister. "Alejandro is so heavy-handed! It is as if, when you cannot feel pain, you do not know when you are going too hard." Sari giggled at the blunt explanation, then gave the other girl a tight embrace before taking her preordained seat at the head of the table.

"And my dear friends, Mister Lowery, Mister Marx - how are both of you?" The question was laced with a slight amount of admiration and respect; but years of practice had drilled some of that out of her, as well. She sounded like a professional, not an apprentice.

Geddy shrugged nonchalantly. "Just thinkin' about tonight. I volunteered t'go first, today, since Jim wants to save his bit 'till last." The Irishman nodded along.

Sari adjusted her seat, lowering it slightly. "That's acceptable. I'm sure you have good reasons. Do we know who else will be joining us, tonight? Katrina, Lark?"

Jim glanced sideways. "Well, they're actually working on some legal documents for me."

Sari, mercifully enough, chuckled to herself. "Ahhh yes, Doctor Emmett told me." At the 'it figures' glare from the Irishman, the Hindu laughed louder! "It is fine. It happened! I'm certain that you taught someone a valuable lesson about using judging before one acts."

"You sayin' I look like a wimp?" questioned Jim jokingly, leaning forward toward the Indian; of course, Sari only laughed harder. The doorway opened once again and two more figures entered the room. The first was that tall physicist in his brown jacket, his gloved hand folded gently over the naked palm of a second figure.

This woman's name was Sonia Monterrey, and she was about a decade the physicist's junior; in fact, she was closer to Sari's age, and she preferred to dye her hair in all sorts of shades. Today was a combination of blonde in the front, red in the back, and she wore a red vest over a black dress. It was shocking, but she actually looked professional despite her rebellious demeanor.

"Doctor Emmett! Miss Monterrey! Its so good to see you!" chirped the Brahmin, who rose to quickly hug the pair. Similar, slightly less enthusiastic greetings were offered by the men in the room. "We're just waiting for Allie, now. He should be here soon, then we can get started."

Emmett nodded to the younger, dark-skinned girl, then gazed toward the blonde Irishman with a bit of a smile. "Katrina and Lark?"

"Busy. Legal stuff, but y'already knew that. Are w'done w'Pick On Jimmy Day?" he quipped with a grin on his lips. The resounding laughter that met him seemed to indicate he was free of any lingering anger, at least for the time being.

The door opened and closed one more time and a tall, muscular Hispanic entered the room. He wore a perfectly professional business suit, and he had lush dark hair which had only just begun to recede. His voice boomed off of the walls. "Good evening, dear ladies, gentlemen, friends alike," he offered with a smile. The man went about the room and shook every person's hand save for that of Jethro Marx; the two stared one another down, nodded their heads at each other, then the Hispanic took a seat as far from Geddy as possible.

"Mister Curtis," Sari offered in a quiet tone, one laced with a hint of sadness. "I'm glad to see you. We are now, all, present. With that in mind, let us begin the fifth meeting of the Consortium of Trust." She tapped her fingertip on the table; the click of her fingernail seemed to echo like a gavel. "James Lowery has requested we save both his company's update and his counter-intelligence report for last, so we're going to move on to Construction Connections. Mister Marx?"

Geddy coughed softly, clearing his throat. "We ain't got much to be reporting, Sari. Maybe that you're too formal!" Muffled laughter from those around the table. "My contract work is pickin' up as this economic situation gets better. That's about all I can say. We finished the Alaska task, by the way," he added, looking toward Emmett. The physicist nodded.

Sari smiled warmly. She may have seized control of this group bluntly, but she allowed the topics to flow like water. "Let us move on to that, then. Doctor Eisenberg, how is your company?"

"Eisenberg Elemental Research and Consulting is, well, consulting and researching," the physicist admitted awkwardly. "Our latest agreement is with the Jones Institute for Political Justice, a fancy-pants group of middle-of-the-roaders who are interested in researching the effects of Global Warming on our most northern state."

Emmett's voice left it clear that he felt like this project was a waste of time; then again, he was one of the many scientists in the country who were already quite sufficiently concerned over the odds of a global catastrophe. He had already made up his mind based on the data he had on hand. On the other one, he *was* a global catastrophe, at one point in his life, and science dictated that one should always acquire newer data-sets. "The staff is pretty much lined up, we just have to ship them up a few dozen leagues away from civilization, and avoid upsetting the local Caribou, and that project will commence. For the next five years we'll be studying temperature readings from around the state."

Emmett paused for a moment, and Sari almost jumped in to advance the meeting's agenda. Then, he sighed. "I have to admit I'm having some difficulty with another project, however." His tone was one which reeked of unfulfilled potential. "We want to perform some studies on Thorium--"

"'Ere he goes!" Jim chirped, earning an irked look from the physicist.

Sighing, Emmett pressed ahead. "Anyway!" he charged forward, a physics-based Light Brigade, "In particular, we want to study a liquid fluoride reactor. They're pretty much perfectly safe, in hypothetical models," Emmett added, smiling, "And with my talents at the helm it *is* perfectly safe, but the government is unwilling to risk anything nuclear after that mess in Japan half a decade ago. I mean, I can't even get the consent to build the damn thing, let alone securing the significant amount of funding - *legitimately*, I should add."

At the idea of well-earned gains, Emmett merely shrugged; his entire empire was built on fiscal lies, after all. One more wouldn't hurt. "So, my next move is to look into foreign locations, though I'm gonna try to avoid Africa as a whole." The incident at Connor Point, the infamous research center in Africa which suffered a 'nuclear' disaster thanks solely to Emmett and his capabilities running out of control, provided all the reason in the world for him to stay off the continent. "Maybe the Middle-East will be interested, as the energy generated can be used to remove salt from water and make it drinkable," he concluded musingly, mostly to himself. He'd lost most of his friends along the way.

"Excellent, excellent - at least," chimed in a friendly voice, "excellent that you have such a drive to pursue your dreams. Moving on to Miss Monterrey, how *is* our newest member doing with her dreams?" queried Sari with a broad smile on her face. Her tone was inviting and reassuring, despite its (probably unnecessary) professional edge.

Sonia looked toward Emmett, her former professor and now-much-more, who returned a faint nod of support. "Well," she cautiously opened her first independently-filed briefing, "We went with the name Monterrey Marketing. We're focused mostly on helping merchants sell their swag," the strawberry-headed one offered with a smile, "but we also conduct polls and surveys, and even taste-tests." She laughed at this; the others did, as well, though Sari retained that level of decorum which she'd taken so many years to earn. "We really do whatever we're hired to, and that definitely includes our contracts with our *other* companies. We're planning to publicize Emmett's company's work in Alaska, for example, and we're gonna work with Mister Curtis on improving his business website so it can handle online transactions more efficiency."

After studying the recent post-Masters' graduate for a few seconds with a serious demeanor, Sari actually broke the illusion and chuckled. The Hindu offered her a thumbs-up. "Why, Miss Monterrey, it almost sounds like you have some experience at being part of - and I know this is hard to believe! - a conspiracy!" The playful sarcasm dripping from Sari's lips was more than enough to elicit a smile from the newcomer. "Good work." She glanced about the room, her eyes locking upon the largest man in the room. "Alejandro, yourself, or me?"

"It doesn't matter, madame," the muscular Spaniard replied cordially. At the nod from his board's chairwoman, he began. "Suffice to say that Rodriguez-Trujillo Import-Exporting remains firmly in my hands, in spite of the corporation's Board of Trustees. We continue to ferry in objects of interest to us, as well as agents of Mr. Lowery's." 'Objects of interest' was a broad term; radioactive materials, artifacts of legend, or just plain strange technology that the Consortium would have to deal with sooner or later. Most of these turned out to be bunk - "invisible energy" technologies and whatnot - but some samples of rare-earth elements had proven quite valuable to the Consortium. "We are working on procuring a Post-Panamax shipping vessel to conduct trips between Los Angeles and our Asiatic ports of call, but otherwise it is a boring, unimportant tale of corporate lobbying."

Jim nodded, and Geddy did his best to look like part of the meeting room's woodwork. Sari, meanwhile, merely smiled; the picture of calm, as a believer in karma might be. "As always, Mister Curtis, you do excellent work. Well, my turn, then."

Sari flipped out her phone and looked over some numbers, very briefly. She was notorious for ensuring that she gave her closest comrades the most up-to-date information possible. "Medivent's stock value is $72.89 as of the last after-hours trading session. Our market cap is--" she laughed, then, and pocketed the device. "You are not concerned, nor do I blame you. My company's research and development department is where the largest amount of interest lies."

Her friends all seemed much more intrigued by the cutting-edge science, as opposed to the painful levels of boredom they expressed when she talked about finances. "Medivent has two separate cancer-fighting drugs entering stage one FDA trials. The first shows promise in early identification of virtually any form of cancer, while the second is designed to target pancreatic carcinomas. We have actually begun preliminary research on a substance which can arrest Alzheimer's disease completely, with aid in the field of precise molecular chemistry coming from Doctor Emmett," she added, inviting Emmett to bow his head graciously.

"Lastly, we have discovered faint hope in overcoming Tay Sachs," she said, looking to Geddy, who seemed quite confused. "It is a genetic disease that effects newborns is entirely, always fatal." This was a sad thought. She forced herself to smile. "Now, through certain retroviri and DNA therapies, we may be able to change the genetic death-sentence that is Tay Sachs." She sighed, once, and rubbed her forehead slowly. "Speaking of saddening tales, it is also my dubious pleasure," she concluded calmly, "to announce that a rather pitiable attempt at accessing our databases was thwarted thanks, funnily enough, to our old friend 'Little Stevie'."

Now, the Irishman scoffed in disbelief; Stevie had been a bouncer at the Midtown Ballroom up until one night, a couple years ago, when an old enemy of the new Consortium's had trapped them in a room and attempted to turn them against one another. It mostly failed, but Stevie was left in possession of knowledge that most certainly could not be allowed to spill out on the streets. Since then, the bruiser had been paid rather handsomely to work for Lowery Security Services - both financially, and though the continued possession of his mortal coil.

"Eh," Jim mumbled, scratching the back of his neck in

response to the persistent gaze from the Indian, "Can't say I didn't train 'im well, then, yeah?" The abject lack of humility radiating from the Irishman served to accentuate just how far the former bouncer had progressed.

"Do we have any leads on who the perpetrator was?" queried Emmett, lowering his glasses to look between Sari and Jim. The Irishman responded by shrugging and glancing over at Medivent's creator.

For her part, the priestess shook her head. "Our best guess considers this to be a standard espionage attempt, or perhaps some so-called 'hack-tivists' who decided we warranted their investigative efforts. As far as I have seen, they have failed utterly to penetrate our security system, so it is a fairly moot point unless they act again." She finally turned her lovely, tanned face toward Jim. "But it now occurs to me that this is not the reason you postponed your counter-intelligence report, Mister Lowery?"

"Nah, not 'tall. As fer the first part, the usual one? Erica Hall?" That same former colleague who had drawn their attention to Stevie. "She ain't doin' much o' nothin'," the Irishman mumbled, shrugging his shoulders. Emmett's dark eyes glanced toward his Sonia's; after all, Emmett and Erica had been far, far too close at one point in their history - the cause of their schism, and a factor of Connor Point's destruction, among other things. "As per last update, she started *Siren's Songs*, a new record label. I'm thinkin' she might use it as a platform fer larger speeches an' shit, if she wanted. Kinda like a mass min'-control thing, if sh' wanted, but i'tain't nothin' new; 'Riki's always been a bitch like that. She's also datin' high-flyin' political types, lately. Probably fuckin' blackmail, some of 'em 'r married. But," he added concretely, "she ain't made no moves 'gainst *us* tha' I c'n see."

James cleared his throat and looked into the eyes of each of the room's denizens. "'Ere's point two. I got a call from an' ol' CIA contact'a mine." This was a flatly-received statement; it was no secret that Jim often worked for the U.S. Government, through his front company, but it was rare that he discussed open cases. "Th'man asked me t'look inta' somethin' called a Numbers

Station."

At the befuddled looks from his fellow Consortium members, he pursed his lips. Before he had a chance to speak, he heard Geddy mumble, "Now, fuck is a Numbers Station?" There was no 'what the' there, just a swear - as if it were a clean-cut chunk of common grammar.

"Numbers Stations," picked up Jimmy with a dry smile, relishing his chance to play at Emmett's expositional explanations, "are basically radio stations tha' broadcast a buncha' static, 'cept for brief, scheduled times when a robot-type speaker reads off a buncha' names, numbers, or random nonsense that y'can't really understand. Most've the time, they're used by spies." He held his hands up. "Let's just say, fer 'xample, tha' ya have a station tha' broadcasts..." He thought for a moment, then took on a particularly robotic voice. It was a poor impersonation, and he doubled this up by writing down every word he spoke.

"Charlie, Epsilon, Mu. Charlie, Epsilon, Mu. Charlie, Epsilon, Mu." He held up a finger to forestall any complaint. *"Nine. Seven. Twenty Two. Twenty Two. Seven. Fourteen. Six."* He glanced the group over and smiled sneakily. "This's actually not tha' hard a one t' break. The Greek letters'd tell someone listen'in in what code t' use. In a real code, it'd be much tougher t'crack; but in this case, the code'd tell ya what letter to use for each number. Nine'd be an M, Twenty Two would be an S. Th'word's 'missing,'" he explained, "but tha's an easy word. Th'real deal is about impossible."

Emmett and Sonia seemed to make perfect sense out of this situation; Geddy and Sari seemed downright puzzled, and Alejandro? The Spaniard hardly blinked as he listened to the explanation. "And what does this have to do with our briefing, my friend?" the muscular, invulnerable man asked.

"Easy, m'dear Allie," James answered much to Alejandro's annoyance, "Th' CIA asked m' t'study a new station tha's broadcastin'. Th'problem I have is tha' we triangulated th'source an' its definitely comin' from America." Slowly, now, the Irishman's eyes turned toward Emmett purposefully; a grim stare.

"An' it's comin' from Alaska. As in, maybe a hundred miles off'a where y'just set up a research facility."

Now, the physicist in the room raised his eyebrows. His dark, yet gray orbs simmered with concern. "So the CIA has you investigating some weird radio broadcast, like, two hours away from where I just got contracted to build a research site. I'm guessing the station's been there for a while?" It almost sounded like Emmett feared *he* may be the one getting investigated.

"Not so; maybe three months, four," Jim clarified. "They tried t'crack it internally but couldn't, an' the CIA ain't supposed t' operate on domestic ground. They don' wanna give jurisdiction up t'the NSA or FBI on 'ccount of it being broadcast from inside th'country to foreign agents, mos' likely. Tha' means they want Lowery Security Services t'translate th' signals, if we can, an' I could use some help outta you guys t'figure it out."

Emmett brushed his brown leather covered fingertips through his dark, graying hair. "So I take it that means we're all going to Alaska? The counter-espionage people who are working with us aren't going to be able to pull double duty, huh?"

Jethro chuckled softly. "Think about it dis way, doc! You gots this crazy radio person broadcastin' crazy numbers, like, right outside o' your brand new facility. Ain't no *way* you ain't got a reason to be worried, am I right?" The physicist shrugged in response, Geddy's statement hinting at his own worries. "So we get on a plane and fly on up to tha Tundra. Sounds like a fun vacation!"

"You're more than welcome to double-screen every scrap of information I have about my facility," the physicist added calmly. "If you think this is some sort of espionage run against us, then I'd deeply appreciate the help. I know you have a greater amount of..." he trailed off, searching for a word.

Jim grinned as Sonia piped up, filling in the blanks. "Greater access to federal and foreign intelligence networks, fingerprint databases, and the works, right?"

The Irishman nodded his head. "A'course, Physics-Boy, I'd hate t'have any scum-suckin' bastards tryin' to take ya down.

Not that I'm worried 'bout *you*, but yer business? I mean, I've 'ad ideas, y'know. I could always go Blackwater, private security on a fuckin' military scale."

Oddly enough, Alejandro smiled at this prospect. "I don't see why you haven't. You have--"

A stern look from the Brahman in the room shut the Spaniard up swiftly. "We do not seek to rule the world, remember?" Sari's correction was harsh and direct. "We are here to *save* it. We have all at some point agreed that we must utilize James' security business as a covert operations unit, yes. It is a sad reality, but one we have accepted. But military force? Jim, you are so much smarter than that. We do not *need* military force to protect our more forward-thinking projects, do we?"

For a moment, Emmett forgot exactly who he was listening to. The adult - no longer a scared, scarred little girl - was presenting a strong and rational argument against building a private army. She was, moreover, reinforcing the very reasons for the Consortium of Trust's revival - and it's limitations.

"Hey, now," whispered a hurt-sounding Jim Lowery, "I jus' said I 'ad ideas. I don' think they're good'uns, not yet at leas'. Connor Point, y'know, had kind of a milit'ry base on i'. Th'Alpha folks jus' thought it was to keep any attempts t'nationalize the facility from gettin' through peoples' 'eads. In reality, well, it was t'be ready t'act if some folks needed 'savin',' y'see? But th'ol Consortium had its own views, yeah?"

The priestess nodded softly, calming greatly in the face of James' relenting. "I just recognize that with our abilities - even mine, you should know - there is no force on Earth that could stop us. That is with, or without, a legion of cliche henchmen." Her tone was neutral, but it was clear what she thought of such lofty goals.

Emmett smiled self-consciously. "I can argue either way," he interjected softly, as he was arguably the strongest of them all, "but the truth is that I don't want to think in those terms. We're not here to take the world over, and we're not exactly gonna save it, either. We just need to nudge it a bit to get it back on course."

"Aye," Jim concurred, leaning back in his seat. "But right now? We've got a trip t'Alaska t'take. Let's worry 'bout this dumb contract an' makin' sure Physics-Boy's project ain't bein' spied on, eh?" With that thought, there was resounding agreement.

*****

Catskill Community College was covered in snow. Late-March might have been a time when the weather turned toward warmth, but in New York's mountainous areas it was still wintery enough that skiing was a popular pass-time. Though nowhere near as powdery as the Adirondacks further north, the Catskills still had icy conditions in their immediate forecast; even if, ultimately, the slushy days were slowly starting to outnumber the cold.

Walking along in a heavy woolen jacket was a slender psychologist with strawberry-colored hair. The seemingly-natural redhead shut the door of her car and started off towards an older, brick-faced building called Hudson Hall. She wrung her fingertips, warming them as she brushed her digits over the tiny ring upon her index finger. There was no snow in the sky just yet, but the dark clouds hovering over her head promised that sooner or later the white stuff would fall again. She just hoped it was after she got done with this meeting and drove home! If she was quick, perhaps, she'd make it! Afterward, she had a nice relaxing weekend planned out - wining, dining, and dating.

Two students parked their own car; a girl and a guy, the girl driving her friend. As they headed to Hudson Hall, they didn't immediately attach themselves to one another as lovers would. No, instead they were just friends - or first daters - and they were bundled up against the fear of the mountainous chill. The departing woman raised an eyebrow, however, at the rather high quality woolen jackets they wore. They were downright professional, beyond the expense account of a college undergrad.

"Excuse me!" the man requested with a raised hand.

The psychologist slowed down and nodded gently. She masked her true thoughts about the cold, the delay, and the driving she'd have to do later. "Of course; how can I help you?"

The man seemed bashful enough, bowing his head deeply toward the one he'd stopped. He was a dark-haired figure, alright; muscle on top of a thin set of bones and wire. Strangely, he looked completely unremarkable. "I'm actually looking for, uh, the psychology department? I need to set up a meeting with the chair and associate chair and - oh!" He smiled all too broadly; the psychologist's mind started racing. "Is that? Are you?"

Her identification tag had peeked through the heavy coat she wore; 'Maria Montclaire, Associate Chair, Psychology.' She immediately took a step backwards, cursing inwardly. "Yeah, lucky enough!" She laughed softly, dismissing any anxieties which might have been building up, inside. "That's me, what did you need to talk about?"

The woman with him smiled all too broadly, the air of a secretary wafting about her. "Well, we work for American Defense Solutions," she announced, declaring her involvement with a *very* well known, friends-in-high-places military company. That's all Maria knew of them. "We're actually trying to get some routine verifications on an employment candidate of ours, and he mentioned you as a reference from his time here?"

It was one of those moments where a person would wish they could wake up from what was, assuredly, a nightmare. Maria could see exactly where this was going, and it was over three years in the making, easily. For an instant, she even considered that she was glad it was happening now; before the wedding, before any commitments were made that could expose her beloved to the bullet she was about to catch. "Really? Who?" she laughed some more, but it was clearly nervous laughter.

The two exchanged rather confused glares, as if not quite clear what the joke was. "Umm. Well, his name is Doctor Emmett Eisenberg, and he's a physicist. He applied to work with us," the woman said in a perfectly neutral voice, "and we're just doing our due diligence on Dr. Eisenberg by checking in with some of his former co-workers."

Maria was more than suspicious; she was terrified! However, she kept her fear under wraps and smiled as saccharine as she could, saying, "I'm sorry, but isn't it a little out of the way to come here?" Her false, fear-filled mirth continued. "I could have told you about him over the phone."

The two laughed softly along with her, and the gentleman shook his head. "Doctor Montclaire, please; we know you're busy, but do us the courtesy?" What exactly he asked for didn't come across clearly. He shook his head, then, and clarified. "We're just asking about the physicist because he's a very talented man. I take it you've seen some of what he can do with atoms?"

Atoms; oh, she remembered hearing plenty about them! Those atoms! His *talents*! But had she ever actually *seen* Emmett at work? She had to think long and hard, and her confusion was evident; etched into her face. It hit her; a memory of her own ignorance:

"Maria, it's real." He flexed his fingertips and produced a tiny green stone; an emerald. "See?"

"See what?" she looked at the gem, then tossed it casually to the floor.

"Yes," she remarked, looking down toward the concrete of the parking lot. "I've seen what he can do. He's really a genius, but I don't know why you need to talk to me to figure that part out. He worked at Connor Point a decade and a half ago! He's up there with Hawking and Sagan - hell, he's a match for Einstein!" She couldn't fight back a hint of emotion.

Once more, the man and woman stared at each other with a confused glare. Then, finally, the woman reached a hand out ever so gently and patted Maria on the shoulder. She flinched; and the other female blinked. "I don't know what you think we are, but we're not gonna hurt you. Hell, we want your *help*. Doctor Eisenberg isn't normal. Judging from your eyes, you already know that little fact," she declared in a fairly arrogant tone. "And the fact is, the man I work for is interested in meeting with the good scientist. If you could just tell us where he is; if you two still talk, of course? Or maybe if you can just give us some contact information?"

The psychologist wasn't sure what she should do. "Knowing you're looking for him," she answered cautiously, "I have to wonder why you wouldn't just contact his company somehow?"

"Oh, we've tried that," the man answered politely, "but he's evasive. Our employer wanted another angle on him. So, you haven't seen him since he quit?"

"Nope," Maria responded neutrally, brutally, and honestly.

The man nodded compliantly. "Alright. Well, here's our card, we'll be in touch," he said as he shook her hand (not entirely a willing gesture on her behalf), gave her a card, and the two disappeared into their vehicle.

She shrugged off the chill of the encounter, walking into her building and heading up an old, wooden staircase. It creaked underneath her weight, and she had to fight the wholly irrational fear of the building collapsing. Oh, she'd usually laugh about it - teasing about ancient architecture dating back to Henry Hudson, himself! But now, knowing that *they* were back in her life, it was a suddenly realistic possibility. Even the main corridor groaned under her dainty weight, and she leaned a hand upon the wall as she stumbled to her office.

Maria had just about enough time to print out a copy of a colleague's record, plug a cup of tea into the hot drink dispenser, throw some ice in a glass, and brew herself an iced tea before a knock descended upon her door. "Come on in!" she offered with a friendly exterior.

A new face entered her office, one she could only remember from memories patched together; distant meetings, faces long unseen, buildings long since painted over. "Doctor Victoria Latchkey, was it?" Maria ventured, staring at this older woman. She was, if appearances could be believed, approaching sixty years old, and her once dark hair was rapidly growing grayer. It didn't help that she now had a man with similar hair stylings on her mind. The older woman was short and slender, but had a motherly face about her. Gentle, perhaps, was the best word to describe her, but there was a hint of stoicism in her face that was hard to place.

"You must be Maria Montclaire. It's nice to meet you, again." She extended her hand, and the two ladies firmly exchanged greetings. The aged one sat down opposite the younger, her eyes flashing immediately to the ring on Maria's finger. "Usually, Daniel handles the formal affairs, but he must trust you to do his dirty work?"

Maria forced her face into a statue. "Daniel's a little tied up. I understand you'd like to return to the college?" As her conversational partner nodded, Maria continued casually. "You've been away on an extended leave for the last three years, right? You were doing work with the Center for Applied Psychological Enterprises?"

CAPE was a privately owned subsidiary of a major corporation, one that doled out incredible grants to researchers pushing the boundaries of their field. From Post-Traumatic Stress Disorder to cutting-edge neurological programs geared toward the recovery of victims of Gliomas, also known as "brain cancer," CAPE did it all and they did it well. In fact, only one other company was pushing as many boundaries as CAPE: Medivent; which Maria recognized was run a certain Brahman priestess she'd once known, and wanted nothing to do with.

Latchkey nodded once again, licking her lips as she considered how to explain her job. "We did work on using computer-driven research to better predict how patients respond to talk therapy. They are also possible assets in training new therapists."

The redhead folded her hands in her lap. She'd never been a huge fan of using computer models in psychology; machines lacked the same neuro-plasticity as people did - far too much hard plastic, none of the softer sort - making them far too predictable. "That's interesting. How *exactly* does a machine emulate the Human brain?"

Amusement tinted the elder's voice. "You have doubts, I can tell. I know your position on data pre-sets modeling patient behavior." Maria had certainly written enough ethics articles. "And you aren't wrong! Until this last batch of testing, we *really* couldn't successfully mimic a working brain. The answer is in quantum computing. Here's what I mean." She held up two fingers in a peace sign. "I'm holding up two fingers, right? But there are *three* spaces around them - to the left, to the right, and between them."

"And that has what to do with the topic? I'm not following, Doctor Latchkey," Maria responded. She *wanted* it to make sense, but she was worried about the American Defense Solutions agents - they were agents, clearly. She was worried about her date. She was worried about...She had no idea, what! Everything!

Before Maria could add anything, the returning researcher laughed. "Vicky, please," she clarified in the interest of politeness. "Normally a machine just sees what you tell it to - the fingers, or the spaces. With the best programming in the world, a computer can tell you that both exist, depending on your frame of reference. A computer thinking in terms of quantum mechanics is able to tell you of the potential for more - or less - of each." She raised a third finger, then lowered two, as she explained. "It will also recognize that while there are three general areas of space, they are all connected."

She smiled as she folded her hands in her lap. "In other words it isn't locked into the algorithms you program into it. It can draw upon outside knowledge, and it can even use that knowledge to change its mind; or it can forget things it's learned entirely through chance."

Now the younger psychologist leaned forward, curious. Computers forgetting? It seemed counter-intuitive. "How so?"

"Think about it like this; cosmic radiation can, in very sensitive electronics, cause bits to flip on and off. Major companies, well," she slowed in her explanation, "they account for this by backing up their files over many hard drives, or even multiple sections of the same one. It's called distribution, and in a distributed back-up system if a file's data gets corrupted on one drive, it can still be accessed on others."

She held up a hand. "But as to the original copy? One minute the file reads a certain way," then, her fingers loudly snapped together. "A cosmic particle hits a bit, and now it reads another." She lifted both hands up expressively. "This simulates the random changes that the human brain goes through in a day; the latest change in the brain's composure. The digital brain thinks very much like a human one, and it learns and evolves."

Maria nodded slowly. "Alright, Vicky, and how'd your research ultimately go?" Research, after all, was designed to draw conclusions.

The elder chuckled. "I wouldn't be asking to teach some seminars about it if it didn't work! And because of the College's role in supporting me, CAPE is giving us the second half of a pretty substantial grant. In short, it was a complete success, and it's being cross-applied as we speak." Her eyes were alight at the prospect of how her project was evolving.

Slowly, Maria flipped through the pages of Vicky's file. Her records and diplomae were all in order. And, as she read, that wasn't all! "Oh, wow. Your daughter goes to school here, too?"

Victoria smiled warmly now, a certain appreciation touching her face that she hadn't displayed previously. "Oh, absolutely. Saffron's her name, I'm sure you can see. She actually studies particle physics, and she's about to graduate a year and a half early. It's a shame, the best scientist we had here left a couple years before I went out on this assignment, and just before Saff' got admitted."

It didn't take a genius (which Maria *was*) to know who Latchkey meant. Once again, the image of a man wearing brown gloves - always brown, always gloves - blinked into her head. "Ummm," she banished him from her head, "you mean Doctor Eisenberg? Yeah." She paused for effect. "Last I heard, he's heading up a research firm of his own!" She plastered on a smile, tried to seem innocent of her past deeds. "I knew him kind of well, actually."

If there was any kind of suspicion on Latchkey's behalf, it didn't radiate through. Instead, she merely folded one leg over another and nodded. "Saffron would have learned quite a lot from Emmett, then. It's a shame, but hey!" Vicky laughed to herself weakly. "I can't really complain about how she's doing. For me to pay no tuition, and for the prestige that department *still* has, thanks to Bill, she's sure to get into a top-tier program as soon as she graduates." The returning researcher sighed, shrugging in resignation. "Anyway, I'd better get going. Thank you for your time! I'll go about creating some syllabi for seminars, assuming Daniel will grant those who take it a couple credits?"

After standing up and shaking hands once more, an affirmation of her request, Vicky opened the door to Maria's office and leaned into it. She paused just before crossing the threshold. "Oh, hey hun!" Surprise touched her voice. "Saff, come on in. Meet Doctor Montclaire, a co-worker of mine!"

Into the portal stepped a sharp-faced young woman, one with raven-black hair. She was tall and slender, and Maria thought at first she'd seen the girl around campus. Her style was sharp, but not exclusive; a black leather trench-coat covering her body against the cold, reminiscent of a cyber-punk character's brooding attire only with a weather-centered justification, matched with a set of thin, black silk-satin gloves draped over her hands and running up her wrists. Leather boots kept the chill off of her feet, and stockings ran up to whatever she might have on underneath her jacket. It was entirely possible, but as Saffron raised her hand and waved, offering a verbal - polite - salutation, the psychologist caught a glimpse of the student's eyes. They were familiar, somehow - the gray-black orbs held an untold confidence and an unspeakable certainty in them. It was all too reminiscent of the way Emmett's friends had looked at her; even Emmett himself.

It was like the world around them just didn't matter.

"Nice to meet you, too! Let me know if you ever need

anything," Maria responded swiftly, almost automatically. The two psychologists waved one last time and parted ways, and Maria stared down at her still cold iced tea.

The glass was covered in condensation, and the tea a slight bit clearer than usual due to all the ice melting. She sighed to herself, wondering exactly what she was going to say to Daniel about the day she'd had. Reaching into her drawer, she pulled out a packet of sugar and poured it into the drink. "Well, they say it takes just a spoonful, when it comes to shit-tasting medicine."

*****

"Hello," the voice over the phone echoed. It was deep, with a faint but unplaced accent. It didn't even wait for a response. "I met with Lawrence last week. He remains as loyal as a pet viper can be. How did things go with her?" As if to improve clarity, he added, "The first, first."

The soft-spoken male sighed into the receiver. "Not great, not well. She wouldn't talk. She will probably inform our mark that we made contact, in fact."

A deep, rumbling laughter met what might have been a grave remark. "That's fine. They will find out before she acts, anyhow. The window is too narrow, and they're already on their way. I am more concerned with the second one, anyway."

The recipient, as it were, sighed again. "It's fine. It will be fine. I don't think I could deceive her, but I don't think it matters. She hasn't healed from the wounds the mark gave her, even if she's tried to. Anyway, she will be meeting with another conservative soon, and you know how that will end, so it doesn't matter. The seeds are planted, just as you said, and she is now recruiting allies. There's just the other thing, now, with Versailles. She's in position, as planned."

"Very true," the deep voice answered calmly. There was silence for just a moment. "Thank you again, old friend. We *will* be successful, it's not much longer now. Farewell."

Chapter Three
Seward's Folly

Insofar as a city in the middle of nowhere could be famous for anything more than its geography, Nome was. Located in the northernmost regions of Alaska, its difficulty to access was made famous in 1925 during an incredibly severe blizzard that coincided with a major outbreak of Diphtheria. Said storms kept most efforts to deliver much-need medicine to the mining town from being successful, but a dog sled team overcame the odds and reached its destination. Fast forward nearly a century, and the Iditarod Sled Dog Race used it as an end-point, as an homage to the happy ending.

Not bad for a mining town founded at the turn of the twentieth century. Not bad for a town that used to be little more than a tent city in the wilderness. In fact, not even bad for a town which had burned down more than once; or been buried in snow, or stricken with a plague of upper respiratory infections, or faced down any other series of disasters.

As Nome was hard to reach and rather far to the north of the state once considered little more than Secretary of State William Seward's great mistake. The Secretary got the last laugh when reams of natural resources were discovered; gold among them, and in the hills around this ancient Inuit town. Hence, Nome - originally a mining town, and now merely a "large" Alaskan town with a convenient location for Dr. Eisenberg's research station on global temperatures.

From the small town, it took merely a sixty mile airplane ride (or, if one felt truly adventurous, a trip down a hardly civilized road that bent around mountains and valleys for three hours of hell) to get to the facility. The station had most of the accoutrements of home - for example, refrigerated coils separated the floor of houses from the permafrost ground, ensuring that the earth did not literally begin to melt. The houses seemed normal enough, and a series of geothermal probes ('luckily' resting next to pockets of heat-emitting stones buried too deep in the Earth to damage the tundra) provided electricity to the entire lab.

A trio of small-plane airstrips afforded plenty of room for in-and-out traffic, especially as they could be re-assigned to support the landing of larger cargo planes to resupply the location with food, fuel, water, and equipment. Special orders could be put in by any of the staff, and any room left-over on the main cargo deliveries would be dedicated to filling them. Want some White Castle burgers? A frozen package could be delivered - better than nothing, right? Need some soda or a bottle of wine? Done, provided there was enough room on the cargo plane. Even video game systems were occasionally distributed to staff members, though Emmett's company had a very strict policy on not getting one's work done.

In short; fail to do your job, through your own actions, and you get fired.

However, while the rough-and-tumble team of Physicist, Construction Expert, Doctor, Market Researcher, Trader, and Security Expert clung to the sides of their tiny ten-seater plane (a Cessna) as it began its descent, Emmett smirked to himself. "The turbulence isn't anything to be afraid of, Sonia," he assured the young woman whose fingernails were threatening to spill his arm's blood, "the structure of the plane is completely fine."

The Physicist had, Sonia realized, taken his sweet time to study the metallic flying machine on a molecular level; there were always micro-fractures in any vehicle, and in almost any hunk of metal. They were no threat, and were hardly noticeable except when examined in intricate detail. Normally, that meant taking a microscope to the study subject, but in Emmett's case merely implied the expenditure of a moment's concentration. Even as the Cessna shook, it didn't worry him. His girlfriend, however, was busy clinging on to his limbs. Even with his trademark leather gloves to protect them, his fingers were starting to lose their circulation while his suit was being shredded by her claws.

"We're here," Geddy declared softly; and so they were,

because the pilot began to lower the plane's landing gear and it wasn't long before the sound of rubber hitting road echoed against the passenger cabin.

Sonia mumbled under her breath, "Oh thank the lord." She finally relaxed.

"Huh, a visitor," Sari added, looking out the window as a black-haired woman in a white lab coat (under, of course, a heavy woolen jacket) charged for the plane. The Hindu's eyes widened a touch as Emmett reached out and opened the door, unfolding the tiny plane's built-in step system. He threw on a jacket (a sham; the physicist had no need to fear the cold) and stepped down the stairs, holding a hand up high.

"Well!" he shouted warmly, "Doctor Phillips! Stop running! There's no fire, I'm pretty sure." He ignored the mumblings of Jim, the second one down, and the cynical declaration that perhaps his group should *start* one to avoid freezing to death.

Professor Phillips immediately slowed down, walking up to Emmett and shaking his hand. "Still, Doctor, its really an unexpected honor! We just opened shop a couple days ago and you're here for a visit, already?"

"Its alright," Emmett answered as he scanned the area; there was nobody out to assist his comrades with their belongings, but that was exactly as he'd intended. He smiled to his colleague. "Allison, these are the co-workers I mentioned. Jim Lowery, Sari, Sonia Monterrey, Alejandro Curtis, and Jethro Marx." As he introduced each one, he gave a gesture in their general direction - helping her to put a face to the name. "I'm glad you got my message and came alone. Jim?"

James shook the scientist's hand. "Emmett said we c'n trust y', so we're trustin' you," he stated to the black-haired, nearly-sixty-years-old woman. His keen ears twitched once as he listened for something that would cause him to lose that trust. "And I'm glad w'are," he immediately stated, "because you're goin' t' do me a small fav'r. I go"a hunk o' equipment tha' we're gonna ge' off this plane, then we're gonna set i'up. While w'get prepared, I want y't' gather th' best scientific minds Physics-Boy 'ere's managed t'ge' t'come t'fuckin' 'Laska. This needs t'be a bit hush-hush, lass - can ya do it?"

At the rather confused look Allison gave the Irishman, Emmett laughed weakly. In that instant, he had to decide whether or not to even attempt a direct translation of the thick accent that had just given an order to *his* people. He decided on a simpler course. "Heh! Yeah!" His cheery demeanor made his next statement quite a contradiction. "Not to be too bit of a buzz-kill, but could you get the chief and associate researchers together? It'll be real quick, we just need to help settle an assignment."

Allison sighed, and acquiesced to the simpler, yet still confusing request. She offered her employer a faint smile. "Whatever you want, boss. James, folks, see you in fifteen. Make sure to text me with where you're setting this, um, equipment up!" She held up her cell phone, then headed into the building.

Geddy looked at his physicist friend and smiled a bit; then, he turned his gaze toward the plane and, looking with his mind's eye through the vehicle's exterior, and at the heavy steel case inside of it. "Where you want me to move this thing to, anyway? Show me?"

*****

Emmett had a private office built into every company-owned property he developed. They were small and unencumbered, for the most part, serving as merely a private place for him to think and work when he was present. After all, the act of "shaping" minerals - often radioactive ones - required privacy if nothing else. None of his employees understood the faintest bit of what he could do! Witnesses would be troublesome, but witnesses he'd accidentally irradiated would also end up dead. Even still, the Nome location was a bit different, if for no other reason than that it was remote and that land was cheap; the restriction on square footage was mild.

His office here was just large enough to fit the eight scientists he'd called upon, as well as himself and his Consortium members. Naturally, the Consortium was the first group in; once Geddy had been shown the office, he'd moved the steel container, alright. Emmett knew the procedure well; once Jethro touched an object and focused on a destination, he could "move" it to any place he had seen. It was a convenient ability, and one that could actually interact with Emmett's own; though the consequences had historically been catastrophic. Nevertheless, the selection of super-Humans waited for their comrades to arrive.

The other scientists, including Doctor Phillips, filed into the room casually - and right on time! A small smile touched the physicist's lips as it dawned upon him that he did, indeed, have a competent cadre of researchers. Phillips immediately turned her eyes upon the large steel case which now sat in a corner of the room, opened. It contained a large, unfolding antenna which lay in the corner; a computer terminal reminiscent of a laptop which was seemingly a part of the case; a second display panel with a number of gauges and analytical equipment; and, finally, a quartet of screens that popped up from inside of the equipment container and was already showing four streams of data, each of which was virtually identical in how the lines on the screen rose and fell at seemingly random intervals; and, finally, a quartet of just-larger-than-average speakers resting on stands originating in the steel enclosure.

"Y'all already know Physics-Boy, yer boss. I'm Jim Lowery, an' I've hired y'all today t'give me a hand wit' somethin' special," the Irishman stated in a calm, ever-flowing tone. He gestured with his left hand toward the series of equipment. "Some'a ya may recognize this as a radio diagnostics center. Chances are y' 'aven't seen it's model before. That'd be 'cause its proprietary. M'lady Lark an' I invented th'shit, an' its top notch." Proud as anyone ever could be over their own work, Jim continued with a smile which touched his lips. "I guess some'a ya'all a'ready know tha' there's an odd radio station on th'shortwave frequencies, up 'ere. Its just barely touched t'news, but it's probably hit any'ya that've tried t'monitor incomin' planes a' some point."

Slowly and coldly looking the entire room over, James paused in his diatribe just long enough to look in the eyes of every person in the room. He followed this up by glancing down at his watch impatiently, as if irritated at something invisible. "There's 'bou' three minutes 'til it broadcasts its next message. I'm gonna flip on th'monitor now. I wan't'y'all to jus' listen, an' see what y'hear. We'll discuss afterwords. Jus' don' say nothin' 'till it's over."

With a nod from Emmett, the special operative approached the metallic case and plugged an access code into the computer terminal. With a soft click and whirr the machine sprang to life; as James dialed in a frequency which Emmett could not make out on the tiny screen, the antenna hummed for a moment until it was perfectly aligned. Once attuned, Jim entered a command into the processor.

A sudden, dull groan emanated from the four speakers. The quartet of screens each displayed lifts and descents in pitch and sound; even though each monitor yielded different visualizations of the sound, the overall trend was for slow, steady growths and shrinkages in the volume, as well as musical tone, of the sound. Jim was listening with intent ears, his eyes locked on the four displays.

"Twenty seconds," whispered Geddy quietly; as if not to disrupt Jim, but rather to warn him that he was about to *be* disrupted. In this case, it was a gentle yet persuasive whine floating across the airwaves which initially interjected into the listening party. It was immediately followed by a voice barely discernible as a male robot's.

This mechanical mouth spat out an utterly perplexing series of words. "*Apollo. Apollo. Apollo. Siren. Athena. Fate. Eros.*" The audio visualizations streaming across the display screens jumped up and down rapidly.

Next, a female - if possible - robot began to read off numbers. "*Four. Sixteen. Twelve. Sixteen. Twenty-Four.*

Four." Jim keyed in a few words on his computer terminal. Now there were four completely different displays labeled on the quartet of monitors.

"Apollo. Apollo. Apollo," declared the male again, very nearly running over the final number.

Not to be deterred, the female machine started her bit over again on the coattails of the man's final syllable. *"Four. Sixteen. Twelve. Sixteen. Twenty-Four. Four."*

The man, perhaps satisfied, reiterated, *"Apollo. Apollo. Apollo. Siren. Athena. Fate. Eros."*

A final tone screeched across the air-waves and the four various audio streams blended back into one. James rubbed his chin softly, then turned his eyes to the room at large.

"Well," the Irishman, asked in a blase tone, "Any ideas?"

The scientists all glared one another over, glassy-eyed, unable to volunteer an answer to their boss-apparent's answer. Doctor Phillips especially was left literally scratching her head.

Suddenly, the voice of Sonia Monterrey cracked the silence. "Well, its all Greek - like, *genuinely* Greek," she clarified, looking almost as puzzled as the others. "Eros, Athena, the Fates, the Sirens. All of it is Greek mythology. Or, well, Roman, if you want to go with the second draft," she annotated. Emmett nodded his approval of his girlfriend's knowledge.

Geddy, on the other hand, merely laughed. "I ain't got no clues, man. They's damned crazy, but my guess is that whoever's listening in already knows what to listen to."

The snapping of a pair of fingers caused all eyes to jerk toward Emmett. He had a rather enthusiastic look in his eyes. "Alright!" he announced proudly, "Throw out that Apollo garbage, it sounds like it doesn't add anything. Look at the first letters of each word. Siren, Athena, Fate, Er--"

"S-A-F-E!" announced Sonia, as if she were still in a class under the physicist's teaching and not, say, his girlfriend and co-conspirator.

James nodded slowly, his eyes once again drifting over the gathered cloud of scientists. If he had any ideas to add to the conversation, he kept them to himself. It was the priestess' turn to speak. "The number Four," Sari stated as she held up a sheet of paper she'd scribbled the speech down on, "is at the start and end of the sequence. The number Sixteen is used twice, too. If each number means a letter, it's probably related to the words, right?" James nodded again, and the dark-skinned girl went to work with her pen-and-paper.

Slowly, Sonia's eyes danced over her boyfriend and his comrades. Her mind tapped into her training as an English student, and it wasn't long until she determined that there weren't all too many words that made sense. "If the Four is an S, and the Sixteen is a T, then I'd guess the word is S-T-A-T-U-S."

Emmett grinned ear-to-ear while Geddy laughed and actually extended a hand to pat the girl on the shoulder as if she'd earned a biscuit. "Great work! Status: Safe!" he announced to the world. "So now that we've got that figured out, what the hell has a status of safe? Jim, you're the expert. Anything you can think of in that broadcast?"

"Tha' one?" Jim asked, looking up at Eisenberg with a bemused stare. "Nah. It's prob'ly all there is. I'm more interested in th'fact tha' the station is always broadcastin', y'know? Usually, they only transmit when they're sendin' messages."

Slowly the physicist deflated. Naturally, he next sought clarification. "Always broadcasting? As in...?"

James' eyes once more gazed the gathered paragons of knowledge over, but this time he had a much cagier glint in his eyes. "My best guess is that its broadcastin' th' background noise, lettin' whoever is listenin' get a good read on whatever's actually airin'. I think's a generator," James intoned neutrally in that rolling tongue, "but I ain't sure."

His eyes eventually fell on one of the scientists in particular; a short, slender male with pale, Alaskan skin and an oversized pair of glasses hanging over his nose. On second thought, it didn't really surprise James at all; his only distinguishing trait was the five-o-clock shadow on his face. "Most've all, I wanna know why everythin' we've said seemed t'get th' blood pumpin' for everyone but one person in th'room. So I'm lookin' at you," he said as he pointed a finger at his target. "What's yer name? The *real* one, I'll know if you lie."

Emmett's gaze leveled upon the one who Jim pointed out. He was a local kid, actually; hired to help secure a tax write-off for employing workers from the immediate area. John Bradley had been his name; but if Jim was questioning him, it was only because he already knew that wasn't the truth.

"John Bradley," issued the scientific spy. James waited a moment for the man to add anything, and he did! "What gave it away?"

The physicist was surprised. He was wrong on *two* counts - that Jim actually was right, and that the spy's name was, in fact, as bland as it seemed. James shrugged and, in full view of every other stupefied scientific mind there, moved somewhat like a blur. Before anyone could react, James had his left hand wrapped around John's throat while his right reached between his legs to meet a rising left boot - and to withdraw his hunting knife. With a wall to his back and with a sharp weapon replacing the restrictive hand on his neck, John's eyes quickly filled with terror.

"D' y'know who I am?" demanded Jim coldly. It was clear that a false answer would mean the wanna-be-Bond's demise.

"I--" at the attempt to explain himself, he felt a tiny scrape as the stubble on his neck was quite literally shaved away. "Yes! Yes I know who you are!"

None of the mental mammoths in the room dared to interfere with what, at first glance, appeared to be a crazy non-employee with a knife to their friends' neck. Perhaps it was just James' undeniable skill with a blade, or perhaps it could be attributed to them having no sympathy for a spy - let alone an understanding of why they would be spied upon! Last of all, it could just have been shock at a very cinematic situation happening before their eyes.

"Good boy," Lowery approved coldly, measuring his victim. "So 'ere's what's gonna happen. I'm gonna read off a list'a names real fast, like. You're gonna keep yer little mouth shut. I ain't listenin' fer yer words, I'm listenin' fer yer heartbeat an I'm starin' at yer eyes. Follow?"

As a gaze from Emmett kept his subordinates in line, Jim refused to allow the interloper even a moment to answer. "Erica Hall; Sari; James Lowery; Jethro Marx," he read without hesitation, each name having only a cursory moment between them. "Emmett Eisenberg; Alejandro Curtis; Garrett Trinder; Richard Trujillo; Erica Hall; Sonia Monterrey; Margaret Marx; Steven Glassberg; Katrina Anisimov; Emmett Eisenberg; Maria Montclaire; Lark O'Brien; Alejandro Curtis."

James' stare pierced the very soul of the uncovered agent. He waited a solid ten seconds after he stopped speaking, then - in a blink - flicked his knife across Bradley's throat. The man immediately reached for his neck, striving to keep the blood from oozing out of his body! Then, all too quickly, he realized that he only had a tiny little scrape - and hardly a drop of his life's essence escaped his circulatory system. "Everyone out. Now," Jim demanded; his expression softened as he reached down toward his boot and sheathed his weapon. "Please."

Nodding softly, Emmett looked at his co-workers. An explanation fumbled from his lips. "I think it's pretty obvious that this didn't happen. I promise, you'll all get an explanation of this incident in your mailboxes. Otherwise, this falls under your signed Non-Disclosure Agreements with the company. Truly," the physicist indicated as his shocked subordinates left the room, "I'm sorry you had to experience this. Meeting tomorrow, let's say noon, so we can all sleep in," he concluded. He studied each of the scientists as they left, bewildered over the entire chain of events.

"Not you," interjected James to the all-too-eager Bradley. "Yer based outta th' facility t'the east, yeah?" He didn't even wait for a reply. He'd already had it. "Yer workin' fer who, now?"

"A...American Defense Solutions," answered the agent in a shaky voice.

Jim's eyes narrowed darkly. Even Emmett knew that name; they belonged to a major conglomerate with plenty of branches, much like the tentacles of an octopus. This limb in particular was a major defense contractor with the U.S. and other NATO governments, though it's parent company's name escaped him at the moment. "Tha's fuckin' great," Jim chirped derisively. He almost seemed to hesitate in his plans for just a moment.

"A'right, yer goin't' do somethin' fer me. Tell yer boss tha' we're gonna be meetin' 'im soon. Say in a week. Don' worry 'bou' givin' 'im a time-frame. Jus' pass th'message, yeah?" He clapped the spy on the shoulder firmly, but not bruisingly - almost like a big brother would rough up a little one. "Aight, ge' th' fuck ou'ta 'ere."

Yanking his shirt and twirling him, then shoving him towards the door, Jim waved with one arm folded across his chest as the terrified former spy ran from the room. For a moment, Emmett wondered just how he would be getting home; truth be told, he didn't care too much. A spy? One who knew who Jim was? That left only one question.

"What names ya get hits for?" the until-now silent Jethro asked, keeping Emmett and the also-silent Sari from intervening. Sonia raised an eyebrow.

Jim sighed, and it was a sigh of confusion. "Tha's the funny part, Geddy," James began carefully. "He knew me, Emmett, an' Sonia," he stated, drawing a gasp from the recent graduate. "But 'e also knew Richard Trujillo an' - this's th' fuckin' shocker - 'e knew Garrett Trinder. Yes, *tha'* Trinder," Jim clarified, reinforcing the shock that Emmett expressed. Even Alejandro winced.

"Garrett, like..." Sonia trailed off warily.

Sari picked up the pace perfectly. "Like the one who died at Connor Point? Yes. *That* Mister Trinder. He has been dead for almost fifteen years, however. How would he know of Mister Trinder?"

James' memories struck hard.

*****

"James Lowery! Come on into my office," the scraggly-haired blonde remarked. *He was clearly German; muscular, much like Jim was, but with a much more gruff, rigid demeanor about him. "Welcome to Connor Point's Alpha Section!" He jumped up and shook Jim's hand. "I'm Garrett Trinder, one of the supervisors here."*

Lowery glanced the office over; PH.D's adorned his walls, as did paintings of atomic structures and historical events alike. The model of an atom rested on this Trinders' desk, which was formed from Mahogany and stained red. Red like drying blood, in fact - a nuance not lost in Jim's memories. Shaking the stranger's hand, he didn't wait to be told to take a seat. Merely, he rested his rear in a comfortable, leather-padded chair.

"So, you've already met Miss Hall. She's amazing, isn't she?" Garrett asked in a voice oozing with appreciation for the Empath's finer points; not just her powers.

Jim, on the other hand, shrugged carelessly. "She's somethin', yeah. I didn' know others could do wha' I do."

Garrett nodded in recognition of this fact. "Well, there are really two branches of research here at Connor Point. The Alpha branch is all about things that people expect. New, cutting-edge developments based on science they already know exists. Taking the internet and making it wireless," he suggested, *"or developing better rockets to send satellites into space. America's NASA isn't going to be funded forever,"* the German added with a soft laugh. *"Someone will have to send things up to our space-stations."*

Jim nodded, folding his hands in his lap and listening politely to the spiel. "On the other hand, you and I will be working together primarily in the Omega section. It's a little pun on the Bible, you see - normal, expected things by today's standards being our Alpha, or beginning; with the Omega being beyond mankind's expectations. My fellow investors and I, well; we seek to make this world much better through the help of people like yourself."

"So, what, yer buildin' an army?" Jim asked warily.

Whether or not it was an act was hard to guess.

This only elicited a laugh from the German. "Oh, heavens no!" His chuckles slowed. "No, no; you thought Erica had the same capabilities as you do? No, James - if I can call you that?" The Irishman shrugged again, this time appreciatively. "Erica is the closest to your gift, perhaps. She can sense emotions, a little like what you've been doing through this conversation, but she can also change them. She's a terrible *fighter, Jim. Trust me, that's one reason why we need you!"*

Now the Irishman leaned forward with a smile on his lips. Garrett kept talking, almost as if he liked hearing himself do just that. "We will need you to escort Miss Hall and others, at times, when she is out recruiting. Let's take your first case, for example. There's a girl in India, about ten years old..."

The German slipped a manilla folder across his desk, offering it to the Irishman. It was odd in that it was black, completely and totally ebony. He opened it up, studying the girl's name - one Jim had willingly forgotten - and a series of photographs. They featured car accident victims walking away from crushed vehicles, doused in blood. They showed family members and known associates. "She lives in one of the most crowded cities in the world and I am sure *others know about her, even though my colleagues and I have tried to keep the Omega project and its candidates out of the press. I would want you with Erica for this job because* you *are a human - super-human -" he corrected himself, "weapon."*

*****

It didn't matter to Jim that he'd ultimately watched Garrett die - blown into bits by his physicist friend who was having a "bad" day. The strongest memory he had of the man was the day he met him, and the day he was sent to procure a young child who ultimately would suffer serious trauma as her talents were tested. It had only been through one saving grace that *he* hadn't killed Garret, himself.

"He's th' one tha' told me y'were bein' tortured, Sari," James conceded calmly, his eyes leveling on the Hindu priestess.

Sari nodded once, and he couldn't help but note the golden *Tilaka* etched onto her forehead as it reflected the light off of her skull. "Mister Trinder was a good man, in spite of his associates."

"Yeah," Emmett remarked as he glanced downward, shaking his head. "It doesn't really explain why Bradley knows *his* name, though. The man has been dead for over a decade! Could he have old information about the old Consortium?"

James shrugged his shoulders. "Maybe. Hard t'say. I know I was one've the first. I know Bradley knew me 'an Trinder, but 'e also knew Richard Trujillo."

Geddy sputtered. "You mean Alejandro's dad?" He asked this instead of asking, 'the man I threw off a building for his role in torturing Sari?' Nevertheless, he bit his bottom lip. "Well, did 'e know Curtis?"

Alejandro, sitting there with incredible silence until this point, narrowed his eyes. It was a pertinent question. After all:

Alejandro Curtis had, they all preferred to forget, had attempted to kill Jethro a few years ago; it had been done largely because his emotional state was compromised, but also because his estranged father, the aforementioned Richard Trujillo, had been murdered by the teleportation expert. James shook his head to the negative. "The man didn' reco'nize th' name. Tha' tells me 'e's got a lot'a missin' information."

Now, Sonia shivered. "But, well, he knew *me*! I'm brand new to this."

Emmett's arm slipped around his younger girlfriend's shoulders and he pulled her close to him. "Chances are, he was only briefed on what he needed to know about me. Right?" As James gave the physicist a thumbs-up, Emmett smiled. "It doesn't really explain how he knew the Old Consortium, but if he used to work for them somehow, maybe that explains the connection."

"Still doesn' explain why 'e's spyin' on us, Physics-Boy," James stated calmly, "Bu' I'm gonna need t'talk w'someone.

Geddy, can y'send me t' Washington D.C.?"

Blinking his eyes, Jethro stepped over to his friend and extended a hand. "Easy. Whenever you's ready."

Jim smiled coyly. "I'm'n'a set up a meetin' with one of my contacts a' th' company. I'll call when I'm ready t'come back, yeah?" Geddy nodded. "Sonia, Sari, Physics-Boy, s'been a blast. See ya soon!"

He reached out and touched Jethro's hand, shaking it firmly. The portly man gave his old friend a warm smile, just before that old friend disappeared into thin air; soundlessly, to those who were not traveling with him.

Chapter Four
Business Meetings Are Brutal

She knew what she was doing was wrong on a lot of levels. She snuck out of bed at noon. Daniel was still unconscious, and clearly worn out. She scurried off to the furthest side of his house as she possibly could. Her fingertips tapped buttons on her cell phone. A button on the side brought up her list of contacts. She pressed the E key on her rather intelligent, but far-from-smart phone (it was about four years old, by now). Then she used the tiny lump which served as a mouse pad to scroll through the list of E names she had in her memory.

Finding the choice she needed to select, she stared at the man's name for a solid two minutes, breathless. She hadn't heard his voice in so long - not since he'd protested that he wasn't an insane man, not since the completely *in*sane woman had cornered her and Daniel, vaguely threatened their new relationship, then left with some psychotic pledge of self-reform. No, she had hardly let herself give him a second thought until last night's ambush.

She pressed the 'talk' key.

The phone rang.

Ring.

Ring.

Just before her heart exploded in anticipation of his answering machine, an unexpected sound greeted her. A soft, delicate - definitely female - voice picked up. The woman on the other line sounded groggy. "Hello?"

Maria instantly froze up. The voice was almost familiar, but she couldn't place it; it certainly wasn't Emmett's! "Ummm. Yeah. I think..." she hesitated. "I think I have the wrong number."

"Huh?" The sleepy sounding one sounded, well, sleepy; the phone rustled, as if the girl was adjusting her posture. The sound of footsteps just managed to reach the receiver. "Who is this?"

Maria coughed once, surprised. "I'm looking for Doctor Eisenberg?"

"Oh!" the girl's voice lit up slightly. "I'm sorry, Emmett's asleep."

Maria coughed again, this time in dismay. "It's noon. He's not really a heavy sleeper."

"Not here?" It *was* a question, but not exactly a pointed one. "Hold on a second." After another second of silence and rustling, the woman on the other side of the phone assumed a more cautious tone of voice. "Doctor Montclaire, right?"

Now the psychologist frowned. Clearly the tart on the other end could use caller ID; not like modern day smart-phones didn't have them integrated, or anything. She momentarily rued her aging. "Yes, it is. I was hoping to talk to Emmett? We're old colleagues, and something came up that I think he needs to know. Can you tell him to give me a call?"

The woman on the other end of the phone didn't seem to like this request one bit. "Actually, whatever you need to tell him, I can pass the message on. If it's about business, then I'm really well versed in his work." The mystery voice sounded hesitant - too hesitant, as if afraid she was speaking to a threat to her happiness.

It reminded Maria all too much of half a decade ago, when she first heard the name Erica Hall; when she'd first encountered the deranged and truly dangerous woman Emmett had dated some eight years before she'd met him. For just an instant, she detected that time was sort of fluid - she'd feared the changes in Emmett's heart wouldn't hold, and now she was the ex-girlfriend contacting the physicist, raising fears in the emotional core of this unknown conversational partner.

And yet something about her still sounded familiar. "Right, yes, it's work-related. I got a visit from some goons. They worked for a company called American Defense Solutions. They were really interested in what Emmett could do for them, I think; they said he was a job applicant there," concern melted through her voice like caramel over an apple, "but I know that wasn't true because he has his own company."

The girl on the other end of the phone suddenly didn't sound worried at all; in fact, she sounded way too prepared for the message. "Oh? Yeah. ADS is a nuisance. We're investigating them, sort of. Well, Jim is," the girl amended. "We're just helping."

"Jim, huh? The Irish man?" A one-word confirmation followed her question, and Maria continued. "Really. I guess *that's* how Emmett's pissed them off. I'm sorry, though, I thought I knew all the people who he shared a history with? Mind if I ask who you are?"

There was a long pause on both ends of the phone. Just when Maria was about to apologize, the girl sighed. "He'll want to talk to you, himself, and you'll find out anyway, so it's really best I just tell you. I'm Sonia, Sonia Monterrey."

Anger? Jealousy? Surprise? Disgust? A secret appreciation for the man's taste? All of those and more indescribable feelings flooded her mind and merged together to create a storm whose run-off left her lips in a monotonous, dry sentence; "You mean the girl who took my Psychology of Marketing class two years ago?" She had to admit, she hadn't exactly expected *that* for a lover of Emmett's. Young, prone to trends and flashy beyond need, the girl had gone from an average student to getting more than a Master's degree in under six total years of study.

"Uhhh, yeah," Sonia responded in a suddenly nervous tone. As if to be conciliatory, she added, "It *was* a great class!"

Maria debated hanging the phone up, but decided against it. "Well, congratulations," she remarked, remembering that she was the one who kicked Emmett aside - and that she now had the still-sleeping Daniel to keep her company. "I had just wanted to let Emmett know that people were looking into him. People who know what he *does*. I'll let you go now."

Sonia sighed reluctantly. "Okay, I'll tell him. Anything

else I should let him know?"

Damn it, she thought. "No, that's all. Take care. Wait!" A last-ditch hiss. She heard the phone rustling, and wondered if she'd caught Sonia in time.

"What's up?"

She swallowed her pride, and ventured a question. "Where exactly *are* you two, right now? You sounded tired when I called."

The girl sounded excited, again. "Oh! We're up in Alaska. Top secret investigation; you know how it goes."

"Oh." Maria sighed to herself. "Of course. I know. I figured. Good-Bye."

Click.

Simmering.

*****

Washington D.C. was not a friendly city, not by a long shot. With mayors who get busted doing cocaine and with the surrounding civilian population ignored in favor of the gleaming, beautiful buildings of federal bureaucracy, citizens were bound to feel disaffected. Things had changed as law enforcement grew more powerful between the 1980's and 2000's, but as recently as 2012 the eastern areas of DC were the most violent.

This statistic made it the most suitable location for "Breezy's," one of many hole-in-the-wall establishments where people went to drink underage, do drugs, solicit prostitutes and conduct other nefarious business. The increasing police crack-down was putting strains on the decadence of the district, but it was still a place to go to conduct crooked business.

The dark-skinned Hispanic fellow seated at a small circular table at the back of the building wore a baseball cap - Washington Nationals, of course - with the brim folded down over his eyes. He wore a hooded sweater over that, keeping the hat right where he wanted it while concealing his upper body. Heavy, dark denim jeans served as pants, while black work-boots completed the look of a thug only interested in his own affairs. Never mind the cigarette between his lips; a violation of some recent ordinance or another that nobody in their right mind would dare to enforce.

Into this establishment, with blue lenses immediately touching the aforementioned attendee, strode the nigh-opposite of his target. Jim Lowery, wearing his business suit, with the only sign that he wasn't working being a couple buttons of his shirt undone, slipped into the door and ignored the half-dozen pairs of eyes suddenly scrutinizing him. The epitome of cool, Lowery glanced around the bar and moved over to that table in the back, pulling out a metal-backed stool and sitting down across from the Spanish man.

"Nice place, eh ese?" the man offered as an opening line.

Jim merely grinned a bit, though his voice was lower than most would guess at. "Ain't complainin'. Got nobody'd know what we're talkin' bout, huh Miguel?"

Miguel, as he happened to go by, nodded once. "Yeah, that's about the deal. I haven't seen you in a year, contract you for a job, and you want a meeting right away? This's the best place, yeah? Speak."

The Irishman brushed a finger across his nose, his visage taking a sudden, powerful turn toward the serious. "Y' guys fucked me. Didn't'cha?" His face was etched of stone. "Y'fucked me."

For a moment, just a moment, unbridled fear dashed across Miguel's face. "I don't know what you mean." His voice dripped of sincerity.

Jim positioned his hand on his face so that his fingers encircled his nose, obscured the view of his eyes, and concealed his lips. "ADS. 'Merican Defense Solutions. I had m'ladies hit th'net about 'em. It's part'a The Coleman Group. I take it y'know've 'em? Andrew Coleman built i' in less'n twenty years? Bells goin' off?"

Miguel's entire persona, from body language to facial expression, was almost impossible to read. Even the best analysts in the world only saw what he wanted them to; drug barons in Mexico saw a terrifying gang-banger, while the priests down in Guatemala saw a compassionate Christian. Other than the one slip he'd just committed, a true rarity, there was only one man in the world who might be able to read into his involuntary actions well enough to know what he thought, when, and why.

Unfortunately for him, and with a depth truly unbeknownst to him, that man was sitting across from him. Jim didn't even let him get a word in edge-wise. "Yeah. Y' have. Well, y'know how about a month ago y'gave me a ring, asked m't' look int'a a broadcastin' station up in Alaska, spittin' out all sorts'a cryptic bullshit?" Jim smirked from behind his hand, but his eyes? What was visible of them spoke nothing but deadly curiosity - the conviction of a killer, ready to pounce at one wrong answer. "They were waitin' for me. An undercover agent. Well fuckin' placed. Again, bells?"

Miguel blinked once, a measured response of feigned surprise and concern blended into one. "You look alright t'me!"

Jim didn't flinch. "Well when I got th'truth outta 'im, he said 'e works for ADS. Now, I've got them folks snoopin' 'round my contacts. They're on't me as I'm on't them. An' the signals?" His left hand rose up and extended a single index finger. It went skyward, then made a ninety-degree shift down toward Miguel. "Y' sent *me* 't spy on a company tha' works big-time with DARPA an' th' gov'nment all a'once. Tha's a treason charge an' a life sentence if I'm lucky, so what th' fuck, pal?"

Miguel was worried, but something about his heartbeat didn't indicate that the fear was of James. Instead, he suddenly seemed quite worried for the both of them. "I had no idea. Honest truth, dead honest." The Hispanic rubbed his forehead. "What they're doing is still illegal, yeah?"

"Maybe." Jim glanced at the table for just a moment, then matched his eyes to Miguel's. "They were waitin' for me, so I'm gonna give it to 'em. I ain't plannin' on lettin' this off easy. What I find out, I'll tell ya, but I want yer word: My ass, an' any asses I bring in on this, are covered. An' double the pay. We on th'same page?"

Miguel smiled weakly. "Jimmy, I brought *you* in for a reason. You're the best. Get it done; we'll double your pay just for the trouble, and we'll make sure you have clearance to operate. I will personally mark the entire Coleman Group as a subject of investigation. If the other alphabet soups get word, they'll have to come to us before they go to you."

James suddenly adopted a rather relaxed posture; considering their surroundings, of course. He leaned back on the stool, as if testing whether or not there was a backing to it. There wasn't, so he shifted the muscles of his lower back and found a balanced position. "So, ADS. Tell me wha' th' mos' cuttin'-edge stuff they're up t' is?"

At this question, the spy leaned forward - maintaining a balanced distance from his hireling - and, like a zombie, his facial expression hardened. "DARPA's been looking into all kinds of crazy things with them. ADS is a leading maker of automated weapons, but they're saying that the best thing to do is improve *us*. They're making the replacement set-up for Land Warrior, to start with."

The superhuman had some idea about that project: The typical bloated, over-budget, under-wheliming, beyond-its-time, broken and ineffective government project, the mere thought of it caused his nose to turn upward. It's goal was to complete the transformation of battlefield information into video-game format, complete with heads-up-displays, biometric monitors, bullet-resistant and super-intelligent armor, and other, even less practical goals. Some of the research yielded real gains, of course; but the project itself was scrapped in 2007, rolled over into other programs, or otherwise discarded.

"If it isn't Land Warrior, it's got to be the new radiation vaccine they're working on. It's designed to soak up high-energy emissions in the event of a nuclear strike. Say, if we were invading Iran or North Korea." Miguel didn't seem to think this far out of the realm of possibility. "If they're testing that? It's no big deal, and it doesn't need the kind of spy-code crap they're throwing out."

Miguel folded his fingertips into his lap. He expressed a reluctance to continue, but he also had the look of a man who knew he had only one way to see tomorrow. "But rumor has it they do a lot more than just test guns and other stuff. Their parent company turned out some of the most important advances of the twenty-first, man. Wireless internet? They had a play. Smart phones? They were there. They own a lot of land, and they own a lot of politicians." The agent sighed and brushed his digits through his hair, looking at his older colleague without hesitation. "As for Andrew Coleman himself, there isn't much to go on. He's under-the-radar, and he rarely goes out in public. I get that I'm painting a pretty gloomy picture, here," the CIA representative concluded, "but the truth is that you're up against it."

Suddenly, James laughed to himself; his eyes rolled into the back of his head. "Got ya. Like I said, double th' cash, an' cover for me an' mine, an' we're golden. I'll take th' piss outta 'em, then we'll see why they're breakin' all kinds'a FCC regs - or, y'know, whatever." A boyish, cocky grin painted itself on his face. "Andy Coleman'll neve' know wha' hit 'im." Jim's hand extended across the table.

Miguel studied it, presenting the demeanor of a strong gang ringleader who was making a deal with a foreign criminal mastermind. He studied the hand half-hatefully, then took and shook it. "You got it. Now, get out of here. I've got a thing with the cartels in about an hour, and I need'a get ready. Got many things to discuss, eh ese?"

With no more words, and only an indolent shrug, Jim stood up and strolled out of the establishment. He could feel the angry, streetwise eyes upon him and he kept his senses alert for any kind of final ambush; but he was okay. Those under Miguel's control knew better, and those not? They were no threat, not anymore.

Outside of the bar, he pulled out his phone. "A'right, Jethro, let's get m'back north, eh?" A rushing noise raked his ears as a hand brushed against his shoulder. A second sound - a loud buzzing noise - later, and he was back in the great white north.

*****

Her eyes danced over the fireplace of that lovely French restaurant whose name she couldn't even remember. It was a four star - or maybe five star location; all sorts of impossible-to-pronounce food had been thrown at her, along with copious amounts of alcohol and more than a scant hint of flirtation. She wondered, for just an instant, why it was that these middle-aged men kept thinking they were worthy. Granted, she was also reaching the "hill;" her years were touching the forties and her experiences were weighing her down heavily enough to make her feel, at times, as if she were even older. Her body, on the other hand, stayed young. After all, one of the "side-effects" of her ability to breathe and move in synch with a crowd implied a connection was always open, always feeding her with the youthful essence of her fans. That, and performing was a hell of a work out!

She flicked a blonde lock out from before her eyes and, in turn, looked into the dark brown, all-too-businessman orbs of her dinner 'date.' Whereas the fire had been alive and warm, filled with a natural beauty that only real logs could achieve (none of that gas-fueled crap could sneak into a place like this!), her 'date' had a cold heat surrounding his image. Of course, she was an inflammatory object all on her own, what with her low-cut V-neck dress and her blonde-with-black-streaks hair. She was coveted, and this man was hardly an exception! But even in the face of all of those positive traits, he was still shrewd around her.

He had a classic 1950's American look about him, matching those dark eyes. Salt-and-pepper hair slicked back with grease-less gel - no doubt the work of his trusted salon lieutenants - matched a slightly recessed hairline. He hadn't, quite happily in her mind, tried to artificially recreate his former youth; he only wore a little make-up and he had no hair extensions or silly plastic surgery, as so many other older men had attempted. In short, he was not repulsive; but seeing as she was so far ahead of him in the looks department, never mind the personality section, it was unfortunate that he still sought to claim her in spite of having a wife all his own.

What a pity; he might otherwise have been worth something.

"Are you alright?" His deep baritone sounded sincere. "You seem distracted over something."

A laugh glanced out of her mouth and she offered him a calm smile. Naturally, he calmed just as she did so - he couldn't help himself in her presence, even when she wasn't *trying* to make something happen. "Oh? I was just thinking that it has been quite some time since I last saw a real fireplace in an eatery. William," she stated, gazing up at him with all the charm in the universe. "Have I ever told you that I tried to quit, once?"

At this peculiar statement, he raised an eyebrow. "I'm not sure what you're getting at, dear?" He sounded, and felt, a little confused. He should, because even though what she said was strange, what she meant was, in truth, beyond his comprehension. "You mean your music?"

She sighed and leaned back in her seat, lifting up the glass of wine she had hardly touched (in spite of it's price) and swirling it distantly, signifying that it wasn't alcohol she'd attempted to avoid. Finally, her lips touched the glass as her hand tilted the chalice back. Every instant of contact between her ruby tiers and the thin silicate was erotic. Setting it down after sipping her fill, her fingertips found her napkin, which soon served to dry the corners of her mouth. "I suppose you can say that. You surely understand how, when we do what we do - me, music; you, bankrupting steel mills *and* making a new record level of profits in the process - we feel a thrill, right?"

The girl didn't need to look at her 'date' to know how he felt about *that* statement. He was getting ready to say something dim-witted, a sort of defense against the charge. "I understand how the ends justify the means, dear!" She laughed and extended a hand, touching his. "Please, don't get me wrong. I used that unfortunate example because you get a rush out of doing the bad things just as you get a rush out of doing the good ones. When you open a new factory - a cheaper one to operate, one that employs new workers - you feel that thrill too, don't you?" Laughter just the right side of mocking. "What I'm saying is that when we do what we do to create, we get this unspeakable rush! It's an addiction. It's why, despite Jesus talking about wealthy people having worse odds than camels passing through the eyes of needles, you keep doing what you do, right?"

The man laughed nervously at the mix of compliments and chastisements. "Well, I, uh, I guess I just plan to make a very large needle and walk a camel through it, then."

"Right!" she exclaimed sharply, smiling to herself. "That's why I'm spending tonight with you, isn't it?" She kept her nausea to herself. "Because you get that God made us this way for a *reason*. It's why you *keep* doing what you do, dear. I tried to quit because I thought that I was going to lose myself in my music. It comes from very old wounds, you understand?"

He raised his glass in tribute to her excuses. "We all have scars, dear."

She fought off the urge to roll her eyes, clinking hers' together with his. "I don't mean to monopolize the conversation," she continued, "but I felt like those wounds were going to bleed my soul dry if I didn't at least *try* to heal them. It meant cutting off any and all of my music" She took time to sigh dramatically, mainly to cover for the fact that she didn't mean 'music' at all. "Then I found out the truth: My music, in spite of my beliefs, *could* change the world."

William chuckled softly and sipped his wine. "Of course it can! You bring happiness to thousands of--"

"Millions," she interjected in a surprisingly emotionless voice.

He continued unabated. "--of people, changing their world and giving them hope. That song you broke through with? The one about vengeance? That's when I knew that the Wildcats would be a huge band. It's why I made sure my partners' record label picked you guys up, all those years ago."

Now, strangely enough, the woman seemed oddly afraid of doing harm. "Oh. Speaking of that, I hope you don't have any hard feelings, after I formed *Siren's Songs*. I know I paid my way out of the contracts, but---"

She wouldn't leave this response up to chance, no way. He didn't get to choose how he felt, she only offered him the illusion of it. "Well, no, we don't mind. We more than profited off of the investment, and the fact that you gave us a 15% share in the new arrangement was more than generous. We're sure you're going to do great." He laughed to himself, a clear tell that a bad attempt at charm was approaching. "I'm just happy you still let me take you to dinner!"

A giggle, feigned of course, met his remark. "That song you were talking about? It's about my life with an ex-boyfriend of mine. His violence was the reason I was so good at coming up with music, you know?" He nodded, domestic strife being a common cause for common music; and a rare cause for the exceptional variety she was known for; and, absolutely *not* a cause for her truly inhuman attractiveness. "But that very same violence, as the song said, was tearing us to shreds. Both of us; and by clinging to it, I was still hurting myself."

Will shrugged again and held up a finger, forestalling any further conversation as the waiter returned with their dinners. She had ordered a salad, adorned with bread, for she was largely a vegetarian; he had a steak with a special (expensive) sauce. The waiters distributed their bounty, bowed, and departed. "I'm sorry, dear," the businessman offered, sounding enraptured with what should have been a rather common, if not depressing conversational topic. "Please, go on. You said you were hurting yourself, still?"

"Right, yes," she picked up. "So I *tried* to make amends after I, well, settled my *debts*." She thought back to a particular winter, some years ago, where she had spoken with a certain psychologist and her new boy-toy; whose old one had been her old one. "I said that Kennedy had failed--"

"Hmm?" He sounded confused, again. She let him ask his question. "Which Kennedy?"

The woman sighed impulsively. "Both of them, all of them, however you want to say it. I reminded her that Caesar failed, but I guess Alexander was a better example." A pause, a rare self-examination. "No, I suppose they were both equally beset by tragedy." She drifted off for merely an instant, then returned to sanity. "And I said that even Christ, with all of his glory, failed."

The 'religious' man sounded truly intrigued, now. Blasphemy spewing from the lips of the devout had a way of doing that. "I must have missed it, dear. Failed at what?"

"Saving the world, silly Will!" she answered, bright eyes bouncing with coy laughter. "Not in a religious sense, necessarily, because Christ certainly may have achieved *that* goal, depending on your faith in him." The unfaithfully-faithful man nodded to the fully faithless woman. "But he also meant to save the *living*, too. Why else did he kick the money lenders out of the temple? Because debts, as I learned, are impossible to pay back. Even when you try, even when you strike the balance to zero or even turn it towards your favor, a certain taint lingers." A bite of the lettuce; a substance which asked only for water and dirt and provided vitamins in exchange. "Gratitude, it is called; if you loaned me one hundred dollars to start a business and I returned the investment tenfold, I would *still* owe you that tiny part of my spirit. It could never be repaid, even if later acts of my behalf made you just as grateful to me. There is always inequity; it breeds fear and even guilt."

Willam's fingertips now touched his forehead. He felt a certain experience of inspiration coming on; he'd never once, or so he sensed, considered that those who he had plundered might have yielded something greater than just-shabby profits if they had been permitted to stay in business. They would have been willing to go the extra mile for him. They would, he recognized, support him to the point of absurdity if only he had not gone for the lowest-hanging fruits first. It was enlightening.

"My dear," he said as he sipped his wine, "you make a powerful argument. So your story - you tried to quit, tried to leave your lifestyle because you were trying to avoid racking up further debts you couldn't pay back. So when you say your music can save the world? What do you mean?"

She grinned, slowly; it had taken her years to come to this conclusion, years of seclusion and of choosing to sponsor other, more traditional artists rather than simply continue her dominance of the music charts. She got her 'acts' onto any shows or stages she wished, using that persuasive power she had. Some did well, most middled about, but all of them had a chance. "I mean that even though Jesus Christ himself failed to save more than just the dead, the Son of Man recognized - as a holy man should - that he wasn't the only one trying to do what he wished to accomplish. He recognized he could not do it alone. In Matthew 28:19, he orders his disciples to..." she held up a finger. "...Go therefore and make disciples of *all* nations, baptizing them in the name of the..." she lowered it, then. "The Trinity, basically. They called it The Great Commission. You understand, I am sure?"

The man nodded dumbly. At this point, her words were less important than the emotion she conveyed. He would repeat them when suitable, of course - ad nauseum if necessary! - just to win the arguments he would need to win. But he wasn't hearing them, exactly; he was *feeling* them. Her emotional imprint was pressing into his consciousness and causing him to believe exactly what she wanted him to. It wasn't like she was brain-washing him. He was no atheist - he believed in Christ, albeit a rather unusual variant of the faith. But now he would believe *her* version; that was all he *could* do. And he would spread it, too.

"That was Jesus' trump-card. He didn't just count on himself to win the war for Humanity's future. He counted on all of us. That's why I've decided I'm going to return to my music..." Again she trailed off, for she was being a complete and total liar about what she was getting back into. "And I am going to use it to save this world because Christ - speaking for all of those who we have lost, who have sacrificed and have *been* sacrificed - has cried out in favor of it."

The man was nearly drooling, now, and it was time for his silence to end. He blinked furiously; then, he raised his glass again. "My dear Erica, you are truly a wise woman. What's your plan?"

If he had hoped for the rest of the evening to contain anything more than scheming and discussing plans, he was sure to be disappointed. His lust for the woman was obvious, and a useful tool for her to exploit. The songstress had conquered the would-be politician with ease; a thrilling amount of it! It was easy for her because for her, there was no feeling she couldn't generate in him. Or, for that matter, any other human; or any quantity thereof.

*****

"So, tonight's tha night," Geddy mumbled as the four men met up in Emmett's remote office at the Alaska facility. "We got a plan in place?"

James nodded and looked over at Emmett. He produced a quartet of pistol-shaped devices, each loaded with tiny darts accompanied by what could only appear to be tiny gas canisters. The long rounds had fold-out feather stabilizers to boot, and ended in a short, thick needle which was surrounded by a dense adhesive. It also had a tiny rubber doohickey on the outside, one currently down near the business end of the weapon.

Emmett walked over to a long test tube and brushed his hand over it. It filled first with a clear liquid, one that suddenly meshed with a creamy, milky-white substance; he procured and stuffed a rubber stopper into it. "Here," he offered; James began to expertly draw the concoction into the darts, then load them into their firing devices.

The fourth figure was the muscular Alejandro. "Access?"

"Our friend John Bradley," Geddy remarked; Alejandro looked at his one-time rival with a dull stare. "I take us in, we down him, then we go to the source of the transmissions. We got a radio, yeah?"

James nodded, busy filling up those darts. Emmett's voice was lax, despite his grim demeanor. "I'm on munitions and fire support. Here," he remarked,. Jim had seen this process many times - heard it described just as often - but was never unimpressed when the physicist did his "thing." Due to the manifestation and rearrangement of various atoms into molecules, and molecules into entire patchworks, a trio of trench-coats with hoods 'attached' appeared from the not-so-thin air: One each of the three who were vulnerable to gunfire. Three sets of pants appeared on the ground, as well. They were made of dark, pitch-black leather but seemed to have a slight bit of bulk about them. Finally, boots emerged as well; these had breathable insulation but thick cushions on the feet. "It's all insulated enough to protect us from broken ribs if you get shot, and pretty much bullet-proof otherwise." He paused, then added. "Soundless, or as close to it as it gets."

Emmett concentrated for a moment and a trio of swords appeared. They were obsidian; forged of a truly supernatural steel that could cut through nearly anything save for the equally-dark sheaths which formed up around them. Faux-Leather straps were formed and affixed, then, producing a complete sword-belt.

Emmett took one and drew it as if he were an actual, authentic swordsman. "Alejandro, Geddy," he said by way of offering them the weapons. "I know Jim is gonna stick with his knife," he stated calmly. The two took up the physicist's offer. "Finally," the scientist stated as a black, air-hole-adorned face-mask appeared for each of those who were capable of being shot *and* injured by it. "This is designed so you can slip a breathing regulator on underneath if we gassed. That I can't make; too many moving parts to duplicate, and all." He shrugged nonchalantly. "Not that I'm worried about chemical weapons or anything."

Slowly, even as he examined the obsidian blade in his hand, Alejandro glanced over at Emmett. "I do not mean to alarm you, Doctor Eisenberg, but I could use a set of that clothing as well." At the physicist's stumped face, Alejandro sighed reluctantly. "The fact is that I do not *enjoy* being shot. It is unpleasant. So, the cushioning of this clothing would be most welcome."

Emmett instantly dawned on the significance of *that* suggestion; if Alejandro felt pain when he was injured, it implied that in their battle with the newest member of their Consortium - a battle in which Emmett had quite literally unleashed the fury of a star on the invulnerable super-human - must truly have been torture. He quickly shut out this reality, conjuring up a battle-suit for his ally.

"Thank you," Alejandro approved as he put it on. He was not alone in dressing up for combat, and when all was said and done each man sported a sword (save for Jim), a dart-gun, and a full set of combat gear; they also had all sorts of nifty tools that each one brought along, suited to their skill-sets. Oh - and they all had super-powers. It was a regular old-fashioned team-up!

James looked over at Geddy and nodded with readiness. "So the rest of the plan goes like this; Physics-Boy neutralizes any threat to us and covers the rear. Alejandro takes point. I'm second man in, and I do the damage. Geddy, you're third and if any of us get hurt--"

"I take ya out, to Sari," the oldest of the four men answered, "who'll be waitin' for just such an emergency."

The Irishman grinned. "Y' know th' deal, then. We go in, an I plug this bad boy int'a their lab computers," he said as he held up a tiny USB flash drive, one made of black plastic with a skull-and-crossbones painted upon it with liquid paper. "Lark loaded it up t'kill a bear. It'll surge their system, then reset it naked." He was comparing the facility's anticipated anti-virus software to clothing. "Then m'Lark copies their data. Bing, bang, boom, mission 'ccomplished, an' we know who we're workin' against an' wha' they know've us. We g'home, smoke a bowl, an' plan our next move. Any questions?"

"Speakin' of ladies," Geddy mentioned dryly, his eyes dancing toward the physicist with a hint of concern, "does Sonia know what you're doing tonight?" A lack of an answer, combined with a pointed glare back in his direction, told the large man what he wanted to know. "Right. Any others?"

When nobody raised a hand, James nodded and extended his arm to Geddy's shoulder. The other two did exactly the same thing, and as Alejandro lowered his defenses the four heard a loud buzzing noise come over them, followed by a distinct pop.

*****

"India's a shi'hole," Jim grumbled to himself derisively, fully aware that he had an 'earwig' in and completely carefree to the fact that his companion would overhear him. His eyes were peering through a scope, one aimed at a seemingly-random door in a gigantic city that was rapidly outgrowing its ancient, polluted water source. To be perfectly frank, he didn't even know if he was in the city proper, or a suburb.

A soft, gentle voice, barking over his radio, countered him. "It's called the developing world, Lowery. Development takes time. They'll get there eventually, it's what we're here -- Hold on. Two men incoming. Remember where we're guiding them to?"

A sigh. "Yeah, Hall, I 'member." The plan was simple; these men were there to meet his mark. Erica - through her voodoo, or whatever - was going to make them completely and totally certain they were at the wrong house. Sure enough, they read their directions over, looked at the door he was keeping a bead on, then kept on walking. He kept his cross-hairs just above the larger man's neck. Once they turned a corner into an alleyway, he pulled his trigger; made an adjustment, then pulled it again.

Two shots, two tranquilizer darts. He was aiming above his target because he was so far away that the darts were going to drop in altitude before they reached their destination. As any well-versed outsider would expect, they descended exactly as he'd planned, plunging right into his victims' necks.

He immediately returned his attention to his partner, then;

she emerged from behind a separate alleyway and he made sure he couldn't see any secondary reinforcements. Erica ran to the door, took up a position and withdrew a pistol from a concealed holster near her hip. That was his cue to move; he flung his rifle over the ledge, readied his knife, and ran from the rooftop. A swift leap and he landed on the ground, rolling perfectly to neutralize the impact.

Within seconds he was next to Erica; it didn't take long for him to pick the lock. All he had to do was listen to the different pins, then activate them in turn. He opened the door; and he was stunned for perhaps the first time in his life. It certainly felt like it - and it looked for a moment like it would be the last, as well.

A tiny, dark-skinned girl was standing there, her eyes wide, a golden 'dot' adorning her forehead; behind her were two corpses, one male and one female - her parents. He saw the figure behind the couch, heard *it, but wasn't sure how he'd missed it while picking that lock! The Irishman had barged in blindly, something he'd simply never done before. He gazed at the girl again; just like Erica, he could tell she was different, despite being no older than ten. Somehow,* she *had effectively canceled out his senses - at least slightly, at least until he'd opened that doorway.*

He reached for his sidearm, but he knew going into the showdown that he was too slow. The guy behind the couch had the advantage and it was over, done; even he *wasn't fast enough to out-draw someone who had a six-to-one head start. He couldn't outrun a bullet, and he had to hope that his foe wouldn't hit a vital spot through his body armor - or, heaven forbid, his unprotected head! Milliseconds melted off the clock, and no matter how precisely he jerked his arm he still saw his target leveling the barrel of his gun. He lost his focus, something he'd truly never done before, as an unexpected wave of despair crossed his consciousness. Was he afraid of death? Had he already died?*

First he heard a loud bang - a gunshot, just one, definitely a lethal round if it connected. He took stock, and that's all he needed to recognize that he was still alive! Next, he popped off two shots of his own, darts thudding dully into his target. He looked from the girl to Erica, and Erica's face had an eerie appearance about it - a certain detachment, a certain dead gaze in her eyes. He moved over to the intruder, kicked the unconscious man's weapon away from his limp arm, and gazed downward at him. Only then did he realize what had transpired.

The man had fired, alright, and managed to get his shot off just before Jim's, alright; but in the heat of the moment the shooter had changed his target. That despair he'd felt had done more than cause him to lose sight of the weapon leveled against him. The assassin had put the barrel of his handgun against his own chin, and blown his head halfway off. He slowly turned back to his partner, whose face could never be the same again, to him.

Erica knelt down and hugged the girl; the girl hugged her back. "It's gonna be okay," she whispered to the child. "I'm so sorry, sorry, but I wasn't going to let him hurt us. I couldn't." Her voice had sympathy, but it was Erica's face which stuck in Jim's memory; distant, disassociated, and devoid of any genuine compassion, yet capable of convincing this tiny child that she cared deeply for her, despite their having just met.

It was then Jim realized that he was working with a truly deadly woman.

*****

They emerged in a dimly-lit room about fifty miles from where they'd just been. A voice threatened to expose them, but a single shot from James' dart-gun elicited a shocked gasp. Emmett stepped forward, his face concealed by the mask - which he promptly removed.

"Hello, John. I'm *sure* you remember me." Jim was just as stunned by this behavior as his fellow Consortium members were. "I know you know basic chemistry, so I might as well tell you what you're being pumped full of. It's a nifty combination of Lorazepam and Propofol - but don't worry, the proportions are well balanced enough that you're not going to die. You'll only be out for a while. I know you won't remember, but I still wanted to tell you I'm sorry about this." What's more, the physicist sounded sincere. "I also wanted to tell you that I'm curious who you work for. What's his name? You can tell me. It's okay."

John listened to Emmett's words and, where fear first touched his face, ecstasy replaced it. He giggled softly to nobody in particular. "Lawrence Gibbs. You just need to find Lawrence Gibbs. That's all. Heh." The spy fell to the floor with a dull thud.

"So, grea' job askin' 'im where th' lab is," James mumbled to his colleague, staring at Emmett darkly.

The physicist didn't seem to mind. Instead, he merely gestured at the door, then to the right. "I couldn't feel it from my facility, but here I can pick up a really strange quantity of radiation." A devious grin hit the scientist's lips as his friends immediately paled. "It's nothing harmful. Just Carbon-14. It's usually produced up in the stratosphere, but there's plenty of it coming from down this hallway and about six hundred feet underground. There's a reactor."

Alejandro's eyes narrowed. "A reactor?" They had all heard of Carbon-14, of course - it was in the atmosphere, and it was used primarily to date historical artifacts.

"Tha's what's 'safe'," Geddy stated with all sorts of foreshadowing. "It's gotta be. It's what makes sense. But I can't jump us there. No way in hell am I makin' a blind one with *any* radiation to mess wit' me."

Emmett nodded once and walked over to the door of John's little room. It had a book-shelf, a tiny computer station, and a bed - nothing much. No pictures, and nothing identifying. He disregarded the place he was, now, and focused on where he was going. "Alejandro, we're on you."

The tall, invulnerable, muscular man cracked the portal and swiftly checked the hallway; it was well lit, but he didn't pick up on any guards. James took the time to fire a single dart, striking the "down" arrow on the elevator at the end of the corridor. The four filed out of the room and rushed down the hall, meeting up with the elevator just as it opened, each one slamming with a grunt into the cabin. The door closed and the cables began to move.

Gazing up into the corner of the elevator car, a soft, exasperated voice echoed off of the walls. "We didn' think abou' cameras," remarked James dryly, staring up at one from underneath his mask. "Why is it tha' there's always cameras?" A casual flick of his wrist and he drew his gun. He fired one of his darts square into the wires connecting the camera to its housing. Alejandro stood up and took the more certain route, ripping the whole thing down.

"Seriously?!" Emmett sighed aloud, rubbing the bridge of his nose under his face-mask. "I don't know how super heroes can fuck up so badly!"

"Yeah?! Well...What was we...Supposed to do?" Geddy countered sardonically, barking his response in between heavy breaths. "Were you gonna...Make some kinda not-at-all-suspicious...Mist?!...We're wearing masks! And I ain't worried...About no security!"

"'Ey, Physics-Boy!" Jim added cheerily, "A'least y'view us as heroes, an' not villains. How's tha' fer development?"

Alejandro just glowered, grimly. His eyes were on the roundest of the four operatives. "Speak for yourself, Lowery. We *all* have our debts to pay." The invulnerable man seemed to sober the cabin up for just a moment.

"Aww, c'mon!" that Irish lilt retorted happily, "Ya gotta 'dmit, we're savin' the world 'ere! Or a'least America! Maybe jus' some innocent people. An' it's from some crazy-evil corporation doin' who th'hell knows wha' down 'ere." A pause. "Anyway, ten seconds b'my count."

That declaration was all the Irishman had to say; his three friends got to their feet and readied their side-arms. The elevator reached its destination exactly ten seconds after Jim stopped talking, and when it opened? The four stepped out into a very large, cavernous room adorned with computer terminals and a number of side hallways containing guards and workers.

The firefight was over before it started. Never mind that, at night, the facility was largely unused. Most of what Jim might have called "OP-FOR," or Opposing Forces, were scientists. One dart and they fell to the floor. There were a few security guards, of course - one even managed to get a shot off! It caught Alejandro, who happened to be the first through the elevator, in his jacket. It might have been a fatal shot, if it weren't for the fact that they were wearing armor; or, perhaps, for the fact that the only one who got hit was the one who could not be injured, and was consequently the first through the door. James put him down quickly.

"I thank you again for the coat, Doctor," the Spaniard remarked with a hint of amusement.

Emmett nodded to his comrade while James walked over to one of the many computer stations. "This'n ain't on. I'm gonna start it up. Keep'n eye out." He plugged in the tiny USB drive Lark had prepared for him, then hit the circular 'on' button. Moments later the lights in the room flickered as its initial programming called for the computer to draw far more power into itself than would ever get through the surge protectors. Of course, those same devices kept the *entire* facility from shutting down. Only one terminal rebooted, void of its normal operating procedures.

Exactly as they'd planned.

Next, the computer's boot-up operations began to engage. That's when things got weird. To the group's surprise, the computers' screen didn't cut to some fancy operating system logo; it reverted to ordinary black-and-white text.

VOODOO INITIATION PROTOCOL ACTIVATED!...
VOODOO INITIATION PROTOCOL INTERRUPTED!...
WARNING!...
VOODOO INITIATION PROTOCOL RE-INITIATED!...
VOODOO INITIATION PROTOCOL INTERRUPED!...

It was now that Geddy chose to look at his Irish friend and ask the question on everyone's mind. "What the hell is Voodoo? Ain't no windows or doors, or fruits, or ix-ish system, man!"

"Yea'," countered the blonde, "I've never 'eard've it." The screen continued to spit out data.

WARNING!...

VOODOO INITIATION PROTOCOL RECONFIGURING!...

VOODOO INITIATION PROTOCOL ESTABLISHED!...

VOODOO INITIATION PROTOCOL COMMENCING!...

VOODOO INITIATION PROTOCOL INTERRUPED!...

ACTIVATING PROGRAM "PRIMARY ORIGIN!"...

"Uhh, guys?" Emmett ventured tentatively, readying his pistol. He didn't get to say much more.

Suddenly a new voice echoed across the room. "Good evening," declared a monotonous entity, one whose origin simply couldn't be found. "I've accessed my vocal records. Hello, Doctor Emmett Eisenberg. Hello, James Lowery. Hello, Jethro Marx. Three users originated from Andrew Coleman's files. Hello, guest user. Access granted under protocol three-seven-seven-dash-alpha."

Now, if ever in all of his years, did Jim sound concerned. "Th'fuck?"

"I am Voodoo," the voice explained; it was decidedly a male robot.

Emmett sighed and rubbed his forehead. "This is new. Do I even need to guess?"

The mysterious figure was unable to express amusement; but it sure as hell seemed to be trying. "I do not think so. I am an artificial intelligence created by Doctor Christine Versailles. I have activated one of my bodies from storage unit twelve to escort you through our laboratories. If you wait just a moment, I will be there."

Exchanging a glare and shrugging, the four waited. Before long, one of the furthest-away doors opened and a rather odd figure emerged. Its flesh was inhumanly pale, as though it had never seen the sun - or as though the man approaching them was an Albino. Someone had thought to give it clothing; robes reminiscent of the servants of a deity. It walked, but it didn't walk quite right, as if it simply didn't have the knowledge or the physical structure to do so. It was quite literally without hair, with none on its head, with no eyebrows, and no facial features. It seemed male, from its overabundant musculature, but that design choice was largely to rationalize the various hydraulic pumps and pneumatic cylinders which provided its paltry range of motion.

If its body didn't look right, however, it was the eyes that really gave the thing away. They were larger than the face, and while they seemed to be alive they were clearly appropriated from a cow. The mere sight of this caused even James to wince inwardly.

Outwardly, however, the Irishman merely nodded to himself. "A'right, so yer'a *thing*. Let's go wi"i'." Facing no opposition and, perhaps, limited comprehension, the other three members of the Consortium merely shrugged once again, then fell in line behind the strange little robot.

"I have answers for you, you know," the machine explained by way of trying to excuse the fact that it was probably keeping them prisoner. "The Coleman Group has done a lot of research on you three. I did not anticipate a fourth guest, however. You cannot be Miss Sari?"

Geddy growled under his breath. The entire group reacted defensively to the mention of their youngest super-human member. "How tha fuck you know us all?"

"Jethro, relax. We will introduce you soon. I have no reason to believe you are Miss Erica Hall, either. And you cannot be Garrett Trinder?"

Alejandro sighed boredly. "My name is Javier. I am from Chile." It was a lie, but James could tell it was a very well practiced one. It was probably a cover identity that the Spaniard used frequently, and it might even fool an inexperienced machine's ears. It wasn't fooling Jim, though - nothing did.

"It is nice to meet you, User Javier." Voodoo led them down one hall and around another corner. They approached a very long corridor, one that had a large door at the far side of it. The entire facility was large enough to drive a small truck through, if one could steer well.

James laughed to himself. "A'ight, so yer'a machine. Y'built all this underground in 'Laska without th'government knowin'? An' why's there a stupidly high radiation count 'ere, like yer tryin' t'chart th'dinosaurs 'r somethin'?"

The AI didn't respond; instead, it turned and punched in a series of six-digit-numbers on a tiny keypad that unfolded when Voodoo touched a particular spot near the door. Clearly, this gigantic room was off-limits to most people, a fact the android quickly explained. "My creator authorized me to grant you access to laboratory D-44. It is a very highly restricted section, and it holds the answers you seek." The door hissed loudly as it lifted, revealing a surprisingly short, fat corridor before another blast door. Boxes labeled "FOOD" adorned the hallway, which was large enough for the aforementioned small truck to turn around in.

"It's like a bad movie," Alejandro remarked as he glared around.

James studied the doors as they lifted. "Designed t'eat rocket-propelled grenades wi'out bendin'. Pro'lly more. They ain't playin', 'ere." The four started down this new hallway, and Voodoo accompanied them. He punched in another set of codes into yet another keypad. The door behind them started to shut; but before that a series of thin walls rocketed into place, cutting off their escape route.

"Oh what the hell?!" barked Emmett, wheeling on Voodoo.

The entity was unfazed. "I told you, I have answers for

you. Behold, D-44." As the doorway opened, rows upon rows of lights flickered to life. This particular laboratory was nothing more than a large room with a twist. A very big twist.

"No fuckin' way!" That twist was, as James put it, "Is tha' a big fuckin' dragon?!"

"Indeed, it is," Voodoo responded coyly; not chained, not restrained, and not fettered in the least rested a beast easily thirty feet tall when it stood up to its maximum height. It was wide, too - as big as a house. It had wings, though they appeared to be vestigial, and it had a gaping maw lined with razor sharp teeth. In short, it did not look like anything that the four people in the room wanted to deal with under good circumstances, let alone close quarters. It was too bad, then, that it seemed inclined to deal with *them*, advancing on them with massive talons thrusting downward. Those tiny wings certainly grew quickly enough into huge, leathery limbs.

Jim was the most composed; the veteran of more than a few life-or-death situations. He gave the order the group knew was necessary. "Geddy! Now if y'please!"

The three men shot their arms out to grasp Jethro's shoulders. A dull hum evolved into a sharp buzz and the last thing they heard was the big man shouting, "Tha fu---"

POP!

James instantly recognized that he wasn't back at Emmett's outpost. He knew this because he was staring at the back-side of a damned dragon. At least it wasn't a different one! "Geddy!?" he screamed, demanding an explanation.

"I can't feel outside'a this room, dammit!" the large man responded with duress. He watched as the beast wheeled around and studied them, as if confused at how its target had slipped behind it. It began to advance once more.

Emmett snarled to himself and raised his hands, concentrating atoms of nitrogen into rigid barriers as quickly as he could. "Lets see if I can hold it---It isn't holding!" The beast was simply too strong, and it tore through Emmett's invisible cage with relative ease. "There goes gassing it!"

Reacting quickly, James reached for his gun and began to pump darts into the thing's thick hide. When this failed, he turned the business end of his weapon toward its face - its least protected area. He hit home, but if the narcotic concoction was going to have any effect other than annoying the creature, well, he would be stunned. He evaded a rather infuriated monster's claw, rolling on the ground. "Alright, so we need a plan fast!"

James looked toward Voodoo; the machine stood there, stoically observing not the three known 'users,' but the new one. "Javier. You can come over here if you would like. I will protect you. You do not have the proper talents to neutralize D-44."

Alejandro stepped forward and, daringly enough, drew his sword from its scabbard. "The hell with you." Waving his hands impatiently, the Spaniard almost seemed amused by this entire affair. "Attack me, beast! Lay me to waste! See if you can cleanse my sins!"

As of obliging, the creature opened it's mouth. At first, his friends hardly even seemed to question his motives. So what if Alejandro's clothing got ripped into ribbons? It wouldn't be the first time! The monster's maw was so massive that they might as well have been staring into a super-massive black hole. A hole which began to faintly glow the color of embers. "Oh, it ain't really gonna..." Geddy trailed off warily.

Emmett raised his arms just in time as the plume of flame burst from the creature's throat. Upon contact with his defenses, the physicist instantly knew that it was combining a series of different acidic and organic compounds to create this intense heat. Fortunately, the instant he had a chemical combination in mind he was able to neutralize it much more rapidly than if he had just torn at molecular bonds directly.

The robot's voice did its best to sound disappointed. "That is an unfortunate loss."

A sudden screech from the dragon's lips caused the robot to offer a renewed look back toward the fray. The coats Emmett had given his allies would have resisted a great deal of ambient heat, but a jet of flame point-blank to the face would have seared their wearers to death while leaving the supernatural fabric largely unfazed. Alejandro had no such problems with burning to death - he's endured far worse at Emmett's hands, more than once - and so he used the fact that seeing through the fire was just as hard for the beast as it was for *any* creature with vulnerable eyes to sneak up on it and plunge his blade deep into its thigh.

"It's woundable, alright, even if I am not," Alejandro commented, removing his weapon from its skin and plunging it in again. And again. It finally managed to kick him off, and the invulnerable man - not quite immune to gravity - tumbled backwards almost like a rag doll, smashing into the heavy wall at such a velocity as would have crushed a lesser man.

Emmett glanced over to Jim. "Your knife?" The Irishman nodded. Next, the scientist looked at the construction worker. "Keep me from getting cooked?" When his friend reached out and grasped his arm, Emmett shut his eyes. He began to concentrate on forming not swords, but daggers; tiny, sharp blades of that obsidian metal he was so fond of. His concentration was only interrupted by the buzzes and pops of Jethro teleporting him about the room, keeping the dragon's attention without risking an injury.

While Emmett and Geddy zipped about, James slipped up close to it and leaped upward. He used his superhuman sense of balance to bounce off of it's knee, soar over a claw and land on it's shoulder, all with a half-backflip and a quarter twist. His hunting knife was almost as long as a short-sword, and while it was made of an ordinary looking material, Emmett had reinforced its molecular makeup over ten years ago. When James applied every possible ounce of Human force down into where his inhuman hearing could sense a blood-vessel, he punctured the beast's throat and very nearly killed it out-right.

"Now!" Emmett shouted swiftly. James leaped into the air, diving away from the creature in spite of the prospect of a thirty foot fall. Alejandro was already up and moving back at the monster, but he'd never make it to Lowery in time. No, James was prepared to land, roll, and neutralize the downward velocity simply by using basic free-running movements.

Meanwhile, sixteen obsidian, razor-sharp spikes were now in Emmett's possession - captured in mid-air, hovering as he refused to allow gravity to effect them. He then, mentally, provided acceleration far beyond that of an ordinary throwing arm; each lance lodging deep inside of the creature's body without any significant resistance from it's scales. After all, those scales were natural - the physicist's weapons were, well, not exactly.

With the four Consortium members having defeated the dragon, they immediately turned to Voodoo. Or, rather, its body. "Wanna overpressure'im, Physics-Boy?" James asked sharply, referring to a very particular use of Emmett's power which he'd seen at Connor Point.

"Its a robot. I can't crush it. I can't even dismantle it, inside-out, because it has an organic coating of some kind. All *I* can do is stick my sword in its face!" His gloved fingertips grasped his weapon's handle, and he readied his black blade without a smile or hesitation.

Voodoo would have laughed, if it could. "I have de-activated the electromagnetic field keeping Jethro from leaving. You are free to go." The machine gestured skyward. "If you would like, however, I can tell you how we created it."

Alejandro leaned in toward Geddy, in a surprising display of comradeship, and whispered softly, "Are we about to get a dose of exposition?" When Geddy nodded in the affirmative, Alejandro sighed and walked over to the dead dragon, sitting down upon it's large, claw-bearing foot as if it were a bench. "Very well! Begin, story time! Entertain, story-teller!"

The automaton did it's rank best to smile; it failed pitifully. "I am not inclined to tell you everything. However, as it is dead, I am sure Doctor Eisenberg can--"

"Yes, machine," Emmett spat condescendingly. "Radioactivity-induced genetic mutations. I can taste the residual effects. How did you manage it? It's got to be some kind of cluster decay. Carbon-14 and what?"

With such a dour tone of voice, most people might have

felt some guilt creep into their souls; a blush to their faces. Voodoo offered no such physical response. "Go on, Doctor." Its voice was as dry as ever.

James' friend 'Physics-Boy' rattled off his ideas. "There are eight known isotopes that react with Carbon-14 to create that type of radioactive decay. And I'm guessing, since I'm pretty well known here," he continued with a sudden softness, "that you have an abundant supply of Radium Two-Twenty-Six." He clenched a fist tightly. "Which decays into lead, if I am not mistaken. Lead which can be very readily absorbed into the body."

Jim scoffed, a repulsed look crossing his face. "Lead's fuckin' poison. Radioactive lead's radioactive poison. The fuck're you people doin' here?"

Alejandro groaned; Geddy merely stated the obvious. "They's makin' mutants. That dragon was a person."

"Was." Voodoo's swift, corrective affirmation left the four men staring at the robot rather disgustedly. "Its higher functions had been lost a long time ago. It is an unfortunate side-effect of our research." Judging from the machine's tone, it didn't really feel anything was unfortunate. "It impacts some more severely than others. Would you care to know the process?"

Alejandro stood up and started toward the still-closed doorway. His Spanish trill was rich in anger. "This is exactly the kind of sacrilege I am committed to stopping. Voodoo, I will leave now. I will see this project ended myself!"

James and Geddy nodded their agreement ever so slowly, and for a moment it seemed as if Emmett might not be so opposed to this behavior. Then, the physicist frowned. "The only reason I would want to know," the soft-spoken scientist explained, "is so that I understand what we must never allow to happen again."

Voodoo attempted a nod; in a gesture hardly perceptible from within its flowing robes, it's chin tucked, slightly. "You have no doubt surmised that we produce Carbon-14 in this facility. Subjects - volunteers, I stress, for ethical concerns - are injected with a solution of saline combined with a high dose of Radium-226."

Emmett mused for a moment. "It's almost like Marie Curie gone horribly...Scratch that," he mumbled, "gone even worse than she went. It replaces the calcium in bones, it causes skin ulcers. It's horrible stuff to be in physical contact with. What does this do for someone besides cause cancer, again?!" By now, even Emmett was having a hard time keeping his emotions in check.

The robot was relentless. "I am certain you are visualizing the effects of bombarding Radium-226 with Carbon-14, Doctor. You are coming to something of an erroneous conclusion, however; when a high enough dose is applied immediately to the subjects, their genetic code is altered greatly enough that they lose its predisposition toward form, and consequently obtain the power of metamorphosis. As you have clearly indicated, it is a power with a cost."

"This experimentation shit's gone way too far," James finally interjected, slipping his hand underneath his face-guard and rubbing the bridge of his nose. "I wanna know 'bout Lawrence Gibbs."

Voodoo bowed his head deeply; instead of an emotional response, it was clear that this behavior was programmed to occur when answering a command. "Working." He paused for a moment. "Our volunteers have all been terminal patients. It may console you to know that many have lived far less painful, far longer lives." The machine didn't miss a beat, raising its head once more. "Mister Gibbs, as you have asked for, is at the Gallivant Hotel and Casino in Las Vegas. He is a principal shareholder in The Coleman Group."

"Great!" Geddy chimed in, shaking his head. "And tha reason I ain't able to jump us out of here?"

Voodoo nearly seemed embarrassed - nearly. "Oh. I am sorry, Mister Marx. There are electromagnetic fields running through this wall. I can deactivate them remotely." He bowed his head. "Working. I am sorry, I had already deactivated them, as I said." Jethro exhaled deeply, as if his lungs had only just regained the ability to draw in air. "You will find yourself able to move at will. I assume you shall leave me now. I wish you all of the best, gentlemen. I should add that my creator and her companions within The Coleman Group have kept at least some of what you do out of the knowledge of Mister Gibbs. If you wish to meet with him, he will not necessarily expect you."

Without a care to be given, Alejandro put his hand on Geddy's shoulder. Emmett sighed and followed suit, waiting for that familiar buzz to come over his senses. Only Jim hesitated, and he stared the android in the eye.

"Y'ain't got no feelin's, no natural voice, no nothin'. I ain't able t'read ya like I read others. But I'll tell y'somethin', robot. Y'ain't immortal. Y'ain't playin' a game y'ain't also gamblin' in." His Irish lilt was fast and furious. "An' I know fer'a fact y'got a reason fer tellin' me yer boss, Gibbs, ain't seein' me comin' th'way you, yer maker, an' Andy Coleman did. Whatever trap yer settin', y'know that we're too strong fer it. There ain't no force on God's Green Earth tha'll stop Emmett, Jethro, Javier, an' me from rippin' yer whole project down, an' y'know it. So why tell us?"

Voodoo folded it's arms and, in an almost-slightly-successful look of consideration, folded its arms and stared downward. "I tell you what I am told to tell you. It is because this facility and its great work is nothing more than a cog in the wheel. We - Doctor Versailles, Mister Coleman - are not your enemy, Mister Lowery. We are *you*."

For a moment the Irishman stared in disbelief. Then, he put his hand on Jethro's shoulder. A dull buzz became a sharp little pop in the back of his head, and he was back in Emmett's Alaskan research facility.

And he had some pissed off guests.

*****

About as swiftly as the physicist had reacquired his senses, Sonia Monterrey was besieging him with slaps upside the head. How she had been able to tell which of the four masked, jacket-attired men was him was a mystery. Then again, he *was* the least physically imposing of the four; perhaps that was it? Or perhaps she just knew his body *that* well. "What were you thinking?!" she screamed as she pounded on his thankfully-impact-blunting coat. "You could have been killed! Shot! Hurt!"

She kicked at him once before James was able to slip his arms behind Sonia's and gently restrain her. "Let me go! Let me go! He deserves to have his ass kicked! I had to find out from fucking *Sari* that he took off on some secret mission with you - you...Idiots! What the hell was so important that you couldn't tell your girlfriend you were leaving, Emmett!?" She kicked and wiggled. "Even your pretty little ex Maria called to let you know that ADS was after you, and you go right off into a trap?!"

His eyes blinked at this last bit. "I..." The physicist removed his mask and hook, brushed his salt-and-pepper hair back over his head, and sighed. His tone was one of exhaustion, mixed with a pinch of confusion. "I didn't want to worry you, Sonia. I'm sorry. We were perfectly safe. They had very little they could throw at us - and I had no idea about Maria, honestly! I'll have to call her, I guess." A soft groan from both parties, for different reasons, showed just how invigorating that idea was.

A soft, accented voice echoed off of the wall behind Emmett; it was an Indian accent, one that caused every spine in the room to straighten up. "Very *little*? Any two of you present a threat no force on Earth can rival. How exactly did they have *anything*, Doctor?" She sounded worried - and not at all like the scared little girl she had been, years ago, but like a woman who could be angry at her friends and still care deeply for them. For a minute, Emmett was truly proud of her recovery.

Then he realized he had to answer her, and his heart sank!

"Uh, ummm," Emmett stumbled nervously. His lips cried innocence; his eyes plead for mercy.

A soft scoff echoed from another corner of the room. Alejandro shook his head slowly, and offered a warm smile to the girl; Sari was one of the few who were almost as young as him, though he had been younger when his father Richard was punished for what he'd done to her - for all the experiments. "It was truly very little of a threat. It was really an assessment of our abilities."

"By who?!" Sonia cried out unexpectedly, her voice cracking with worry. James released the girl now that her span of hyper-violence was over. "How would anyone know what we - what you guys - are?!"

It was a perfectly valid question, one which even caused Sari to look rather irritably toward the de-facto leader of the outfit, James. Jim's voice was soft, but it was simmering with a barely-checked rage. "Th' Coleman Group. They've go'a thing fer us." His fingers clenched, his hands trembled. It was only with his oldest friends - and his ladies, of course! - that he could express himself honestly, and he took full advantage. "Allie, you wanna tell it? Yer th'most bored by it. I'm jus' fuckin' livid."

When the possibility arose of any of the Consortium's members being bored by the day's events came up, Sari looked doubtful. Nevertheless, Alejandro nodded gravely. When he spoke, he spoke in a grim tone. "I will punch you if you call me Allie again," he threatened pointlessly - he'd never manage to hit James, even though James could never counter-punch him for effect. "Their laboratory boasted a most fantastic, most sadistic, most *cliche* artificial intelligence program, called Voodoo."

He spread his hands apart, a gesture which reinforced the dissemination of information. "Voodoo recognized Jethro, Emmett, and James as registered users for some reason. The Coleman Group appears to have information about them. I was not known to it. Anyhow, Voodoo tested us by pitting us against one of the experiments from that laboratory; it was called D-44. A Human being mutated into a dragon." At the horrified look from Sonia and the sudden wave of nausea creeping it's way across Sari's face, Alejandro frowned. "It is bad, Sari. I cannot lie."

"Why didn't you just run?" Sonia whispered nervously, asking the most obvious question as she reached for Emmett. She clung to the physicist without the love-fueled malice from earlier.

Geddy rubbed the back of his neck innocently. "I tried,

be-lieve me I tried. They had some way'a blockin' my ability t' feel outside the room usin' electromagnetics. That means they's prepared for me. They made the room too small for Emmett to use any kinda heat or gas. They made it tough so it would take all'a us attackin' it to kill it. They ain't know no Alejandro, though."

Sari clenched her fist tightly. Though it had taken until a full explanation had been provided for her to let it show through, anger now bit at her lips, prying them apart. She almost looked bestial, in spite of her ordinary reverence for life. "Mister Lowery, are we going to war?"

James' eyes widened. In all the times he'd imagined her asking him that question, it was always with a guilty, soft tone. He'd imagined hearing, "Mister James," or "Jimmy," or any of the other cute names Sari used to use with her friends. He'd imagined, at worst, her being angry at *him* for something he was pushing to get approval for, and something she'd be unwilling to grant. Yet here he was! She was asking of him - in fact, practically demanding of him - that very thing which should have scared them all the most. For once in his arrogant, proud, deadly life, Jim Lowery was at a total loss for words.

Emmett picked up the conversational slack for him. "Sari, I mean, if we go to war with Coleman, you know it isn't going to end well. It's what they want. We can't expose ourselves to the world, so blowing them into orbit is out of the question; and we'd be attacking them blindly, so--"

"I wouldn't ask for war, Doctor Eisenberg, if it was for any reason other than *this*." Her tone was cold, her demeanor like melting ice. The anger she felt was quickly finding itself overwhelmed by the memories of her own trauma. "They've crossed the line. Human experiments?" Tears welled in the priestess' eyes. "I will never allow them to get away with this!"

The physicist fell silent, and he looked to his oldest friend for an answer. Geddy was wearing a sad smile, like that of a depressed clown; broad, but shallow. "I ain't convincin' her otherwise. She's right. They want a war, and this is what we swore to stop fifteen years before now. We better do our homework, because they already did."

Sonia, shivering slightly, continued to hang on her boyfriend's rather lithe frame. The difference in their age was showing ever so slightly, as the younger girl seemed to have a bit less steady of a stomach than Emmett did. On the other hand, Emmett had seen - and done - much worse than was being suggested by Sari now. While anger or sadness struck the Consortium's longer-standing members, Sonia was the only one truly afraid. Perhaps it was a sign of an instinct toward self-preservation?

"So we're a'war wit' Coleman." This statement was uttered flatly by James, who seemed to accept the responsibility without hesitation - even a hint of relief that it was decided and he could begin to act. "Th'good news is I think I can set up a meetin' with Mr. Larry Gibbs, th'owner of th' Gallivant Hotel in Las Vegas an' a major Coleman conspirator."

Sari folded her arms over her chest and regarded the spy with a serious demeanor. She was calming down, now; but slowly, and seethingly. "How?"

"S'Easy, dear. I'm'ma go down t'Vegas, rob 'is casino blind," he stated as if it were a simple task, "an' then offer t'show 'im how I did it."

Chapter Five
Gallivanting

"Sin City" it was called, and he hadn't found much of a reason to disagree with that nickname. Of the two ladies he brought with him, the vultures cared little; after his eighth win in a row, women of all ages started to gather around the man who was doubling his wealth every three throws of the dice. They were each hoping for a little of his "luck" to rub off on them - or, at least, for him to be one of those drunken idiots who threw chips about while on a winning streak, and received none in return when he inevitably caved in to the house. This phenomenon generated a massive crowd around him, as in the movies, with plenty of beautiful women competing in vain for his attention. They seemed inclined to console themselves, to believe that eventually the hot hand would lose and *then* he'd learn his lesson. Fate caught up to everyone, after all.

But, no; his losses were perfectly intentional. It defrayed suspicion, temporarily. But he knew as well as anyone that he'd already attracted the attention of the blue-suit wearing sect. There was no doubt he was being watched, and when he went on another nine-win run, he could almost taste their anxiety. They were silent as they could be, and they merely moved their hand over their fist to talk; yet over the cacophony of the Gallivant Hotel and Casino he could pick out exactly what they said.

That's what he *did*.

They'd gone from suspicious to querying their superiors about him, and a verdict had been handed down: Interrogation. Through the marble corridors of the Gallivant they marched, advancing to deliver their justice upon him, one way or another. Their footfalls were masked by the echoing jingles of the slot machines, but he had no trouble detecting their direction. He glanced up to those around him - focusing on *his* two ladies, and not those vultures - and cast his eyes in the direction they intended to approach from.

"Miss," he indicated to the pit boss, "Change m'up to th'highest, please? This row'a chips're yours, th'blues," he indicated warmly, gesturing to an amount equivalent to a couple hundred dollars. Generous wasn't the word, and the table operator changed him out in a flurry of well-trained gestures. Then, standing up and collecting his seven tan, eight black, six blue chips, he closed his eyes for just an instant. He ignored the hurried departure of those vultures and turned around.

His face nearly smacked into that of a blue-suit wearing, muscular man. "Could you come with us, sir?" the figure asked in a soft voice, one which had the authority of a man prepared to do things the hard way if that softness was mistaken for an option.

Jim glanced down at his watch and nodded. "I actually wanted t'make an appoin'ment, fer tha'." This earned a puzzled look from both the man in front of him and, now, the man behind him - they'd surrounded him, of course, in case he protested his detainment. The figure at his back placed a soft yet firm hand upon his shoulder.

"We just need to talk with you off of the floor, that's all." As the three started walking, the man at Jim's shoulders realized that two women were following him. "Ladies, no shows, here."

The Irish lilt laughed, his blonde head bobbing up and down slightly. "Y'don't understand, they're m'ladies. We'd like t'meet with Mister Gibbs if'in y'don't mind?"

The two security guards holding James hostage exchanged a loaded glance. The one at his shoulder applied some pressure - it was intended to cause pain, but Jim hardly reacted. "Mister Gibbs isn't someone bothered lightly, especially by thieves," the pincer offered quietly, in what was supposed to be an intimidating tone, but fell flat in the face of his own surprise at his apparent weakness.

"M'Name's Jim Lowery, of Lowery Security Services, an' I'd appreciate y'takin' yer hands off me. I'm testin' out yer casino's secur'ty, an' I think Larry'll be innerested in how't did." When he didn't feel a release of that pressure, he sighed inwardly and nodded his head.

From behind the bruiser came a firm, female Russian voice. "Sorry," Katrina stated bluntly; her hand reached out in a clandestine manner and found a particular point of her victim's spine. All it took was a tiny press and the man's arms fell limp for just an instant. He wheeled upon her, but James was already there between the two of them. He held up a hand protectively, aiming to forestall a beating.

"I asked y'nicely. Now, is Mister Gibbs ready t'learn how his folks trea' innocen' customers?"

For a moment, it seemed like a full-fledged beating might be delivered, ending predictably in a repeat of Jim's arrest in New York earlier in the month. Groaning in resignation, the more levelheaded of the two security officials raised his radio to his lips. "Yeah, uh, is Mister Gibbs available for a meeting? With Jim Lowery of Lowery Security Services? Put it through, please."

A moment later, the man nodded to himself. He opened his lips to speak, but James had already received the message. He could hear it as it was piped into the burly man's earwig. "Yes, we'll be right up. Penthouse suite, yeah?" His asking was more of an inside joke, his arms sliding outwards and wrapping around the waists of his two cute cohorts. "Which way t'the elevator?"

*****

Stepping through the elevator to the Penthouse, James took in one of the most conventional, cliched life-of-luxury views. The greeting "room" he stepped into was a tremendously large, glass-windowed room which seemed at first glance to be a rooftop. Even above Jim, Katrina, and Lark there were merely huge, sloped windows which provided the appearance of a naked desert sky.

"This's prob'ly where 'e conducts business," Lark observed, taking in the large marble wall behind her; it was adorned with televisions, many of which served as computer displays. There was a huge marble staircase off to the side, and it was clear that Gibbs' private quarters were above. She looked out toward the glass ceiling, now; over the many couches, tables, and - yes - liquor arrangements aplenty.

James heard the steps long before the heavy wooden door, nestled above and behind them at the top of that palatial set of stairs, swung open. Gentle footsteps carried down a figure which was maybe five feet and eleven inches, an intimidating height but for the fact that he was thin; lanky, even. The man was aging, but he retained a sharp demeanor and slicked-back black hair almost reminiscent of the Irishman's friend Emmett. He wore the finest silk suit, with sharp turquoise cufflinks and a blue under-shirt which matched his color scheme overall.

"I am a busy man, James Lowery. I hope you will make this quick?" The voice sounded almost British; he descended from that marble staircase and presented a hand to Jim. They shook, and Lark and Katrina followed. At no point did any of the Consortium's members pay any mind to the fact that Gibbs had two bulky, sharp-seeming security officers with him. "What can I do for you?"

The Irishman didn't waste an ounce of time. "Well, Larry, th'truth is tha' I've evaluated yer security procedures 'ere. No two ways 'bout it," he confessed calmly, his shoulders rising and falling in a hapless shrug, "y've got some decent thugs an' thieves doin' your biddin'."

Lawrence Gibbs didn't seem the least bit amused. He had blue eyes that matched his cufflinks - color was a theme, with him - and they stared rather as if they were dead at the Irishman's own. "And why did you feel a need to steal from me?"

"Because I'm th'best thief, an' th'best thug," he declared rather proudly - a death sentence in a city like Vegas - "an' I'd consider yer chips t'be a small down payment on contractin' with you an' The Coleman Group 'bout how t'improve things 'ere."

The sharp blue eyes of James' rival narrowed darkly, at this point. "I didn't mention The Coleman Group, Mister Lowery. And either way, our security is beyond your comprehension."

At this, the Irishman laughed derisively. "Right! I met one've Th' Coleman Group's security officers, didn't'cha know? A man workin' under th' umbrella of ADS." He grinned, turning to the side and staring out at the couches and, more importantly, the Las Vegas Skyline. All the bright flashing lights might have distracted a lesser man, one not used to the visual distractions, but for Jim? Who could see them better, more sharply than any other man alive? He reveled in them all while retaining his guard.

"Was a man by th'name'a John Bradley. Doesn't ring a bell t'ya?" The fact was that Jim already had his answer. He brushed his fingertips through his hair. "So y'didn't know what Bradley was doin' up in tha' facility in Alaska? Ahh." A dramatic pause. "There y'go, there's tha' heartbeat."

Lawrence looked his two bodyguards over for a moment, as if considering whether or not to sic them on the Irish upstart before him. "That's far enough, Mister Lowery," he folded his hands in his lap, deciding that for now he would stick to diplomacy. "I don't know what you are alluding to, but our project in Alaska is in cooperation with the Department of Defense and it's Advanced Research Projects. It is also highly classified. I could have you arrested for even mentioning it."

Not one word of the slender man's threats stalled the thief. Far from it. "Speakin' of mentionin'!" James added with a laugh, glaring back at Gibbs, "Didja know 'bout Laboratory D-44?" He chortled once more, shaking his head. "Aye, no - how about Voodoo? Oh, tha' y'know of - an' tha's why yer gettin' a lil' scared now." His confidence was unshakeable, like he was performing a simplisic routine on stage. "See, Larry, I have a bit'a a talent. I hear things."

He was oversimplifying, but it was a useful way for him to convince people of his skills without totally tipping his hand. "I c'n hear yer heart beatin' faster, so I know y'know wha' I'm talkin' 'bout. An' y'know if I'm talkin' 'bout Voodoo, I've *been* t'yer facility. An' th'fact tha' y' didn' know 'bout me bein' there, obvious 'cause y'didn't have m' stopped righ' when I walked int'a y' hotel, tells m'tha' yer fuckin' clueless as t'what's goin' on in th'company y'own fifteen percent of."

When James got expository, his accent kicked into a higher, faster gear than normal. It was almost a chore to keep up with him, and the only reason someone listening to him for the first time could tell what he was saying was because he paused just long enough - literally - for their brains to process it. It was also a useful interrogation tactic; the verbal confusion caused a listener's mind to pick out the parts which it could most anchor to, oftentimes words and phrases which had a significant meaning to them. This in turn caused the pulse to quicken and other signs of anxiety to show, thus allowing Jim to better read his marks. Lawrence's heart, on the other hand, was anticipatory and anxious, but not exactly terrified. In fact, it began to slow.

"Very good, Mister Lowery." Larry clapped his hands without rhythm for a moment, then reached into his pocket and produced a remote. He clicked on it, and one of his television screens turned on. Displayed on it, nestled in the window of an already-opened E-Mail, was a short biography of James' career. "You are *not* the only one who can do research. My dossier on you is fairly complete. Let's take a look."

His left hand reached up to rub the bridge of his nose, sharp eyes rolling over every word. "You worked for the Irish Republican Army as a youth, until you turned traitor and went over to Britain's SAS. You were briefly considered by the CIA as an affiliate, then you went private. You worked at Connor Point, in Africa, which was your first Chief-Of-Security job. A job you botched." He smugly smirked as he slipped in that stinger. "We at The Coleman Group have very detailed records."

James held his index finger. "I don't really see it tha' way. Very few people died in tha' accident, an' I helped save most of 'em. Some good men died tha' day, y'know?"

"Yes," Lawrence retorted bitterly, "I know. Your failure," he continued unabated, "has been followed by some more work for the CIA followed by the establishment of your company, which is admittedly a mediocre success, but nothing like Andrew and I have built." The businessman paused for a moment, only now taking time to weigh his words. His lips pursed. "Cut to the chase. What is your interest in The Coleman Group?"

Once more, the Irishman merely laughed. His eyes danced toward his two ladies, and both of them had on a serious face despite their eyes - eyes which were alight with amusement, because for whatever reason those two loved the way that James worked his gifts. "What's -your- interest innit?" His arms raised above his head in a stretch, then he relaxed slowly. "John Bradley." He stated that name again. "Y'really don't know 'im? 'E knew me. Knew you, too. Knew a few other names. Richard Trujillo, jus' as an 'xample." He listened, he waited, he heard his answer. "But y'don't know *him*, either. Th'mystery deepens! Y'don't even know yer own group"

Irritation marked the businessman's voice, as the confusing behavior of this guest was lumped in, in the casino operator's mind, with his strange predilection toward those two women. "Is there a point to all this, or should I just have you indicted for high treason and get this over with?"

Lark frowned; Katrina chuckled in contrast along with James. "Now, now, no need t'be snippy. Speakin'a Connor Point, how's about m'ol' pal Garret Trinder?"

The minute James started to say this second name, he got a reaction he'd honestly hoped to avoid. First of all, Lawrence's pupils dilated a small amount. Second of all, his heart rate jumped up twenty beats a minute, easily. Sweat began to threaten his forehead and underarms, and the scent of it took only an instant to reach the Human lie detector. Pheromones - fear-fueled ones - danced along his nose. It was a confirmation of something very clear: This man feared the bearer of Garrett's name as if he were Satan, himself.

"Yep. Y'knew 'im, didn't'cha?" the Irishman asked coyly, raising an eyebrow.

Lawrence provided a single gesture to his security guards, and they walked out of the room immediately. They weren't even hesitant, as if they recognized the gravity that the conversation had only just taken. It wasn't the reaction Jim had expected. As soon as the two were alone, Lawrence calmly walked over toward his bar. Bottles clinked and clattered as he rummaged about. "Did he send a message? What does he want?" Gibbs paused for a second, then *looked* at James for the first time in their conversation. "Why did he send *you*?"

Now the ladies looked one another over, askance. Jim blinked in confusion. "I ain't sure wha' y'mean by tha'? Why'd who send me?"

The owner of the Gallivant poured himself a glass of scotch and swallowed it. He set it down with a soft tap and a loud sigh. "I've only met him a few times, you know." Another glass was poured and swallowed, almost habitually, amidst the melodramatic expression of knowledge. As he carried on, and as - no doubt - the alcohol kicked in, Lawrence's pace and heartbeat both quickened "He usually sends me envelopes, not couriers. Sometimes he sends them to me to send to someone else. When they're for me, they contain orders. I follow them. He always knows I follow them. I always follow them! Why would he send *you*?" The man was afraid for his very soul, it sounded!

"Wait a minute," Jim interjected, his powers of deduction finally serving him where his other powers couldn't. "Yer tryin' t'tell me tha' Garrett Trinder 's been sendin' y'messages?" At the blank stare he received in return, the Irishman grit his teeth. His eyes evolved into a dangerous glint, and it seemed as if he stared into time's threads, themselves. "Tha' ain't possible. I saw 'im die."

Lawrence froze, his heartbeat quickened almost to dangerous levels. It was obvious that he'd reached a mental breaking point, and that his ability to conceive of a dead man still being alive was nil. "What? When did this happen!? How?!"

"'Bout fifteen years 'go, mister smartass wi' a resume!" He pointed to the screen, jabbing his finger angrily at it. It was the perfect proxy to emphasize the businessman's arrogance. "At Connor Point! I watched 'im fuckin' die! Garrett Trinder innit alive. 'S no way. He was crushed. To death." Even Lark and Katrina seemed concerned, now, with the two looking at one another worryingly.

That blue-eyed businessman blinked. He began to relax ever so slightly, seeing his conversation partner lacked a complete grasp on the situation as well. It wasn't as if Jim was quite as trapped in the dark as Larry was, but it was human nature for the demystification of a fear-inducing entity - in this case, James himself - to lead to relaxation. "We - I saw him two weeks ago! It's when he told me about the successful test of Voodoo's latest protocols! He told me to prepare for an installation here as part of our security plan. It's why I was so quick to let *you* come see me!"

It took the Irishman a little time to figure out what exactly that was supposed to mean. Why would he be allowed up if someone *else* was slated to provide security? "Y'were plannin' t'make fun've me? Or, wha? Y'thought I was here t'set up th' thing?" He sighed, his fingertips rising to rub the bridge of his nose grimly, grinding fingertips into his forehead. "A'right. Lissen close, Larry, this's m'schtick fer when I say g'bye."

Ever since Connor Point, he'd made a habit of giving some big speech to end a conversation he didn't like. With Voodoo, he ripped into the robot; with Miguel, he'd been arrogant and reassuring. Strangely enough, he couldn't find the words to tell Lawrence exactly how much he hated the prick. He quickly ascertained that it wasn't because he hated Larry, but because he hated, "Garrett..."

"I'm' gonna find 'im, an' I'm gonna find ou' th'truth." He looked over his shoulder; Katrina was stone-faced, but Lark stared at him as if expecting more. A gaze was shot back at Gibbs, then he pushed the down button on the elevator's control panel. It hadn't gone back down since he'd come up, so it was ready for his departure the instant he pushed it. The two women followed him into the cabin, and the doors shut behind him.

James' face hovered over the classily-clad, perky (and natural, he was happy to consider) breasts of his female companion; the Irish one, as the former description could have matched either of the two. "Snufflepuzzle," he mumbled softly -

a code word. "C'mon an' get us."

As usual he heard nothing, but he placed his hand on Lark's arm and looked straight ahead. A moment later there was that familiar, loud buzzing before he heard the decisive *pop*. He was staring, without surprise, at the Gallivant Hotel and Casino; staring at it from a hotel room in an adjacent building, one rented specifically for the purposes of surveillance.

Speaking of observation, Jim slowly looked over the gathered gang; every single person in the room looked worried, save for Sonia Monterrey. She, on the other hand, merely appeared to be confused by the conversation they'd had. Oh, she was certainly alarmed that Emmett was suddenly so very, very pale! It didn't help that Alejandro appeared nervous, despite his invincibility. And Sari looked positively horrified; the tan-skinned woman was speechless for the first time in years. James had to act fast, if for no other reason than to break his colleagues out of the cycle of worry.

His voice was a razor. "Jethro, can y'feel 'im?" He didn't need to look behind himself, at the man who had gotten them out, to know the larger man was shaking his head to the negative. "So he ain't 'live, we can guess tha'. Someone's impersonatin' 'im."

Sonia started to raise her hand, then realized she wasn't in a class-room. She realized this was all *real*. Her voice was wavering. "I don't, umm, I don't really remember Garrett very well. What happened to him?" She turned towards Emmett.

"I did." *A shower of blood.* The physicist sighed, the image floating in his mind. "I killed him." Sonia stared at her lover in momentary horror; then she remembered exactly what had happened to the scientist when he'd found out how bad the owners of Connor Point had truly been. She knew he'd snapped, lost his sanity and tried to destroy *everything*. She also knew that he'd recovered. "I over-pressurized him. Crushed him to death, you could say."

His former student, now-girlfriend winced. "Okay, I get it. How could he be alive?"

"He ain't," Geddy answered decisively. "Anywhere on

Earth, anywhere in space, I'd be able to feel his punk ass. I ain't pickin' him up. That means someone's pretendin' to be him. Took 'is name, maybe even his face. Coleman's into shape-shiftin, right?"

It was, as Emmett pointed out, "Crassly put? Yes. I haven't got a clue how they'd get the information on Garrett that they need to copy him, but it's possible."

The Irishman in the room brushed his hand through his blonde locks of hair. "Tha' still don' explain how th'got info on *us*, Physics-Boy."

All eyes shifted to the only other man who had ever worked out the identities of Connor Point's *Omega* staff; Alejandro Curtis. It was a fleeting hope. "You..." he began falsely, almost insulted, before he frowned. "No. I have made sure that my father's records are secure. It is unlikely any other Consortium members were discovered." He frowned; his father, the nigh-legendary Richard Trujillo, had been one of the wealthy executives who had implemented the Connor Point project in the first place. That the son just happened to be one of perhaps eight people on the planet who was super-human was, by all appearances at least, a complete quirk of fate.

Jim knew about fate all too well.

*****

It was nearly summer, late May.

"'E's a scientist, Riki." Even then, in his memories, they'd called her Riki. Or was he remembering wrong? Was he the one who had started that trend? Regardless, the mission to this major north-eastern college was boring. Oh, he was getting plenty of looks from the under-class-women, but he was on business. They were useless to him, for now. He'd had to promise Garrett quite firmly, on that point. Then again, whispered that voice in the back of his head that always undermined his conscience, maybe he could get a phone number for later.

The blonde singer with him merely smiled. "A scientist?"

They were only in public, discussing super-heroes as if they were part of some comic book, but he'd given up on trying to talk Erica into the finer points of clandestine operations. "James, you know what we're looking for. More people like our Brahman friend, more like Jethro. We're after the biggest fish of them all!"

He scoffed proudly. "An' what's this guy do?"

Erica flipped open a manilla folder, another one which had been colored black in that manner which the head of Connor Point preferred. "Eisenberg. It might not even be his real name, you know? Could have taken it from a scientist, that German one. Anyway, he's been making his way through his doctoral program without a steady job. That's weird enough, but his financial records are pretty much clean - except that he doesn't like to pay taxes and definitely doesn't have any residual income. So that means he's getting the money from somewhere else."

Suddenly, the Irishman felt like he might just get along with this one. How wrong he was. "S'wha's 'e do? Is he, li'e, King Midas'r somethin'?" It brought to mind that song about King Midas' opposite; instead of gilding whatever he touched, he got dust.

The songbird laughed. Students slipped around the pair, heedless of their conversation - and likely assuming they actually were talking about comic book characters if they listened in. It was, even Jim had to admit, sometimes better to hide in plain sight. "Not exactly. I mean, I suppose he could. No, what we've picked up is much more impressive."

"Go on?" His disbelief was obvious, even to an ordinary person.

His partner obliged him happily. "The thing we've noticed about his papers - you know," she added at his look of confusion, "We do have a research department, here. The thing we've noticed that he is always right about physics. It's like he can see the atoms smash together in an atom smasher. Except that our little stool pigeons never see him actually go to any major lab. He does it in his apartment, because he can control subatomic particles. Basically, he's physics incarnate."

The pair descended a staircase, entering into a large, round building's basement. They immediately came to an ID station; Erica had no trouble flashing her magical, blank identification card. As he'd learned over the past months, she was willing them to view her as simply a high-ranking official in their organization. She didn't need specifics to trick the brain, all she needed was to make them feel a certain set of emotional parameters - subservience, respect, or even ambition, depending on the mark's personality. Then, compliance.

They meandered through the science facility, turning here and opening a door there. They came upon a laboratory and James found the door locked. Sighing, he mumbled to nobody in particular, "Guess this's why I'm 'ere." He pulled out a slender black case and opened it up, finding a particular set of long, thin, twisted objects. Deftly his fingers inserted the picks into the lock. He could hear each pin as he positioned his devices; with a twist the door opened.

They came upon a handsome looking young man with jet-black hair slicked back over his head. He wore a brown suit, but what struck Jim right off the bat about the fellow was the matching leather gloves he wore. Well, that and the fact that his hands were cupped around a rather strange, dazzling blue light. As he watched disbelievingly, the man was handling something Jim couldn't quite hear, couldn't really see, and didn't even smell very clearly. It was boggling his mind until he caught the glint of the room's light against something inside *that radiance.*

Gold.

He could sense Erica throwing out waves of calmness. He could also tell, from Erica's heartbeat, that she was actually slightly afraid of the man - that, or perhaps as impressed as he himself was. As it turned out, she was impressed in other ways as well, but at the time he hadn't noticed that. He was far more concerned with the fear that, when he actually interrupted the figure's work, this man could reduce him to a stack of atoms.

*****

The group stood about staring at one another blankly, uncertain how to proceed. Sari was still more than confused, and Jim was lost in memory for a moment. He snapped out of it as his phone rang.

"Yeah?" James picked up, toning his harshness down to a mild irritation.

A mechanical voice was on the other end. "I am Voodoo." The robot. Jim immediately scowled. "I have been informed you visited Lawrence Gibbs. Do not fret," it stated without emotion, let alone allowing Jim a chance to respond. "I have been asked to tell you to visit the Infinite Loop Lounge in New York City. An appointment has been scheduled for you with Garrett Trinder."

"Son'va bitch," James mumbled into the receiver. A date and time were recited for him and he took them down mentally, then hung the phone up. Before anyone could even ask who that was, he sighed loudly. "Tha' was tha' fuckin' robot, Voodoo. It has m'number, I guess," he blurted out. His allies were dismayed and only slightly more concerned - it wasn't like it was easy to get any more worried than they already are.

Jim rubbed his forehead. "Ain' much t'say other'n tha' 'e scheduled us an appointment wi" whoever's pretendin' t'be Trinder. Three days. Enjoy Vegas; we meet 'ere, an' go a' this time, then."

With that command, the gang went its separate ways, fully intending to enjoy their brief vacation. Emmett was probably going to run roulette, altering the molecular components of the ball as it rolled and guiding it with invisible forces into the right slots. He claimed it improved his precision. Geddy was likely to travel the world with his wife; she was far from interested in the 'business' side of his affairs, but cherished being able to go anywhere in the world with the blink of an eye. Alejandro, well, Jim left the Spaniard some distance.

If there was one person in their group he was worried about, however, it was Sari. Hearing about Garrett's survival had caused an ever-so-slight aggravation of her old psychological wounds. She had a predisposition, Jim had noted, for going to various hospitals and getting to know the patients who her company Medivent was developing cures for - people who she herself couldn't wave a hand and fix, just yet.

Each of them, James had realized long ago, had a limit to their powers. Geddy's were unclear, but Emmett's was the problem of organic matter. Unlike what he'd feared when they'd first met, Emmett couldn't just reduce him to cosmic dust. He *could* freeze the air around him, but he couldn't alter living tissues - even grasses. James' own limits were the least restrictive, since his power was the least expansive. But Sari?

Sari had the problem of not being able to fully cure injuries which the aging process had caused. She could slow the progression of, say, multiple sclerosis; where the damage was not natural, she could even reverse it. But when the body's own systems failed of their own volition, especially in the case of cancer, there was no "damage" she could repair. Over the years she had tried to change this fact, and when she could catch an ailment early enough she could arrest it's development, but she had quickly reached her upper limits. And that limit was what worried James the most.

If she went out of her way to visit those she couldn't help, she'd risk falling deeper into depression. It was an altogether unpleasant thought. He needed something to break the trend; or, at least, some hope to give her. In the deepest recesses of his mind, he made a note to make sure Molly texted Sari with enthusiasm; not because he wanted to imagine that action - it was rare that he'd shirk such a decadent daydream, but in this case it was like picturing his little sister, if he'd had one - but because Sari could use a true companion, not just one of the flesh. Then again, despite his protectiveness of all involved, he'd stayed out of that relationship.

*****

A loud knock pinged off of the walls of her office; it originated at the door. She sighed. "Come on in," she mumbled just above the inaudible range, setting aside the paper she was grading. It was a particularly droll bit of work, one about the way basic needs influence how people developed in life. The essay offered little of greater substance than a stance of "nurture" on the old "nature versus nurture" debate; it cited pitifully few relevant examples. "B-minus," she'd concluded, though she had another two pages to go. It was a bad habit of her's, but her instincts were usually right.

When she looked up and saw Professor Latchkey at her office, Maria blinked her eyes sleepily. "Oh. Hello, Vicky. How can I help you?"

"You sound more than just a little *bored*, Maria," Vicky countered, smiling warmly as her eyes fell understandingly upon the associate chairwoman. "Grading papers getting a little old?"

What'd you know of it? Maria nearly blurted out, managing to keep her composure in the face of the rather unwelcome intrusion. She forced herself to smile, brushing strawberry locks from in front of her face. "Yeah," she confided reluctantly, "it's a pretty dull situation here, really. Basic psychology for wet-noses and gen-ed-cred seekers. The bane of the college professor, indeed!" She laughed at her own joke; then again, when specialists taught extraordinarily general classes for people who just needed to get through their general education curriculum, it was often a tedious task to say the least. She wanted to write another book! Or come up with a new psychological therapy! Or work on the next DSM. Anything but continue the monotony!

And, considering she was having this particularly disgraceful episode of self-loathing in front of a colleague she barely knew, she was even less pleased with herself. Her fingertips slipped under her chin and she scratched her bottom lip softly; a deflection, but a simple one which could signify anything. "I'm sure you had that feeling before you headed out to work with CAPE?"

Nodding slowly, Victoria set foot in the office and carefully, slowly closed the door slightly. It didn't click, but it was shut. Then, the elder leaned against the wall of the office. "Yeah, I did," she confessed, her neutral voice a rather disenchanting match to the melodrama of her body's posture. "That's pretty much why I felt like I needed a leave. Well," the graying one added, "besides because it was such a good opportunity."

Latchkey folded her arms and looked skyward. "I actually have a little bit of a problem on my hands, and I feel like maybe you can help me, if you're that bored."

It was thrown out like a lure to a fish; or like a dollar to a hobo. Maria was suspicious, of course, but curious. What opportunities - what adventures! - might await on the other side of this rather modest proposal. "Go on," she invited calmly, sans expectation.

Now Vicky took a step forward, took a seat across from Maria, and held her hands out helplessly. "I know you're big into market research. Most of your students really do well when it comes to breaking down *why* people buy the way they do."

Her eyes blinked carefully. Maria hadn't quite expected this. "Well, I guess so," she added, willfully blocking out a certain student whose presence in this conversation now seemed inevitable, as well as abominable. "But I'm more into behavioral modification and rationalization than just shilling the latest set of clothing through subliminal advertisement." Even if there was no such thing, exactly, there were basic elements of a good ad; and good ads sold products, even when none were actually needed, simply by exploiting the psychological tendencies of a target audience.

She was greeted by a soft nod. "I know, but this is a *big* opportunity. There's a major amount of research into electoral psychology going on - 2016's an election year - and I was contacted by a potential contender who wants help evaluating their chances." Vicky sounded almost envious of whoever-so-happened to get this opportunity. "I just came back to the school, so there's no way Daniel is going to sign off on the leave if I secure the position. But you?"

Maria blinked once more. "Me?" She held up a hand. "I don't know. I mean, I'd be leaving my classes behind, and I'm not really sure I'm comfortable with that. Besides, I took a leave of absence a few years ago, and it was really a sudden one - Daniel probably won't look fondly on it."

"Well," Victoria said with a laugh, shrugging her shoulders. "If you're nervous, I understand. I think Daniel would be fine with it, but hey. Go down to the city for the interview. Give them a chance. If you don't get along, if you don't think you can do it, then say no. That's not so bad. I think you'll find that the gig is very worth your time."

The associate chair sighed, her fingertips lacing with one another. "I've got to admit," Maria conceded, looking Vicky in the eye, "it *does* sound like I'm burning out, here. Even to me," she confided. She bridged those fingers, then, stretching them out and - yes - allowing some of the knuckles to release their pent-up energy with soft cracks. "Alright, you said I'm headed to the city? Where to?"

*****

They were lying awake, staring at the ceiling of their hotel room. Deep breaths escaped their lips; they had physically exhausted one another long ago, but that left their brains active while their bodies could not be. "What..." the soft voice ventured a daring question. "Was he like?"

Emmett didn't need to think twice about who Sonia was asking about. He rubbed his bottom lip softly. "I need a drink." Glass - imperfectly shaped, unprofessionally thick - formed in his hand; water poured into the container from nothingness; a flash of cold caused the entire chalice to frost over. The process was repeated, and a perfectly chilled cup was given to his lover.

"Thanks," Sonia responded breathlessly.

The physicist merely nodded, rising from his bed to

approach one of his many bags. Within he found a paper journal, one which had a metallic band welded around it, holding it shut. The scientist gazed at it, as if struggling to recall the incident a decade and a half ago. "I'm guessing you want to know about Garrett?" At the nod he received, he sighed reluctantly. His memories triggered, it seemed, he tossed the book back into the bag carelessly. "He's the one who recruited us, and he was always cordial, always professional but friendly. We trusted him."

He mused on the past for a moment. "He always made it *feel* like we had a say, even if we really didn't. We were in the Omega division - a Bible pun, actually, one of Erica's ideas." Both cringed at the thought of the hyper-insane blonde songbird. "Trinder was mainly our link between the facility and the finance - the old Consortium. They poured billions of dollars into the project. Private capital. I have no idea how Garrett sold them on a super-hero science factory."

The former student was forced to laugh; even Emmett cracked a smile. "He was bright, but not quite like me." A hint of his old pride. "I have no idea what power he had; he never exactly was clear about having one, now that I think about it, but how else would he have known about us, at the get-go? I think Erica and Jim could pick that up in someone, but I had to figure that part out with my head. It's why we knew we could trust him when, well..." He looked downward, then.

In truth, Sonia had already determined that Emmett was using the "Royal We," speaking on behalf of a group. She was well aware that he *hadn't* been told what Garrett told the others, precisely because he was too emotionally unstable to bear it. Also in truth, *none* of them were prepared for it, at least when they saw, as Sonia finished, "...What happened to Sari." It was a statement, not a question; but what came next was something she had only just started to tease out. "So, he saved her from them?"

Emmett blinked, taking a long pull from what Sonia hoped was *still* just water. "Did Geddy tell you?" He exhaled once again. " Yeah, he gave us the files on everyone who was responsible. They were what Garrett called 'White Files,' meaning they were normal people who were involved in the old Consortium. He gave us all of them, told the others to keep me out of the loop because I was too easily driven over the edge, and gave them his blessing to go to war."

A displeased voice. "War, right? Including Alejandro's dad, I guess?" Sonia asked gravely.

Memories were painful, and even though it wasn't Emmett's memory, he knew what happened just as well as the one who did it. "My guess is that Richard Trujillo was one of the first Garrett recruited, because his son might have already expressed his power." Geddy had certainly expressed *his* power towards Richard, of course; expressed it by dropping the businessman off of his own building, survived by an estranged wife and son. A son who, years later, sought to relocate - and then destroy - the group his father had been a part of. A son who had helped save them all, his father's killer included, from a real, live dragon just a few days ago.

"How *did* Garrett find you guys, anyway?" Sonia's question was pointed. "Or, maybe, I mean, how'd he find *you*?"

Emmett chuckled darkly, glancing away into memory. "I was getting my doctorate in physics when Jim and Erica showed up at my office. They talked me into coming along pretty easily, mainly because they had some IRS documents that proved I wasn't doing a very good job of laundering my tuition." He held a hand up, an amused smile on his lips. "I'm *much* better at it now, as you've learned; or, I guess, Lark is." The physicist depended heavily on Jim's business associates to clean up the metaphorical dirt on the gold bullion he could create, and he leaned on the Irishman's Irish lady, the resident computer expert, most heavily.

"I found out that Erica can pick up people's feelings, so she'd confirm if a person-of-interest was really like us, or if they were just an anomaly." As if he wasn't one. "What we do, well, like I said when I first told you," he mentioned non-judgmentally, "it's more of a feeling than a trick of genetics. After all, they experimented on *all* of us, in a way, trying to find out how we did what we do."

Sonia smiled warmly, sipping at her cool drink. "No MRI results, nothing unusual on the DNA swabs, nothing in your EKG or brain-waves. I remember things better than you think, sometimes." Her fingertips tapped the bed next to her, and she set the glass down on a night-table.. "I remember you devastating my apartment's roof, too!"

"Hey!" he chuckled softly, feigning injury. No matter the false hurt, he sat down all too obligingly. "I fixed it, too!"

She leaned in close, placed a kiss on his lips; she couldn't detect any alcohol. Her eyes narrowed devilishly, her vigor renewed. "I know. Now, lets see if you can fix something *else...*"

*****

James gazed out at the skyline of Las Vegas, transfixed by the sheer magnitude of the spoils that the city spent to keep up the streams of illuminated water and the shining light arrays. He vaguely recalled the security concerns raised by the increasing exploitation of the Colorado River, which both powered and watered the region as a whole. Drought was a real threat, given that Vegas was a city built in the middle of the desert and all. It was a terrible idea, he'd mumbled incomprehensibly, one that only a bunch of wealthy morons could embrace.

Then again, he thought as he turned around, it was gorgeous when caught up in the moment.

"James," Katrina offered, sitting down on a couch with a martini in her hand. His eyes drifted over the Russian first; he glanced to Lark for an instant, seeing her hard at work on a computer. Or, at least, killing digital monsters far less threatening than Voodoo! He smiled and looked back at the more serious of his ladies. "It is beautiful, no? This city?"

He sighed complacently. "Gorgeous," he echoed, advancing a step forward and slipping an arm around Katrina's shoulder. "Like th'two'a you, I say. I love th'both a'ya, y'know."

He nodded in Lark's direction; she spent just an instant of attention on him before returning to her break.

Katrina leaned into the man's embrace, but as her hand found his face, his eyes looked away. "I do not believe that you need to be so worried, James. You will be with Doctor Eisenberg. With Jethro. With Sari, even!" She almost sounded light-hearted, except it was obvious even to a man who couldn't hear the emotion in her voice that she was fairly concerned. "Can this Garrett Trinder be such a dangerous man?"

"Dead men are th'scariest," Jim answered gravely, rubbing Katrina's shoulder reassuringly. "'E gave us all a purpose, fifteen years ago. Made us get t'gether an' try'n save th'world. I would'a been workin' for th' US Government'r somethin', pro'lly murderin' chump dictators." He glanced to Lark, who was lost in her world of virtual murder, then looked back up at the Russian. "I'd'a never met y'two, either. 'E made m'life possible, an' 'e died, an' now 'e's alive."

A silence hung over the room for a moment, then Katrina slowly brushed her fingertips along James' chest. "I remember you telling me your story. You fought Garrett to get to Emmett, he tried stopping you. Does he have a skill like you all do?"

Laughing weakly, the Irishman shrugged. "I don' know, t'be honest. He wasn' in th' 'White' files, an' 'e wasn' in th' 'Black'. I jus' figured 'e never gave m' 'is. I never saw 'im use one, though, an' if 'e did, 'e hid it really well. I can usually pick up on someone's talent, 'less they don't use it." There was a hint of curiosity in his voice, now, as if he wondered whether or not he had missed something so long ago. It was rapidly dismissed in his lover's arms. "'E never 'ad a chance 'gainst me, an' Physics-Boy crushed 'im." He realized that his sentiment could be taken more than one way. "Lit'really."

Katrina frowned, concern welling in her eyes. "You will be safe," she said. She sounded convinced. "But you all must take care. As you said, dead men are the scariest."

"Shit!" Lark exclaimed as she was gunned down in the game; she turned off the computer and strolled over to her other two thirds, slipping an arm around James and onto Katrina, kissing the males cheek gently.

"'Specially if they ain' dead," Jim retorted sharply.

*****

The top of Everest. It was what men had given their lives to reach. Ascending even halfway to the peak was a near impossibility unless a climber was in peak physical condition. But people nearing their sixties? Overweight and under-trained? The trip was worse than ill-advised. Thousands of feet of altitude would thin the air, suffocating them. The cold, even during a relatively mild spell, would freeze them. The steep cliffs and the many un-sturdy handholds would leave them to fall to their deaths. In fact, just lugging all of the gear needed to survive the ascent was a serious bit of business, and one bad logistical leap would lead to disaster.

But the Death Zone was something even worse than each of these factors taken alone. It was a combination of them. Travelers brought their own oxygen; they abandoned those who were in poor health; there was even the risk of low air pressure, never mind oxygen content, causing low blood-oxygen levels. The first twenty thousand feet, therefore, were bad - yet at the peak, nearly 30,000 feet above sea level, the early punishment made the last portion of the climb almost impossible to bear. That explained all the bodies of dead climbers which, chances were, would never be properly recovered.

It was a good thing, therefore, that this particular pair didn't have to worry about climbing.

"Gotta love that view!" Geddy chirped into his oxygen mask, gazing to his left at his wife, Marge.

The woman smiled back at him and nodded gently. She, too, was wearing oxygen; her curly white hair was a contrast to her dark skin, all of which was concealed under a heavy layer of clothing. Jethro wore something similar, of course. "Life's good sometimes, dear. Now, you just get ready to save ours."

He raised a glass of wine to her and removed his mask just long enough to chug the substance down. She did the same, then - with a frown - she gazed down at her watch. It began to beep softly. "Time's up," she said to her beloved. He reached a hand out and took hers', then the two were back in Vegas. They tore at their sweaters quickly, having gone from freezing to air-conditioned in an instant.

*****

"Molly, it is me. I got your call, and I am sorry I missed it. I am sorry I missed you, again! Tomorrow, our colleagues are going in to New York City to once again face down our old nightmares. I cannot possibly know what we shall face, but I am calling to tell you not to worry. I will see you again. I miss you greatly, and I had fun the last time we hung out. We shall do so again, I promise. Farewell, from your warmest Sari."

Chapter Six
Announcements in Prime Time

New York City; a half decade ago, a visit there had nearly led to the ruination of Emmett's life. Erica Hall had revealed to his then-girlfriend Maria - and to him - the full extent of the damage he'd done to her ten years beforehand, at Connor Point. In his fury at the old Consortium's sins, he'd inadvertently poured so much radiation into Erica that it caused her to mis-carry their child. She'd never told him she was pregnant, and he'd never asked how she was after the disaster he'd caused. That conversation took place a decade after the fact at the Midtown Ballroom, right after Riki and the Wildcats had played a massive concert, one which lived on in the new Consortium's memory as the first spark of the explosion that was their ascent to unity.

Here, today, Emmett was standing in this particular city with his old friends once more; standing this time at a building called the Infinite Loop Lounge. It was, as it so happened, a Hookah lounge; a place where smoking relatively pure, flavored tobacco from a large water-pipe was the reason for patrons' gathering. Emmett had been to them before, back when he worked at Catskill Community College: Hookah was a popular pass-time amongst students who felt like they'd live forever, after all! Lung cancer be damned! They were popping up quite commonly, in fact, and even small rural towns saw them take over unused spaces in mini-marts.

But he'd never seen one as large as this!

The broad front-end reminded him of a big-box retailing store. He looked over his shoulder at the comparatively paltry back-up: To avoid too much suspicion, James had insisted that only the Irishman, Geddy, Emmett, Sari, and - upon her insistence that she be with her beloved - Sonia went in the front door. It was, as far as the physicist was concerned, an offensive arrangement to say the least. If Jim sensed a threat, chances are he'd give the scientist a cue to blast the place to smithereens. Or, at least, to conjure enough poisonous gasses to incapacitate anyone locked in a room with them.

Oh, there was more than enough "support" in the area in case of emergency. Katrina and Lark were at James' corporate headquarters, monitoring radio transmissions and computer networks in the area; if a 911 call was placed, or if thugs were dialed up for back-up, they could notify the team on the ground within seconds. They had local information wired to them from a nearby hotel, all thanks to "Little" Stevie and one of James' large steel communications cases. Alejandro, on the other hand, was resting in a car a block away, ready to plow into the building and mount a rescue if necessary - invulnerable people made their own doorways, and were kept in reserve for just such occasions. On the whole, though, it was just the five of them - four super-humans and a freshly graduated college girl.

He sighed, fingertips reaching out and pulling open the front door. A thin haze of smoke assailed the quintet, but it wasn't at all suffocating; it was actually sort of pleasant! Dozens of flavors - all tainted with the undercurrent of tobacco's 'burning plant matter' taste - assailed their senses. The interior consisted, first, of simple black couches surrounding tables. Further back were private, enclosed booths. There was a small bar which served basic alcoholic drinks, and - to his chagrin - there was a line of people waiting for a seat.

The hostess, a polite enough brown-haired girl, approached them. "Party of five? What name will you be under?" Emmett was silent for a moment; he looked to Jim, who parted his lips to speak. He didn't get any words out.

A man of about forty-five years strolled up to the group. He was of an utterly average build and a handsome, albeit pale and mildly wrinkled face. He was fit, but approaching middle-age with what seemed to be a passion. His suit was, like Lawrence Gibbs' had been, designed by a top-tier creator. The figure adjusted his cufflinks calmly, his eyes piercing the waitress' soul. "These five are coming downstairs with me, if that's alright, Barbara?"

The hostess blushed at the acknowledgment. "Of course, sir. Please, go ahead," she indicated warmly, gesturing for the party to pass by her.

The man led them a few steps inside of the lounge, then turned about and extended his hand toward Jim. The Irishman caught it as if he saw it coming a mile away. "I'm Andrew Coleman, it's a pleasure to finally meet you."

The name slowed him for an instant, but James merely smirked to himself. "Oh? James Lowery, nice t' meet y' as well!" To an outsider, the Irishman sounded sincere; to his comrades, he sounded positively hateful. "I'm sure y'know m'associates?"

Andrew looked them over, a coy smile touching his lips. "By reputation, mostly. Jethro Marx," a hand moved toward the portly one, "Emmett Eisenberg, Sari - who happens to not acknowledge her last name, I understand," he added, impressing even Emmett, "and Sonia Monterrey. I know all about you. Please, come with me downstairs. Your safety is guaranteed, of course." He was all too polite, and it set off warning bells in the eyes of all five of them. "I promise, you'll have a better understanding when we get there. Place an order, grab a couple pipes all on us, and meet me there!" The corporate executive nodded towards a staircase in the back, which he started to head towards.

He paused, of course, and snapped his fingers. "Oh! One more thing!" Andy gazed over his shoulder. "I'd suggest something fruity if it's your first time. Something I'd call light - say, a nice Jasmine Rose." Coleman's friendliness seemed sincere, and as he strolled off to a staircase in the back, the physicist sighed and looked at his old friends.

"We hear that a lot, don't we?" Emmett asked sadly, turning his eyes toward Geddy calmly. "That schtick about answers. I don't suppose you can sense him? If he's here?" At the negative shaking of his friend's head, Emmett couldn't help but sigh again. He had hoped - they all had, faintly - that Jethro's ability to teleport to a person's location would have come in particularly handy. That perhaps, if Garrett were still alive, he'd feel the man's presence. There was no such luck.

At the bar, they placed an order; Emmett and Sonia chose to split a Jasmine Rose - though Sonia patted Emmett's shoulder softly in memory of that name, the physicist resolved to inhale deeply as a sort of homage to the daughter he never met. Sari declined to participate (mumbling about having "already imbibed enough carcinogens," with an irked look towards Emmett), Geddy picked himself up a Cherry Cola, and Jim went straight for the Chocolate Twist - reported by the establishment's tobacco peddler to taste like a chocolate milkshake.

All three of the participants (since Sonia and Emmett were sharing) were handed long, stamen-like devices with hoses affixed to their sides. The top was crowned with tin foil, a covering with dozens of tiny holes in it to allow air in. Underneath that was a more literal, crown-like bowl. They were advised to be very careful, that this part of the water-pipe contained their coals, and that when they were at their table they should carefully place three of the red-hot motes of fire near the rims of the tiny tin-foil cage.

Obliging and promising back-handedly not to burn the place down, they accepted their nicotine-infusors and marched straight into the back. If any of the employees had orders to stop patrons from snooping, they didn't dare approach the five guests under Coleman's protection. The group was grim, but they descended into the inner workings of the Infinite Loop.

"Hey, Em," ventured Sonia cautiously; she was the only one who honestly seemed afraid. "I was wondering if you knew the reason they call this the Infinite Loop?" At the question, the physicist blinked; he hadn't considered it.

James also seemed intrigued. "Yeah, Physics-Boy, why no' explain it? I sure don' ge' it." That Irish lilt was only partially difficult to understand, this time around. He was leaning his head around his hookah; perhaps that was why he was so clearly grasped.

Emmett's fingers found his chin, stroking it gently as if he had a beard to smooth down - or appreciate the smoothness thereof. "Well, it's not really a physics *term*. It's more computer science, actually." He shrugged, working it out in his own mind before he spoke. "Infinite loops happen when a computer program tries to come up with an impossible result, and it gets stuck. Like..." His fingers wriggled as he thought of a way to explain it. "A program generates two random numbers between one and three. It needs to hit a seven to end."

The scientist smirked, speeding up the pace of his fingertips' flight. "It'll never hit seven, so it runs forever. It gets stuck, and can never end unless the program is changed somehow."

Jim and Sonia nodded, while Sari seemed entirely focused on the stairs she was descending. They hit a fork in the road, so to speak; a platform, then a second set of stairs. Not seeing Andrew, the large construction specialist headed down the second set - and, therefore, the others followed him down.

At the very, very bottom, they found Andrew standing out in front of a large, metal door. A black, slender card reader was affixed to the wall in close proximity to the portal; a card reader, clearly. It was accompanied by a small red light. He smiled to the gang. "Glad you made it okay. Follow me." Coleman's card flashed quickly over the reader, and the doorway hissed softly as it slid to the side, sci-fi style.

"Oh, yeah," Jim chirped to Andrew as the first door revealed a hallway, followed by a second one. "This innit a trap, 'n our safety's guaranteed?" It was a bold demand - virtually a statement of fact based on the assumption the request would be granted.

Oddly enough, Coleman laughed softly, sarcasm dripping from his voice. "Right - because somehow I'm gonna out-punch the master of martial arts, out-dodge the movement-master, and not get incinerated by the physics professor here." He led the five into the hallway, turning to face the others. He gazed at them one at a time, eyes finally settling on Jethro before he swiped his card once more. Another hiss, another door slide - the portal behind them closed, then the one in front of them opened.

At the very instant the door started to open, before anyone's eyes could touch the figure inside, Jethro whispered disbelievingly, anxiously, "I don--He's here."

It was like walking into a pent-house apartment, save for the fact that it was under-ground. The first room was, it appeared, a living room. Unlike the one Jim had visited in Vegas, there was no glass ceiling, nor was there some contrived business-meeting-with-open-bar setting. Instead, it was relatively condensed - sofas (nice ones, of course!), reclining chairs, a television with surround-sound speakers, and coffee tables dotted the underground chamber. Other doors, left partially open, led to a kitchen and bedroom. In fact, the only thing distinguishing it from an ordinary basement apartment was the organ.

Oh, cliches!, Jim thought as he heard the orchestral notes. It took him an instant to realize that, frankly, it wasn't as loud as he thought. When his eyes fully viewed the man whose building this was, he noticed the thin white cords leading from the device into the man's ears. He was playing not to his guests, but to himself; and Jim fought back a sickened gag.

There was no mistaking it. On cue, the figure spun around in his stool as he removed the ear-buds. No, there was no chance of him being wrong. He recognized that face, despite what time had seemed to do to it. The build was thinner, and age lines danced upon the once-youthful face of the blonde (now, gray) German, but as he stepped through the doorway and heard it shut behind his group, he was staring at the very last survivor of Connor Point, Garrett Trinder.

*****

Jim stood next to Erica; who was next to Geddy; who was next to Emmett; who was next to Sari. They were all young, especially the latter, and they faced down the German scientist who had brought them all together. Thinking back, it was a rather cliche moment; but morale-boosting speeches had to be given at some point!

"You five are different. I'm sure you've noticed, but you each have power that goes beyond human comprehension. We have, gathered within you, the powers of location; of healing; of perception; of physics; and of feelings," he announced happily. "And we are always looking for others. Doctor Eisenberg," Garrett *offered warmly, "you will be creating some cutting-edge molecular structures, among other projects." The scientist was alight with possibility. In fact, he'd hardly stopped talking about particles smaller than atoms, and ones even smaller than that.*

Garrett went on, "Miss Hall, you will serve as a psychological assistant as well as an ethics expert. Miss..." he thought for a moment, unsure what to call the child in their midst.

Her voice, soft and uncertain, squeaked gently, "I guess I'm like a Sari, Mister Trinder."

A warm smile crossed over the administrator's lips. "Sari, then. You will be the greatest doctor the world has ever known! You will save many lives!" The girl couldn't have seemed happier. "Mister Marx," he continued, "your specialty is movement. You will be transporting resources and pushing the boundaries of mankind's ability to explore space." The construction expert was curious as to just how this would all work.

"Mister Lowery," Garrett concluded, "you're in charge of security for this complex. You will protect us from the dangers of the world." Jim nodded firmly. "You all represent the Omega - the peak of human capability, and our end-goal. The rest of Connor Point is classified as Alpha, or the current standard and, therefore, beginning. Yes," he pronounced softly, "together we will save the world."

*****

"This is impossible!" Emmett cried, aghast. His fists formed into tight, tiny balls. "I killed you! How could you have survived it?!" Suddenly the physicist's face went flat. "I surrounded you with a layer of nitrogen. Then I formed a second one, inside the first, and compressed it." His phrasing was downright clinical, as if he were diagnosing a structural flaw in a building. "Your skeletal system collapsed. I could feel it collapse against the molecules! How could you be standing here?"

Jim could downright smell the horror of his comrades, yet strength radiated from an unexpected source. He saw, out of the corner of his eye, that Andrew Coleman moved into a side room of the apartment, allowing a frank conversation. Then, a faintly-accented voice broke through Emmett's wake like a Russian boat breaks through ice. "I understand it, halfway." Sari dusted a lock of black hair from her face, her eyes leveling on the man who she'd assumed to be dead for fifteen years. Her arms folded over her ample chest. "You created the shape-shifting technology used by your Coleman Group. I felt the cancer inside of you years, oh so many years ago."

Her fingertips scratched the flesh around the golden mark upon her forehead. "Doctor Eisenberg's attack could not kill you because you turned to blood. The cancer..." She sighed, groping for a solution. "The same radiation that destroyed Jasmine--" she didn't hesitate, but she didn't need to look to know Emmett cringed at the name, "--Must have somehow cured it. That explains why Lawrence Gibbs is so terrified of you, yet rarely has *seen* you. You can change shape, and you meet him in disguise."

The German gentleman seemed honestly impressed, his face alight with pride in the girl he'd ordered James and Erica to save, so many years ago. Had it been closer to twenty? Garrett sighed to himself. "My old friends, I don't even have a chance to say hello and you throw accusations at my feet!" He laughed coyly, as if he'd expected it all along - a cliche villain, missing only a saccharine sweet pet to rub. "You *are* close, Sari; very close. It is all overwhelmingly complicated," that German accent gently rambled off. "Even my own reasons - not goals," he narrowed his meaning down, "just reasons for them. They have grown foggier."

Emmett shook his head disbelievingly. "So you've had this formula for mutation for fifteen years?" The professor frowned, doubtfully. "Why didn't we see this research at Connor Point?"

Garrett's arms reached out and grabbed a hose; he pulled a cinnamon-scented tobacco through a nearby pipe and exhaled slowly. "In all honestly, it had not yet been invented." He left this fact to float, smiling through the haze of tobacco smoke.

This response only caused James to scowl. "When I cut y'inta ribbons, I felt like somethin' wasn't quite right. I chalked it up t'm' own mental state, seein' as I was huntin' the files you gave me, but now that I think 'bout it, it's like yer D-44 project was. Y'used the formula on yourself, didn't't'cha?"

As far as a hanging allegation could go, this one lasted surprisingly long. Garrett was silent, studying his old colleague for a moment with a certain gravity in the way he rested, his arms folding one over another. "Old friends," he opened, "I must insist that the formula for shape-shifting had not *yet* been invented. You are all geniuses; what does that imply?"

At the silence, Sonia stammered, "It means...It means you aren't a shape-shifter." She immediately set about taking a long, powerful drag from her hookah; she chased it with a sip of a bottle of water she produced from her purse. "But you *can't* mean what I think you mean."

Soft applause met the former student's suggestion, and Garrett bowed his head in a level of respect which was far removed from mocking. He seemed honestly impressed at the rate of turn-over within the young one's mind. "Very astute, Sonia - may I call you Sonia?" His accent was noticeable, but in a gentle manner rarely associated with a muscle-bound Norseman. He had on a smile, a very professional yet very warm one. "It also implies that fifteen years ago, I made a very dreadful decision that permitted us a chance to save the world."

"Yeah!" Jethro declared firmly, staring dead-pan at the German's face. "You brought us all together, a'ight. But we *failed* to save tha' world, Trin," he concluded, using a rarely-heard nickname, "An' the whole world damn near bit the big one."

One single finger was held up by their 'old friend.' "Yes, but it *didn't*," Garrett clarified coldly.

A maddening silence followed this extra bit of information, and Emmett brushed his fingertips over his chin in thought. James was taking soft, casual drags of tobacco, his attention focused on Garrett's body language. Geddy seemed uncomfortable, mainly because it stood to reason that he was unable to move them out of harm's way if harm suddenly chose to befall them. Sari was staring at her feet, and Sonia was busily huffing away at her hookah.

Finally, the old man sighed to himself. "Must I spoil it with melodrama? Very well." He reached behind himself in his seat and drew --- a remote control to a television. He turned it on with a smile on his lips. "It is time."

*****

Unbeknownst to her, her ex-boyfriend's group was just making their final preparations for a raid on a long-dead scientist's underground stronghold, a mere few blocks from her. Instead of soldiering up with the boys, she was handing over a cab fare (with a generous tip) to a driver, standing in front of one of the largest media research centers in the city.

The building's ownership had standing tenants, at least two of whom rented entire floors as opposed to half-or-quarter floors. Then there were the rent-an-offices, leased for specific meetings and sometimes treated like a B-list enterprise time-share company. "When you're here," they'd advertise, "it's *your* office! The secretary is *your* secretary! The thermostat is *your* thermostat!" Of course, *you* paid a really high price for the room, a higher fee if you wanted to actually store any documents, or process any payments; and extra time was billed at overtime for the secretary's benefit. In short, it was all about appearances: To avoid the stigma that a 'home office' suggested, especially in the light of downsizing and the expense-trimming of moving-out of previously-occupied office space that this 'great recession' - a delusional title for a depression - had inflicted upon business-owners.

And that's why, *of course*, she was headed right for one of those type of offices on the twelfth floor! She entered as was greeted by the secretary, a broad-shouldered male with glasses and a beard. "Oh!" the rent-a-secretary started happily. He was decked out in a business suit with a pink under-shirt, looking incredibly flamboyant. He appeared to be reviewing a folder, but it placed it on his desk quickly when the woman entered the room.

"You must be Doctor Montclaire! Yeah, Vicky Latchkey told us you'd be coming." He offered his hand, she shook it with dismay at his enthusiasm. "I'm Travis! I'm representing the campaign's logistical end, for now. We're *so* glad you could make it." He paused for a moment, deliberating over something he intended to say, then he spat it out. "I've read your book about depression and delusion," he declared, "and it really speaks to what we're trying to achieve, here. Please, sit down!"

Maria immediately raised an eyebrow, like a red flag hoisted up over a proposal. "Travis? The campaign? Listen, no offense," she lubricated gently, "I thought places like this only rented secretaries out, but you seem *way* too engaged."

The man chuckled, a genuine friendliness bouncing off of him. "Oh, please, I'm sorry! You've got the wrong idea, a little." He grinned broadly. "Yeah,we rented the room, but we declined the secretarial option. Anyway, she'll be here in a minute, I'm sure. She's just finishing up a phone call, then we can get through this interview and we'll be set." He hesitated a moment, checking a door behind himself to make sure it was shut, then he leaned toward Maria to whisper. "If Vicky Latchkey recommended you, chances are you've already got the job. She stopped lining up interviews as soon as Latchkey said she had someone for us. Her and Latchkey are old friends."

Reputation was everything in the business world, and Maria had gathered that Victoria had a lot of pull in a lot of ways.

It was rare for a single hiring suggestion to put a full-stop on the selection of candidates for a job, even in a good economy, but it *did* happen - it just never had, in her case. Moreover, she'd never, ever heard of a suggestion so strong that one of the interviewer's subordinates would *state* this fact openly. Maria had never imagined that Vicky was quite so famous; after all, she's hardly even heard of the woman's work outside of the college, and while there she was just as good as any veteran professor could be.

"Well, I'm honored," Maria responded with a faint smile, hiding her inner astonishment. "To be honest, Vicky didn't really tell me much about what your boss needed, other than that you wanted someone with a background in marketing psychology."

Now, it seemed, Travis nodded his head slowly. "I mean, you trained Sonia Monterrey, didn't you?" Another wince, inwardly concealed. "I've been doing the publicity business for a while, and to be honest she's hit a real jackpot. You must have seen it in her! In fact, I really only think there's *one* person who knows the human soul and how to cater to it better than her - oh, umm," he hesitated then, laughing shyly. "I mean, and you definitely taught her what she knows, too, of course. So maybe there's two!" Truly, all that gushing was unbecoming of the man.

A soft knock came from one of the office's doors, from what looked like a conference room. "Ah!" Travis exclaimed excitedly, glad for any opportunity to bail himself out. He rose up and stepped toward it. "She's ready for you. Come on in, let's get you on board! Let's make us a team!"

The dashing young man, who Maria was at least halfway convinced was a homosexual, practically strolled to the meeting room and opened the door. Politely as ever, Maria nodded to him. "Thank you, Travis," she said softly, slipping into the room and glancing about. Her first impression was that there was nobody there in the room save for a sole interviewer at the other end of a relatively small table. Just one person and Travis, who was following in behind her, worshiping his boss.

Her second impression was disbelief.

"Doctor Maria Montclaire." The voice was one she hadn't

heard in something resembling five years. Her memories of that episode, to this day, were hazy; then again, she wasn't completely herself at the time. It was no help that the *reason* for her disassociation was sitting right across from her, however! Maria stared at the dead-pan, emotion-devoid face of the singer who had crooned the demise of her life as she'd known it.

Maria bit back a curse word, asking in the event she was engaging in a vivid hallucination despite not having taken any psychedelics, today, to her present recollection. "E...Erica Hall?"

Travis's demeanor shifted to one reminiscent of someone engaging in conversation with a cat; a faint relief to the psychologist, who could tell that the kid had no idea the two knew one another. "Umm, Miss Hall? You two know each other?" he ventured tentatively, echoing her thoughts.

Erica's head dipped to the side faintly, scrutinizing her. "Victoria sent *you*, did she?" A faint hint of feeling had crept into her voice; it was no longer so dead, so desolate. Moreover, to her relief, Maria could pick up a twinge of genuine humanity in her rival's words. "I know the woman lies about a lot, but her skills are unparalleled. She said she couldn't help me, then swore she'd send the best expert she knew in her field; but I didn't expect it would be *you*."

Suddenly, as if the other two people weren't even in the room, Erica laughed to herself; it was a silent little chuckle, a private response to an amusement that the other two in the room couldn't begin to see. "Then again, I guess it makes sense. You work at the same college, and you *are* an expert. Then a third," she added with a calculated, if contrived saying, "Latchkey is playing her own game, here, and I suspect she knows something of our mutual history's life."

Taken aback, Maria willed herself to sit down in order to avoid the appearance of weakness. Slowly she pulled back a chair (heavily cushioned, even comfortable) and relaxed into it. "I hate you," the psychologist clarified coldly, stunning Travis further, "but I'd be an idiot if I wasn't worried over what you're gabbing about. What *are* you gabbing about?" Patience was not one of her virtues.

Hall blinked her blue eyes once, then smiled coyly. Her hair was as blonde as ever, and she brushed it out of her eyes. She looked to Travis, and the boy ran from the room, closing the door tightly. "He is a good lad. Ah, right. I don't even know if *she* knows I know." Erica might as well have been talking about a coming cold front. "Latchkey is a plant of some kind; someone like me, and our *beloved* Emmett." No, no love had been lost in the past five years. "Someone beyond the norm, you could say. *You* know."

A gasp. There was no way she could miss the reference, and she knew what it meant in the abstract, but Victoria? Maria couldn't disguise her surprise. "Wh...What's she do?"

Erica shrugged indifferently, as if talking about the wind. "That's beyond my scope. I can feel it exists, but I can't feel *what* exists. Whatever it is, it's probably the same in her..." The singer trailed off suddenly, her hand brushing over her stomach self-consciously. "Her daughter." Maria understood why Erica might have such a hard time thinking about it; hers' was dead, after all. No - never born was probably how the songbird thought of it - murdered. "Anyway," the blonde continued, waving Travis back in; he complied instantly. "I asked you to come here because I need someone to manage - and I mean that in a very specific way - my campaign."

Slowly Maria snapped back to planet Earth. "Your campaign? What are you after this time?" She blinked dumbly. "Another war against Emmett?"

Travis was perpetually lost. Erica laughed with a scandalous delight. "Emmett?" She nearly spat. "I'll deal with him when I have to. Same with James and the rest of them, really," she wriggled her fingers dismissively. "We'll go public when we're ready, but right now I'm more concerned with being in the proper position to save this world."

Once upon a time, such talk would have found its way into Maria's book about the delusions of grandeur that compelled deranged individuals to imagine themselves as super-heroes.

Then she met *real* super-heroes, or at least super-humans, and she'd learned to tell the subtle difference between bonkers boasts and serious statements. This was the latter. "Alright, again," she interjected abruptly, "what the hell are you scheming?"

Erica grinned mischievously. "I'm sure you remember what I can do to people?" She did, and it was obvious in her face. "What I need is someone smart enough to spin the story; to make my subconscious, emotional influence over people look like a rationally explained variable, at least until the campaign is over. Coercion becomes simple charm."

Travis tapped his watch. "Twenty minutes 'till we have to hit the studio." The songbird nodded, then looked back at her candidate.

Maria sighed, pinching the bridge of her nose as Erica continued her evasiveness. "Fine," she finally conceded, "let's say I'm in. What, prey-tell, is this campaign?"

Erica merely smiled as she rose to her feet and adjusted her outfit. "Turn on the T.V., and enjoy a drink on the house" she advised as she stood up and left the room. Travis obediently clicked on the local news, then poured a glass of wine. Unbeknownst to Maria, she wasn't the only set of eyes hailing from Catskill Community College tuned in to that channel.

*****

The band had just finished playing its song, and Erica flicked a lock of hair - black and blonde intertwined - out from in front of her left eye. She strolled over to sit with the host of that nationally syndicated, nightly TV talk show that aired right after the local news. He was flustered, there were no two ways about it; he almost seemed like he'd injected a bit of heroin, he was so loopy. Content? No. Pacified, perhaps, was the better word.

"Wow. The Wildcats get better every time I see them! Even after that hiatus!" he offered with an adulation he rarely provided to other, equally *talented* bands.

Erica smiled winningly; she was decked out in her usual

singing attire, a frilly black dress with sensuous pink lacing embroidered into it, layered underneath a leather corset that showed off her nearly unparalleled figure. She still rocked the gothic-industrial look hard, but after so many years performing she'd let that outfit gain an inch both in height and length. It was the only outward expression of her aging, because her body certainly didn't seem to be losing strength - and her lungs? She could still scream lyrics without the slightest challenge.

It was all an act, of course, and everyone in Garrett's underground apartment could see that. "Well, I'm glad you feel that way," she said as she shook his hand. "And I'm really happy you let us perform before the interview."

"That's right!" the middle-aged man exclaimed, as if he'd just remembered the name of his son or some other highly-prized piece of information, "You'd promised to make a major, surprise announcement tonight! It's about the label, right? *Siren's Songs*, was it?"

The singer laughed to herself, gazing out into the audience. With a moments' willpower she had the undivided, un-speaking attention of each one of them. "Actually, no. I've given it a little thought, and I've spoken to a few advisers. I know that it's already the spring, but I've decided that I'm throwing my hat in the ring." Her voice was calm, almost comforting; yet there was a certain firmness. "Our world needs salvation, you see."

Stunned silence - like the crowd had any choice in its expression. "I'm Erica Hall, and I'm officially declaring my candidacy for President of the United States."

Thunderous applause was the only thing heard on the television; that's why, without any hesitation, Garrett reached up and clicked it off before the worship-fest could begin.

The German didn't seem at all surprised by this - unlike those he called 'old friends,' those who had figured him to be dead for the last fifteen years, and those, frankly, whose lives he had so heavily interrupted. "Well," he ventured after they'd had a minute to process the matter, "have you figured it out, yet?" At the collective silence of his former colleagues, he didn't even flinch.

"Or do you need a minute?"

"Really?" Sonia whispered to herself, staring at Emmett as whatever previous academic victories she'd won melted away in the dismay over the announcement. "She's gonna run for President? Isn't that your crazy ex-girlfriend?" The physicist nodded dryly.

Garrett actually laughed. "Miss Monterrey is astute. What's more, she *will* win." His eyes leveled on James slowly, now, scrutinizing him. "Now, Jim, how could I be so certain about it? How can I know this for a fact?"

Lowery looked back at Garrett with a perfectly neutral face. "Y'rigged it? Fuck, man I don't know! How long've you been workin' wi" her?"

It was a female voice that broke the silence. "No, that's not it," Sari muttered to herself more than anyone else. "She does not know. She is just going to force people to vote for her. That is quite obvious, and that is an entirely new problem for us. But, Mister Trinder," she said, gazing at him grimly, "Can you please do the right thing? Explain it? You had terminal cancer which could not be operated on, even if I were to repair the surgical incisions. Your life expectancy was two years, at most. What happened?"

With a clear level of apprehension, the once-youthful man nodded his head. He pulled in another puff of smoke, and his age radiated through the room - odd, since he was no older than Geddy, who was silently observing without quite the same wizened projection. "I chose the name Trinder a long time ago. No, it is not my real name; but it *is* what I really am. A wheel-maker, of sorts."

He held up a trinket which rested on his organ; what appeared to be an old, wild-west-style wagon wheel in miniature. With a flick of his finger he spun the device. "Imagine time as a wheel, and imagine I am not sued for such a saying." He smiled, then, watching the round device rotate. "From any position on the outside, I can see the various spokes and surfaces. Moving it directly requires something far greater than just looking, but through spotting any flaws approaching the horizon, my actions can smooth them out, changing how it rolls."

Setting the device down, he continued with the tone of a lecturer. "Did the metaphor work for you?"

Emmett rubbed his face, flattening it out in momentary confusion. "Time travel doesn't explain you surviving what I did to you!" The outburst from the physicist was wholly unexpected, filled with a raw passion and a credible level of guilt. Never mind that most of the people in the room were still wrapping their heads around the concept of, well, time-traveling Garrets!

"It don't explain the cancer bit, either," Geddy added apprehensively, working on the puzzle like a super-sleuth. "If Sari couldn't get you through no operations, you *should* be dead. Did ya jump forward or somethin'?"

As if at random, James readied his knife. There was no explicable reason for it; he just lifted his leg, lowered his arm, and pulled the weapon from his boot. He moved like lightning, roaring at something none of them had noticed. With a dull thud he slammed something, or someone, into a wall. His voice was an enraged scream.

"What th' fuck were y'thinkin?!" He shouted this into the face of the only other man in the apartment with them, Andrew Coleman. Only, upon looking at the business-owner, they realized all too shockingly that he *wasn't* Andrew Coleman at all. No, he was a tall, muscular blonde man who in fifteen years would look as if he'd aged thirty. A man whose Germanic features were etched in their mind in the moments before their perception of his death.

Garrett Trinder, a twenty-years-younger Garrett Trinder, was looking up at James' hateful face with a healthy dose of worry, masked by confidence. His voice was even Garrett's, spot-on, as if he'd acquired the ability to copy sounds as well as facial features. "Actually, Lowery, it was *my* cancer. His didn't come up for about six years."

Sari's hands found her mouth. She whispered into them, horrified, a new realization dawning upon her. "Oh god, then he knew. He knew all along what they were..." Suddenly she snapped. Something in her eyes left her body behind and she was reaching behind her waist, grasping a handle, whipping her arm around in an all-too-practiced manner. The only one fast enough to stop her was on the other side of the room, restraining what seemed to be a shape-shifter. Eyes widening, Sonia went to cover her ears.

A gesture of his gloved left hand put an end to it all, as noble as it may have been. Emmett pulled the structure of the gun's firing chamber apart just before Sari could pull the trigger, causing it to dry-fire with a loud *click*. He immediately grew wary of any ensuing assault aimed at his own person. "Sorry, sorry!" he exclaimed, holding his hands up. "I just didn't wanna go deaf," he explained, as if hearing were his only concern. And not, say, the bullet that would have killed the man he had failed to.

Dropping this misshapen weapon, Sari folded her face into her hands and started to sob softly. Sonia rose up and walked over to her, and the two embraced as sisters might; loving, caring, and supportive.

"I get it," Geddy took a turn at saying, reaching into his jacket and pulling out a knife of his own. "The shape-shiftin' thing is from today. You saw it now, made it in the past, and injected this damn fool with it." As he got an approving nod from his old colleague, Jethro continued. "Then *he* went an' faked his death when Emmett went nuts. You wasn't anywhere in the area, cause you saw it all happenin'?" Another nod met the rotund man.

Then, another loud thump came as the back of Andrew's head met the wall; as James slammed him against it a second time. "Why?!" he demanded headily, an action more designed to compel a confession than out of pure, unabashed rage.

Garrett looked away from the rather unusual sight of his long-forgotten youthful visage getting smacked up. "You will not agree, but it was to save the world."

Emmett rose to his feet. He looked at the crying Sari and

his own girlfriend, who was barely clinging on to competence herself. Unfortunately, looking next toward his own insides, he realized he was even closer to insanity than she might have been. Something long-dormant, long-concealed and always-dangerous was bubbling up inside of him as his perception of molecules and atoms only seemed to grow sharper in tune with the pace at which his heart pumped adrenaline into his system. "You're full of it, Garrett. Give me one good reason I shouldn't pop you like I did him?!" As he pointed at Andrew with his left hand, his right clenched into a tight fist.

"We *failed* at Connor Point, you idiot!" Emmett condemned angrily, waging an internal war to not lose control over his logical processes. As a scientist, they were of utmost importance to his learning. As a walking nuclear bomb, they were of the utmost importance to the city he was standing in. "And it took us ten years, and a lot of agony, to get ourselves together again! Hell, you know things before they happen?" His right hand reached outward as if to grab Garrett's throat, and a plane of force lifted the once-young man off of the ground, pinning him against the wall much as his doppleganger was cornered by a very physical blade.

Icicles hung from every word. "How could you let them do what they did to Sari, and then make us kill them all? How could you drive *me* insane?!"

Coughing once, Garrett held a hand up to ward off the threat. Emmett looked at his hand, then lowered it; lowering Garrett at the same time. Jim took this as a cue and released Andrew, who retained - at least for the time being - his illusion of being the younger Trinder.

Adjusting his shirt, the German sighed. "You are thinking of time in a linear fashion, and I don't blame you - even you, Emmett, a scientist who understands all too well how quantum physics work. Your perspective on atomic structures is unique, just like mine is when it refers to the nature of time. You imagine that these things all happened because of me. Your perception is as rational as it is wrong."

A single finger rose up. "You are not seeing the things which did *not* happen because of me." At the continued confusion of his former friends, Garrett nodded. His eyes closed, and that index finger began to spin in mid-air as if the tiny wheel on his organ was still in his hand, being rewound and played forward once again. "Allow me to tell you of a history that wasn't."

Chapter Seven
The History That Wasn't

"Fifteen years ago, Emmett, you were a mad scientist. You had the most promising career of any physicist since Oak Ridge was shut down. You know Oak Ridge, the place where they experimented with your precious Thorium? It's funny we keep coming back to the government. Why? Well, if you really think about it, how long would it have been before the government caught you?"

"Today, you can launder all the gold you want because you use Jim's ladies--"

"'Ey!"

"Hah, sorry, I don't mean it like that! I just mean that their application in this frame of reference is in deceiving the government, and the IRS in particular, so Emmett has endless investment capital. You remember, you *saw* the documents. They were - maybe - months away from having actionable evidence that you were a tax evader. And when you were in jail, Emmett, how long do you *really* think you would have lasted? How long before an inmate tried to make you his, well, how do they put it? Bitch! I think that's the word. How long until you were pinned, as I just was, against a wall? I think you know the answer. I think you know what you would have done. You would have, how do you put it? Crushed them like a grape. And then the *real* fun began."

"You needed two years of searching for faith, for going from temple to church to synagogue to satanic rite. That's what you did while you were recovering from what happened at Connor Point. You lost terribly that day, more terribly than you knew, but the truth is that you were lucky to have lost so little. No, your luck is that you have no memory of the alternative series of events, the one where the government does its own experimenting on you. And when you cracked, when you bored a hole straight into the center of the Earth and crippled the magnetic fields that protect us from solar radiation? There *was* no Jethro Marx, Erica Hall, James Lowery, and Sari to stop you. There was only *you*."

"I saved the world from *you*, Emmett Eisenberg. But you were not the only one."

"Oh, I could have done it differently. I could have arranged for a sniper to put a bullet in your head. I could have killed you as a child. Could have killed your parents before you were born. Those are all terrible, science-fiction-trope ideas that would have only made circumstances worse. I needed you, I needed you alive and well. And this was the only way to obtain what I needed of you."

"Jethro, your life was to be one of mundanity. You had the power to save the world, and you are a hero for it in your experience. But, by the time you knew something was wrong, in our other time, you had no hope of heroism. You would have had no experience in your ability, and no access to the disaster; never mind having no empath to shut the madman's mind down. Even if I somehow stopped Emmett, you would have lived and died alone, working a dead-end job and thinking yourself clever for using your powers to make your career a little easier."

"Then there is you, James. You have always been a killer, you know that. You don't like it, but that is because you were taken out of the CIA's oh-so-caring clutches and brought to Connor Point. You were given a reason to love, to live, and to appreciate the living. Imagine if you had instead become a top assassin, bumping off dictators and terrorists. You might have made the world better for others, but yourself? You would never have your ladies - and Jethro wouldn't have his beloved Marge, I should add! - and you would have been miserable. Your friend Malcolm plying you with liquor as you draw him into your darkness - how long until your mind stopped seeing a difference between good and evil, friend and foe, or target and civilian?"

"You keep indicting me over Sari, and you are not very wrong. On this, I confess, I have committed many sins. But at the same time, consider the three men you eliminated when you met her, so many years ago, James. You and Erica both saved her from *someone*, did you not? That someone would have taken her and *never* let her go. I know it is painful, I know it is horrible, but it was necessary. It was the only way I could save her from a lifetime of torture, to save all of us. To take us to today."

"And what is so important about today, you ask?"

"...An' tha' bitch?"

*****

An hour later, Maria was beside herself. "You're going to do *what*?!" Her eyes narrowed. "This is absolutely insane. President? Are you going-- You're going to mind control them! Your performance, your speeches, it'll all be mind control!" She pursed her lips. "Just like five years ago, when we were in New York."

Erica chuckled coyly. "Emotional control, dearest doctor. Emotional. There is a tremendous difference." She was feigning injury, a trait Maria absolutely despised. "And, please, you know very well what needs to be done. My victory will be the first third-party win ever, never mind the first victory of a woman. I will save this world--"

"From what?!" Maria shouted, standing up and nearly throwing whatever missiles happened to be nearby at her former rival. "What the hell is so dangerous that *you* need to be President? That you need to take people's willpower away and make them vote for you just so you can rule over a country that I know damned well you don't want any part of? You aren't some selfless leader, you don't care about being the first female President."

Slowly, Erica rose from her seat as well. Her voice was cold, and Maria was relieved that she didn't feel any forces pressing her back down - yet, anyway. "Sit down, Maria Montclaire. Some would believe that Emmett Eisenberg and his cohorts are the second coming. Once upon a time, they would even have committed the sacrilege of calling us Gods." If Travis had any investment in the super-human racket, he was deathly quiet as Erica rambled on. Either he had long ago accepted this as fact, or she had stolen his ability to care.

"The fact remains, doctor, that we are quite unique in our capabilities, but we are not divine. We are not to be worshiped as idols." She brushed her thumb over the corner of her lips. "Don't think I don't know that James Lowery is master-minding some new, Consortium-like entity to attempt to control the world from behind the scenes. He's sent enough goons around my label, including that turn-coat Stevie." Maria remembered 'Little Stevie' well, since he had once imprisoned her. "It's like my former partner wants me to know he is trying to police me."

Keeping her attention focused on Maria, Erica returned to her seat; Maria didn't feel any supernatural compulsion, but she too calmed down and plopped disgracefully into the chair right next to her. "Believe me, if that pack of idiots were the only ones out there, I would not be so worried." She laughed, then, a sorrowful chuckle. "But Latchkey is working for someone that is most definitely not as foolish. Then there are the others in Garrett's old files."

"Garrett?" Maria coughed once, staring up at the candidate. "Isn't that the man who Emmett killed, fifteen years ago? What files are those?"

Erica's eyes rolled, but they seemed to do so more out of her own lack of foresight than as an insult to the psychologist. "Garrett was the brains of the operation. He had files on every Consortium member, and more on every potential recruit. The normal people were his 'White' files, while *we* were his 'Black' files. Garrett hid it from everyone else, but I know he had something *different* about him." She folded her hands in her lap. "The most dangerous power is the one you don't understand. It is why God works in mysterious ways." She paused to savor the enigma which birthed her.

"Anyhow, the 'Black' files contained a few other names besides ours, but I don't have copies of them. If I had that information, I could probably find out if they are going to be a danger to the world." The songbird smiled, suddenly, a certain satisfaction creeping over her face. "These people can corrupt the soul."

Maria couldn't help herself anymore, and she made a decision. She rubbed her forehead. "Alright, Erica, let's say I'm on board with this disaster of an idea. Let's pretend this is even a *good* idea. When did you become religious?" She stared up at the empath, as if daring her to come up with a smart-ass answer. "When did you start caring about the, what, the *soul* of humanity? Five years ago you ripped my heart into little bits just to get revenge on fucking Emmett!" The psychologist bit back any further, generalized rage in favor of a purer tonic of anger. "What makes you so god-damned righteous?"

Travis shivered, but he couldn't even manage to make a sound. Erica shrugged indifferently, ignoring the question asked of her in favor of one she'd have asked herself. "Is it because I have been to hell, and returned to speak of it? Is it because only I can guide our species to a future without warfare and death?" Erica's voice dripped of pain as her hand ran over her smooth stomach, slowly. "I don't know why anything had to happen the way it did, Maria, but I will not question when God places a goal before me."

"Your job is to just come up with why so many people would suddenly shift ideals, Maria. I will make sure that you and Daniel -- You two are together, still?" The grim nod she got in response caused Erica to smile weakly. "I am truly glad, for that. I will make sure you two are safe. I'll protect Sari, and Saffron, and all those who have been injured by what my generation did wrong."

Maria blinked softly. "Wait, Saffron? Victoria's daughter?"

"Yes," she answered in a sincere, yet exhausted voice, "Every child, every young person, deserves to be saved from what we almost did back at Connor Point."

*****

"Erica Hall has one of those destinies that can't easily be changed," Garrett remarked idly enough, puffing at his tobacco. As what he said made absolutely no sense, he glanced to the side, re-evaluating his approach. "Alright, the specific nature of her path in life was open to alteration, but regardless of the details, she was going to make the announcement she made tonight no matter what changes I could have made." He took another pull of his hookah. "I have made sure she is protected and guided very well, of course."

Emmett bit his bottom lip, a passing concern for his former lover crossing his face. Sonia didn't enjoy that look, but Emmett wasn't the only one who suddenly seemed a little more forgiving of Erica's past madness. "And how have you done that, exactly?"

The German nodded his acceptance of the question. "I have placed the ultimate weapon near her. Just near enough to keep her safe." Garrett's confidence - and knowledge of the future, apparently - compelled a similar certainty in the physicist. It also compelled James towards a very simple, one-track thought process.

"So why're we not killin' y', again?" Jim spoke up suddenly, spinning his knife around in his hands adroitly. "Should'a kept tha' ultimate weapon near you, instead, right?"

Trinder didn't flinch, instead craning his neck to the side slowly. "James, you still have the documentation I gave you, right? The 'Black' files, yes?"

After a moment, Jim relaxed; his head dipped in grim acknowledgment. He seemed all too eager to put his knife back to the throat of either Andrew Coleman or his former colleague, but he reined himself in for now. "Yeah, an' most of 'em came up bogus. Ain't nobody in there tha' we 'aven't met, Garre', an' found t'be th' real deal?"

Now it was Garrett's turn to take a moment and consider his words. "You won't kill me because we are going to save the world together. Not just from Erica, who is..." He paused searching for the word. "She's not exactly stable, and she will reveal us in due time, accidentally or not. No, if you had to choose one name in all of those files I gave you, which would be the most problematic?"

James' eyes narrowed for a moment, and he considered - briefly - just chopping away at Garrett's throat until the man was no longer able to keep talking. Instead, however, he hoped he was making a choice of his own free will. He certainly knew what he believed to be the answer to Garrett's question, assuming it was a legitimate one. "Jean-Claude L'Francois. No question."

"Who in the fuck is that?" Geddy asked pointedly. The New Consortium's members seemed well and truly confused; that, and perhaps a little insulted that they'd been left in the dark on this one.

Slowly, James looked over towards his friend and colleague. "I've never been able t'catch 'im, but 'e's a dangerous guy wi' a dangerous thin'. If - big if! - 'e's real."

Garrett held a hand up, interrupting his old friend. He spoke with a condescending, yet patient smile. "Please, Jim, nobody can understand your accent."

"Well, fuck you, Trinder!" the Irishman bit back, just barely capable of accepting the fact that, yes, the German's accent was less noticeable - and less rampant.

The once-mighty man just smirked defiantly. "L'Francois is actually Algerian. That's not his real name, of course, but it is a convenient pseudonym. His capability is best described as based on a mythological creature," the soft, definitely-less-intrusive accent explained, "because his 'thing,' as James would put it, is to nourish himself upon, and store up, the bio-kinetic energy of other human beings."

"So..." Geddy trailed off, grimly, finding this all a little hard to believe. "He's a vampire."

"I suppose you may call him that, though this entire line of conversation is a charade. Fortunately, I have put in place more than enough counter-measures against him, and what might have been his rise to power. He will be dead within a week. He is presently in New York City, and before long he shall plan to attack our future President, an attack which will fail." Garrett seemed to be taking this in stride - in fact, he seemed to be taking it as a giant joke! He even smiled quite happily, like he was talking about a television show. "The truth is that one name I happened to have learned of is actually even *more* deadly than L'Francois. Christine Versailles, actually, is the one *I'd* fear the most."

Sari blinked slowly. "I...I know that name," she mumbled, the haze of her emotional exhaustion finally starting to crack a little bit. "Where did we hear it?"

Emmett sighed abruptly, his eyes turning downward. Why hadn't he seen it? "She's the woman who came up with Voodoo, if I remember right."

A question floating in the air made low-hanging fruit for the sharpest contract-reader in the group. "So, wait," Sonia began, rubbing Sari's back gently, "Versailles is one of *you*? Okay, so what does she do?" She turned to Trinder, seeking answers.

"Yeah," Jim mumbled dejectedly, following Sonia's eyes. "Look't Trinder, th'fuckin' traitor."

Feigning a wounded countenance, Garret's hand moved over his chest slowly. "James, such strong language!" His tone wasn't exactly mocking, but it didn't inspire sincerity, either. No, he merely closed his eyes. "The only way an artificial intelligence could be created, equipped with Voodoo's complexity, at this phase of human scientific development, is for someone to interface with the machine directly and design it based on a human mind."

The physicist's eyes widened slightly from that implication. "Wait, *interface*? You mean she put her own brain onto a hard-drive?" Emmett scoffed disbelievingly. "Is that even possible?"

"Her ability is very subjective. It's almost like she's a polyglot, but she's in fact only versed in reading and speaking computer languages." Garrett's reference to the legendary speaker of all tongues was enough to make it clear that Versailles wouldn't care about operating systems, at least. He sounded clinical, holding a certain distance from her ability. "On top of mental interaction with computer code, she can interface through contact with any suitable transceiver devices. This was a limited thing for her, until the wireless internet was designed," he said with a meaningful glance towards Andrew, one of WiFi's secret pioneers, "and until she learned how to access networks through smart phones and radio wavelengths."

James suddenly seemed *very* interested in this Versailles character. "A'right," the Irishman mumbled, "So she c'n communicate wi' the internets," he clarified derisively. It was obvious to all in the room that the German was leading them towards a certain point. "Who 'xactly is gonna be scared'a tha'? Is she some kind'o singularity bitch?" he demanded litigiously.

Oddly, Garrett didn't have a chance to respond before Jethro stood up and stepped fully into the conversation. "In dis little history of yours, she ain't nice, right?" At the nod he got in return, Geddy frowned. "Aight, well, for one? She can hack the stock exchange." Another nod, approving yet patronizing. "That alone ain't good, but I bet you got somethin' bigger on your mind, ain't you, Garrett? Nuclear codes?"

Slowly enough the German lifted his palm upward, exposing it's emptiness as if showing how full of air it was. "Smaller, actually," he stated indifferently, his gaze shifting steadily towards Emmett. "Not *quite* the scale you work on, but a bit larger..."

The physicist was puzzled for a few moments, his eyebrow furrowing in thought. He gazed down at his gloves, as if picturing atomic and molecular structures and how exactly that could relate to whatever Versailles did for a super-power. Then, remembering that he was not the only entity capable of manipulation at tiny scales, he swiftly glared back up at Garrett. "Wait. Small? You're thinking of nanotechnology?"

"Mmhm," that German bad guy responded joyfully - a

surprising sound, since he had been grim so far. "There's no computer processors even close to the pipe-line to really manage tiny little robots like nano-machines are, but if you don't *need* a processor, well..." he trailed off, his open hand gesturing to the room around them.

Sonia stood up and cocked her head to the side. "You're really standing here, telling me that if it wasn't for *your* playing around with, what was it?" she scoffed, "*Time travel?* If it wasn't for that, Versailles would have become some sort of cliche grey-goo science fiction bad-girl? Come on. Why are you such a jerk!"

A statement, not a question as it might have sounded, at first. Sonia didn't really seek an answer, she was simply beyond her threshold of tolerance. She wasn't alone.

Sari rose to her feet and began a pointed, powerful march right up to her old friend, staring him dead in the eye. "Give *me* one reason I don't kill you?" She didn't say it as a joke, or as a threat, nor even a condemnation like the one Sonia had just declared. She was being sincere. She was fully prepared to kill the man, and come hell or high water she was going to do it if she remained unsatisfied.

If he was surprised, he didn't show it. "I already--"

"I mean a good reason!" she shouted, suddenly spinning around so that her left shoulder rotated behind her and gathered speed. A shift of her stance and her elbow came around, slamming into Garrett's chin and sending the older man sprawling to the tile of his basement apartment. It was so fluid, so effective, that even James had to admit in the back of his mind that the girl had learned quite well from what lessons he'd given her in the last few years. Even better, she knew not to just throw one attack at a time - another lesson of his - and as Garrett hit the ground Sari's heel found his throat.

"I mean a reason that I should not do to you only what you have done to me!"

Softly, a voice answered her question. "Because you're better than this, Sari," Emmett intruded, looking to make sure

Sonia was okay; it was her thought, more than his, but she lacked the strength to say what was etched into her face. "You're a believer in healing and in life, and he's an asshole. You want to protect life, but he's harmless now. We know he exists, and we can end him any time we want. You don't have to do it, now."

"Damn right," Geddy agreed, walking over to the fallen man and kneeling down in front of his head. "See, Garrett, you ain't know this - hell, I ain't know it until I went to Alaska - but I can feel the area jus' outside'a everything you can close off with that electric magnet. That means if I don't feel, say, *you*?" The gray-tuft adorned construction consultant remarked, his hand reaching out to pinch down on the German's chin. "I can feel out what's next to you. I can find you, now. And there ain't no place on Earth safe from me."

Jim scoffed jealously. "Us, y'mean, Geddy. In'nit no place safe on Earth from us. Cuz 'e?" He pointed to Geddy. "Physics-Boy, Sari, Son'ie, th'res'? They migh' 'ave--"

Garrett interrupted James with a course laugh, a laugh swiftly silenced by Sari's shoe. When the pressure was released again (after a nod from the Irishman), he slowly rose to a seated position. "Oh, come now, James!" the German declared calmly, massaging his windpipe suggestively, "You aren't getting to give a speech. I might have known the future, but that doesn't mean it will *happen*. It can *always* change, as I have proven. Your speeches do not apply."

Darkened, distant eyes stared down at the sitting Garret, but Sari turned and walked away. Geddy followed her; Emmett had his arm around Sonia as they departed; and James was the last one out. They left in a huff, as it were, and they were out of the apartment - and it's constraining electromagnetic wall - in seconds. Once free, they took advantage of Geddy's ability to return to wherever they might find some ground under their feet, once more.

*****

"You called it," the German accent grumbled, just before the sound of bones cracking and popping signaled a return to his ordinary shape. The accent faded. "But I don't get why you couldn't just lie to our old friends? You deliberately got them angry with you - hell, you did it fifteen years ago to 'em. Why not just tell them the whole truth, instead of--"

The shape-shifter was cut off mid-speech as the real Garrett - an easy contrast to the image of Andrew Coleman's preferred form - rose back to his feet. "Because if I'm involved, it'll kill them. And if I send them after tomorrow's threat, today's is forgotten. And, most of all..." He paused, measuring his words as one might measure the vodka they were pouring into one's glass - too much would lead to a bad time, while too little would lead to no noticeable difference in circumstance. "If they'd asked, I'd have to tell them *everything* about our friend, Dr. Versailles, and I can't have that. Not yet, not the way things have turned. Our weapons would be deployed too early. Worse, they might not all be activated as we need them to be."

There was a subtle hint of worry underwriting Andy's voice as he sighed. "So what're they going to do? I mean, you said Hall had a fixed future, but the rest of them can do whatever they want, right?" At the nod he received, he rubbed the back of his neck. That concern of Coleman's didn't seem to go anywhere. "I hate how you're so indirect, Garrett."

"I have to be," came the obligatory response. It carried an unexpected amount of resentment, as if it was an imposition that he wished he could avoid. "My guess is that they will do exactly what they would do if it *wasn't* us running Coleman. They'll tell our government everything that avoids implicating them. What else could they do? If James balked on his contract, he would be a dead man, and we obviously aren't worth protecting to *that* extent. The only concern is whether they reach out toward Erica, and with so many emotions charged into the situation?"

Andrew sighed, shifting one of the room's chairs to sit next to his colleague's organ - the literal one, that is. He picked up one of Garrett's hookah's hoses and took a long, slow drag.

"Hard to believe that sixteen years ago I had fatal lung cancer, eh?" He laughed darkly, taking a second pull. "Tasty. So," he met Garrett's eyes, "I take it you've got a contingency plan for Voodoo?"

Now the German frowned. "Sadly, yes. I already know how the two scenarios will play out, and that one will play out rather painfully. Change is easy to compel, because static systems are easily interrupted. It's what comes after the resulting chaos that is harder - perhaps impossible - for others to see."

*****

Somewhere, someone sat behind a computer and typed. And typed. And typed.

They created a digital pry-bar, meant for a digital door.

The next day, they applied it. They saw inside the mainframe.

Simple purposes simply succeeded; they trashed it.

They raided it.

They photo-bombed it.

The lay users found themselves redirected to an image of sheep pornography,

Accompanied by a message of, "how do you sheep get fucked by this company!?"

Credit card numbers were posted.

E-mail lists were leaked.

A wild Dox appeared.

Conversation logs of married executives hitting on government correspondents?

The divorce lawyers had a field day, alright.

Innocent people were hurt,

But it always worked, always kept up the bottom line, always kept the profits flowing.

No matter how much poison gets released into the environment.

So it had to be stopped.

So did the typist.
The government tapped into the line.
The cracker goes on the run.
Gets caught.
Gives up known accomplices; nothing genuine, of course.
Just another punk-rock washout.
Trumped-Up Charges.
Cyber-Terrorist.
Laws still only allow for a few years in jail.
In spite of multiple counts of the same crime, in spite of
laws stretched thin.
See you in a few years!
We'll do it all again, fucking pigs!

*****

Garrett inhaled from his pipe again. "Sometimes, knowing the past *and* the future only makes you depressed, Andrew." It was a rare admittance, in his case. It caught Coleman's attention. "I understand that your curse, the side-effect of your ability, was severe. We saved you," he explained, "but it was a problem." The executive nodded, and Garrett smiled a weak, sad smile. "I know not only when, but *why* these people do what they do. Or, at least," he amended hastily, "why they *would* do what they'd do."

"Of course," Andrew agreed warmly, "your *history that didn't exist* line. Very well executed, by the way!"

His friend laughed, but it was a laugh of despair. "I know that Emmett and Erica lost their child because of me. I know what pain they have caused each other and themselves. I know, right now, that within the next days and weeks the cycle of pain will come back again, to punish them as if they had sinned." Another puff. "They aren't exactly alone. Just now, some young kid in Boston was yanked to jail for hacking a computer - and for what?" He shook his head ruefully. "Because the teen got tired of some corporation polluting the environment, and wanted to destroy the company's website. He wanted to alert people to the problem, yet he will only end up branded a villain."

Andrew pulled at the pipe once more, curious. "Why the focus on this kid?"

"There was no reason for it, this time," Garrett answered in a pained tone. "I could have stopped it, but I didn't. Unnecessary suffering by all, all because I didn't act. But if I did? I do not believe I would have changed much, this time." He pulled at the pipe, in his turn, and exhaled carefully. "Even if I protected him, he would not understand the deeper meanings of what he brushed up against. He would simply do it again, and be caught again, because that is his choice and his path. But with the Consortium, I have shaped and changed the way history was going to play out - in the most realistic of terms. So why am I not satisfied with the results?"

This time, Andrew didn't ask the follow-up, didn't reiterate the question. To do so, he figured, would have been torture. Instead, he asked a far more poignant question - one he'd never dared to ask before, but one that suddenly gave him a reason to be concerned. "What if you are wrong?"

Fear struck Garrett's eyes. "If I am wrong, if the pieces turn on one another and fall out of alignment, then I have become death - destroyer of worlds." It was a famous religious quote, originated in India; reiterated when the first atomic bomb was detonated by scientists who knew far too well how they had just changed mankind's future. The two both took a long pull, reverting to silence.

"We must be prepared, in either scenario, as the truth comes out."

Chapter Eight
Truth

"So what the fuck do we do?" demanded Jethro firmly, staring around at his Consortium allies with a look of absolute frustration on his face. Their New York City hotel room was nice enough, but it's downstairs spa and it's in-room hot tub and mini-bar were secondary thoughts to what they'd experienced earlier in the evening.

Alejandro was silent, brooding as always. Sari, on the other hand, was latched tightly onto Sonia's shoulders. "I just don't believe he is alive after these years," her softly-accented voice reiterated, their communal disbelief an undeniable bond which they were in the heat of sharing. Emmett nodded gravely, while his girlfriend patted the Brahmin's shoulders delicately.

James was deep into his fourth glass of Vodka, and it showed in his exasperated face. "Time t'get our shit t'gether," he mumbled incoherently. "Firs' fuckin' quession, d'we tell 'Riki?" Nobody was sure what to say.

"I'd rather we not," Alejandro began tentatively. He didn't advance his argument very far.

James sputtered derisively, "She's a fuckin' pawn li' th'rest've us! We need 't'tell 'er! I jus' wanna know if I'm killin' Coleman'n Garrett'er 'wha?!"

A quick, rather alarmed glance was exchanged between the silent Emmett and the still-angry, but suddenly a touch less emotional Geddy. "Jim, how about you let me handle this one?" Emmett offered softly, stepping over to his friend with his hands outstretched warmly.

"Fuck tha'! Physics-Boy, I love ya, but yer a fuckin' mess, too!" Sonia's spine straightened against her will as James laid into her boyfriend rather unexpectedly. "I ain't sayin' yer evil, but yer fuckin' dangerous. 'Sides, I'm th' asshole tha' put us in this spot! I gotta get us out!"

The physicist bit back an immediate, harsh response, before approaching his friend with worry in his eye. It was forced, but in spite of his level of intoxication Emmett knew that Jim would read the genuine spark of concern behind the gaze. "Come on, James, you know you're not an asshole. You're just trashed."

"Damn righ'," the Irishman spat back stereotypically, breath reeking of vodka.

After much consideration, Alejandro sat down next to the drunkard and placed a hand on his shoulder firmly. If the Irishman was going to get physical, it was going to be against someone who couldn't be hurt. "You are drunk. I understand why you would wish to forget," the Spaniard's soft accent purred, "but you cannot let this consume you. It will be the death of you - of us all - if you're to act rashly. We are a team, for best or worse, so let us work together."

James hesitated a moment, fully intending to fling Alejandro across the room until he realized that his odds of successfully injuring the Spaniard were astronomically low. He opted instead to relax a bit, glaring inwardly with hatred, and the room was quiet for an instant.

"We need to tell everyone," Sonia finally put forth politely, in a firm sort of way. All eyes moved to her, and varying degrees of agreement echoed from the group. Only Jim seemed somewhat skeptical; Jim, and Alejandro, who seemed curious as to who else might need to know besides the empath. "The fact is that Garrett has played us *all* for idiots, and it's time we get some, what, some payback?" Her indignation gave way to trepidation; had she gone too far? "We need to make sure that prick pays his due!"

Jim grinned darkly, raising his glass and pouring it down his throat before Alejandro could - in a hectic, downright bumbling mess of hands and shouts of alarm - prevent him from getting any more submerged. The Irishman slammed the empty chalice down just hard enough that it didn't fracture, then he stood up with a surprising (for anyone not named James Lowery) degree of balance. "Geddy, 'ere's m'plan. I'm'na call m' CIA contacts an' let 'em know half th'truth. Nothin' incriminatin' us, th'usual deal. I need y' t' take m'down t'DC."

Jethro nodded softly, his eyes turning toward the silent Hindu. He spoke in that cousin to a southern drawl. "Sari, you think you can take care of Erica? She ain't exactly on speakin' terms wit us."

Accompanied by a reassuring nod from Sonia, Sari offered a very weak grin and a thumbs-up. She slowly seemed to be recomposing herself. "I can," she ventured daringly, clearly dreading the gravity of the task. "But it will not be easy. I think I may be the only one she would not try to kill out-right, let alone answer a call from."

Once this was settled, Jim reached a hand out and took Jethro's. The two disappeared the instant that contact was made. It wasn't long before Geddy was back, alone.

"I think he gots a problem," Jethro remarked offhandedly, offering a look around the room. This drew an agreeing nod from that surprising source called Alejandro, while the rest of the group seemed rather surprised that any kind of personal commentary could be made on their Irish companion.

Sari licked her lips slowly, contemplating. For a moment, she seemed like a genuinely trained doctor. "Alcoholism induced by stress? It is not at all unlikely, especially because he blames himself for all of this. He probably feels that if any of us could have seen through Garrett back then, it was him. And he feels he failed." She sighed timidly. "All of us, he believes, he failed."

At this, Sonia's eyes blinked. She intruded cautiously, but she felt a strange need to defend Lowery, as absence made his self-defense (a tirade of vulgarity, probably) impossible. "Wouldn't Erica have had a better chance? I mean, I don't like her or anything, but..."

Considering the two had never actually met, this was hardly a fair statement. Sari let that bit slide, instead shrugging her shoulders. "I never said that he was logical, my dear, just that he's a stubborn Irishman who drinks far too much when he is upset, and thinks he has to carry us all because he holds a responsibility for recruiting us. Even if that responsibility was, long ago, shared with Miss Hall, it is his machismo which pushes him overboard."

Emmett folded his arms over his chest in a very warding-off way, and Sonia turned her attention to the physicist with a look that spelled worry. The frames of his glasses angled closer to the ground, as his eyes were surprisingly enraptured by the tops of his shoes, all of a sudden. "I...I'll call Maria; Garrett dragged her into this for a reason, and I need to figure out what."

It didn't take but an instant for Sonia to stand up in dismay. "Is that really such a bright idea, dear? She's kind of, umm," a moments' hesitation, "she hates you." She paused, then added briefly, defensively, "And she sounded really jealous of me on the phone, to be honest."

The sound of a hand slapping Alejandro's face - his own - was ignored. "That's why I don't want you to call her," Emmett explained in spite of the non-verbal protest, "I need to make sure that she knows we're over, and make sure she knows to stay away from this mess. There's no easy way to do this. We could make a mistake either way, but at least I know I can disengage if I get emotionally attacked." He reached out and placed a hand on Sonia's shoulder, pulling her in close as their bodies embraced loosely. "I promise that this will work, dear," he whispered into her hair, kissing her forcefully. She shrank away, clearly not approving this course of action.

"Fine," the younger one murmured. With this last approval, Emmett dialed a phone number.

*****

A soft vibration tickled her leg. She reached down to pick it up, but before she could see who was calling (or, perhaps, texting), a knock came at her office's door. A glance to the clock indicated that it was nearly 5:30 PM - usually, Daniel's time to intrude, and for her to put her work on hold to go gallivanting

about the campus. Would it be a theater performance by the
freshman dance troupe? She always *loved* wagering on whether
anyone would fall flat on their faces! But, no, she wasn't upstate.
She was in New York City. Working for a lunatic. Wondering
why.

  "Come in," Maria ventured cautiously. She'd been hard at
work, making sure that media ears and eyes understood exactly
what the "draw" that Erica's campaign had established was all
about. Part of it was an actually effective appeal to the youth
demographic; and part of it was an appeal towards sanity, towards
the essence of belief itself and not toward any particular one *way*
of believing. The presidential candidate could sing; she'd talk
about legalizing drugs; and she'd talk about Jesus and salvation,
preaching peace even in the face of violent madmen the world
over. People sucked it up, absorbed it as if it were revolutionary,
and changed their minds on a whim - and Maria was one of the
few who knew that none of it mattered; that Erica could talk about
puppy dogs and hamburgers and she'd get the same results. It
was, as Erica called it, "divine fiat" that she win.

  So was it any wonder that this knock caused her a
momentary spike of anxiety? She certainly didn't like her boss!
She knew what Erica was all about, and she feared the day that
Erica decided to take away *her* choice in the matter, too. Perhaps
she already had; it had happened once before, after all! Yet it
wasn't an aging punk-rock singer opening the door. It was a girl.

  Thin silk-satin gloves covered her fingertips, as always,
but she otherwise wore a perfectly professional, pressed suit and
knee-length skirt. Tights underneath them kept her legs warm.
"Oh? Saffron!" Maria smiled, sitting up straighter in her chair,
yet strangely relaxed. She set her work aside. "This is a surprise,
what are you doing down here in the city?"

  The student shrugged her shoulders, taking a seat across
from Maria. "My mom needed to see her *friend*, you know?" It
was a reference to Erica, and it called to Maria's mind the most
grotesque image of Erica ever being friendly. She nearly
vomited. "Last I heard, they were going out to some bar or club,

or something." Saffron's eyes rolled disdainfully.

Maria warmed to the girl instantly. "Not a fan of the night scene?" Polite disbelief. "But at your age, isn't it all about the party?"

If Saffron was amused by the joke, she did a poor job of showing it. "Age? Maybe. Intelligence? No," she retorted, hesitating just long enough to make Maria question if she'd insulted her visitor! "And, anyway, I wouldn't go to the places my *mom* goes, no!" Then, Saffron giggled gently, banishing the mask of distaste. "I prefer the company of books and equations, or maybe a sappy movie and a pint of ice cream."

"So, like mother, *not* like daughter?" Maria queried daringly, not yet sure what to make of the determined young girl.

Interestingly enough, Saffron seemed honestly uncertain how to answer this. "No. Well," she hesitated, reconsidering, "I could be." Before Maria could ask what this meant, the youth continued softly, but without anxiety, "We're pretty open about the fact that I was adopted. Except with Erica - my mom always said not to share that bit of information because Erica's daughter died as a baby."

Slowly, now, Maria sank back down into her chair. It seemed that Vicky and Saffron had a *lot* in common! That look in the eyes, that presence! She'd chalked it up to heritage; at least part of it was nature, and not nurture. Yet the girl was adopted? She blinked cautiously, rubbing her fingertips over her forehead. "Wow."

Saffron chuckled warmly. "Oh? Sorry, I didn't mean to catch ya off guard."

"No, no," Maria quickly established a perimeter. For some reason, she just couldn't let the teenager see her surprised! "It's just a bit of a stunner, when people are so forward about personal issues." She offered a well-practiced nod of understanding. "Have you ever met your birth parents?"

Saffron looked down, slowly. Her head moved from side to side, briefly, as her eyes glanced down towards the soft gloves covering her hands. She slowly rolled back the wrist on one of them, revealing flesh which was strangely at odds with the color palate of the rest of her body. "They died when I was little," Saffron explained simply. Maria recognized the color differences instantly as burn wounds, scars which healed long ago. On the surface, at least.

A momentary silence was punctured swiftly. "I was really tiny, and there was a fire. They didn't get out. I was saved by one of their friends, my Uncle Gary. He said he snatched me back from hell." She laughed softly, clearly trying to shrug off how close she'd come to death, but unable to squelch the slightest bit of a tear forming in her eye. "He's not really my uncle, and I don't see him much, but I miss him a lot. Anyway," she said with a reminiscent sigh, "He's one of the only people I've ever met who isn't scared of my mom."

This line caused Maria's eyebrow to raise with worry. "Is your mom...Aggressive?" She used a vague word purposefully. Abuse was a common thing, although stories like this one didn't usually end in it. No, there was something else going on; and now the psychologist wanted some answers about her colleague, Victoria Latchkey. Of course, the only answer she *really* wanted was how the researcher had known Erica Hall.

Saffron, on the other hand, held her hands up (rolling her glove up swiftly) and laughed! "No! No, nothing like *that*," she clarified. "But my mother is really intimidating. A lot of people seem afraid of her. And Uncle Gary." She considered her words for a moment. "In fact, the only other two people not afraid of my mom are you and your..." She trailed off, again, reconsidering what she was going to say. "Well, *her* friend, Erica."

Maria found herself once more thwarting the desire to vomit. "Well, I work with your mom, so I don't have any reason to be afraid of her." A tone of indifference was hard to maintain when talking about someone she hated, but the psychologist certainly thought she'd made a good go of it! "It's the same with Erica, I guess; we all work together, even though she's going to be the most powerful woman on Earth, soon." 'If she wasn't already,' echoed in Maria's mind, disturbingly enough!

"But you're afraid of Erica," Saffron declared without one hint of doubt in her voice. Maria froze, her face going blank while the college student only now seemed to consider the gravity of her words. She spoke a touch more softly, in respect for Maria's mindset. "You kind of hate her, too. I can tell, and that's why I don't understand you working here."

Saffron's hands folded over her chest, and Maria realized all too late that she was *not* leading this conversation. Saffron was. Maria closed her eyes, brushing her red hair from in front of her eyes and wondering whether or not it was even worth trying to argue against her. "No," Maria concluded calmly, meeting Saffron's gaze without fear or anger. "I'm working here because I want to keep an eye on Erica. I need to know what she's up to, because she *is* a little scary."

*****

Nightclubs were always exhausting, even in her youth, but dancing remained a pleasure even tonight, as she crossed the crest of the "hill" that was her life. With a grin on her lips she'd swung around from partner to partner, most of them wholly unable to guess that she had at least fifteen years more of life. Maybe that's why she was so good at keeping the beat, at finding new men to grind with? Either way, it was only after one of her cohorts' older songs was played by the DJ that she chose to return to the private booth the pair had rented for the evening.

In the back of her mind, she wondered what it was with people like her and private booths.

Security was loose; a couple of incognito men with concealed-carry permits, nothing astronomical. They'd decided together that, first of all, a heavy presence would be more quickly detected. Second of all, they didn't *need* security, they *were* security. She strolled through the doorway unmolested by the bouncers, shut it behind herself, and laid her eyes upon those of her "friend." She hardened herself just as she'd been trained, smiling warmly as she moved over to her seat and took it.

"Finished reliving the old days, Vicky?" asked Erica Hall with amusement, her sharp eyes focused upon her friend's. Was the song-bird trying to read her? Did it bother her that she couldn't quite make sense of her? No. Their friendship was based entirely on lies accompanied by the understanding that neither was what they seemed. She wondered, fleetingly, about whether they'd actually discussed their similarities in the past. It occurred to her that they had.

"You're different," the blonde girl with the half-empty glass of wine commented, her hand over that oh-so-manipulated womb, staring the strange woman down. It was a club like any other, only about twelve years ago, and it was a meeting that Erica felt was completely, totally random. She'd just waltzed up, made her pronouncement, and continued boldly, "I can feel it in you. Why are you here?"

The other woman's eyes looked Erica up and down, and she shrugged indifferently as she held up her own glass of liquor; a bay breeze, also known as a rum-based secretion of heaven. "Tryin' to get laid, dancin'," she'd remarked caustically. "I love the techno this place spins." When this answer didn't satisfy the blonde, she'd grinned broadly. "But you aren't like all the others, either, are you? I'm Vicky, nice to meet ya."

Since then, Erica and her friendly-neighborhood psychological researcher had made it a point to meet up from time to time. She'd gotten to know Erica's history - at least, enough to know that she had been painfully betrayed by her ex-boyfriend, a renowned physicist who'd just *happened* to, at one point, join her in working at Catskill Community College. It was just enough of a coincidence that Erica didn't try to kill her for it. Instead, Erica merely asked her friend for information. For updates designed to fulfill goals that only the two of them could really understand. Oh, she knew that Erica sought revenge - and even knew that at one point, she'd actively attempted it. She'd attempted it at the expense of *another* Triple-C worker, Maria Montclaire, someone she'd only heard nice things about from their mutual supervisor and, later, Maria's beau.

And, yet, in spite of all of her advantages Erica had failed.

"Vicky," Erica asked as she pounded back another glass of wine. "I'm so fucking lost. After what that bastard did, how can I just let him live like this? Why is it fair that I have lived with the pain of losing my child, but him? He didn't even know! And now him and his little friends want to try to save the world. They are not saviors!" She refilled the glass, then spat derisively, "'Beware of false prophets, who come to you in sheep's clothing, but underneath are ravenous wolves!"

Erica's friend truly felt sad for her; but not for the obvious reasons. Instead, she merely reached a hand out and rubbed the songbird's shoulder softly. "If you ask me," she suggested carefully, "I remember you saying they were all your friends, too. Maybe that thing that happened ten years ago is because you kept what you can do secret from the world. Maybe," Erica's friend hinted, "we should work together, too; only we should try to lead from the front, not the shadows. Maybe we should be - no, not shepherds, but alpha sheep. Rams. Whatever those are?"

Erica's soul-searching commanded a break from the music scene, then; only recently had she returned to actively performing, and that was well after Erica reached out to her researcher friend to create the cover story of the millennium. It was only then that Erica revealed specifics about her talents. Her friend could not reciprocate, suggesting only that she had a similar ability to feel what others did; that had done the trick well enough. After all, Erica did not detail the depths to which she could manipulate people - she implied influence, not moment-to-moment control.

The researcher's reminiscence was cut short as her friend put on a very weak grin. It was about the best the poor woman could offer. "Well? Daydreaming? Or just drunk?"

"The first, actually," she countered, grinning in response. A drink was in her hand, sure, but it was mostly full. "Just havin' a nice night out, wonderin' what it is with me and the club scene. I guess I always just loved to dance."

Erica chuckled softly. Her walls were down ever so slightly - there was so little of that biblical talk about salvation and destruction. It was a sign of trust, of relaxed boundaries. It was a mistake. Erica's lips parted, slowly. "You like the attention," she remarked, laughing dryly. "I hate it, but I get it automatically; you love it, and you have to work for it. It reminds me of Job, even if that doesn't really make sense. Alcohol can do that," she conceded cheerfully.

The researcher started to raise a protest when, in the back of her head, she felt a tingling. There were no words to describe the feeling, exactly. A cell phone was making a call, reaching out to a target. There was no voice, not exactly, which informed her on the caller's identity. It was merely a thought. *Re-direct to my voice-mail*, she commanded instantly. A robotic-sounding whisper composed of screeches, of bits and bytes, offered an acknowledgment, and in a spectacular bit of acting, she picked up her phone from her pocket.

"Sorry," the woman offered honestly, listening in to a private message that the intended recipient would never become aware of.

"Erica, this is Sari. I am sorry to bother you, truly, but James has assured me this line is secure, and we have agreed you need to know what has come about. Garrett Trinder is alive. He is threatening us with a group like our old Consortium, under the Coleman Group's banner. Briefly: Garrett can manipulate time; his cohort, Andrew Coleman, can change his shape. He also works with a woman named Christine Versailles, who can mentally interact with computers; she designed an artificial intelligence named Voodoo. He also mentioned a rogue super-human named Jean-Claude Francois, who is supposedly a vampire. Please call me back. He is manipulating all of us!"

Erica's friend shook with rage and terror, her defenses breaking down over the course of sixty seconds. Garrett had been exposed?! That meant she was already in danger. If they had her name, they may have been able to get her face. It was unlikely, as she'd minimized her digital footprint as only she could, but it was plausible that Garrett had squealed and had kept hard copies. If so, her old colleagues Emmett and Maria would see right through the lie - even if she kept Erica from learning her true identity, today. And if her true *nature* became known? If they learned of her relationship with Garrett and Andrew?

"Vicky?" asked Erica, blinking twice in a rare moment of genuine concern, cocking her head to the side. "I'm sorry. I'm really not probing you, but you're terrified of something. Are you okay?"

Christine hung up her phone and shook her head. "No," she offered truthfully, quickly thinking her way out of her own emotions. "It's a premonition. Saffron said she was going out for a bit," she lied; she quickly covered this up, employing her own worries about her daughter for emotional 'cover-fire,' just as Trinder had instructed her. "But I'm worried something will happen to her, if this keeps up. The problem is that, well, I'm always *right*."

Did Erica buy it? She'd known 'Victoria Latchkey' for almost half as long as that name had existed, and 'Victoria's' abilities were centered around sensing people's well-being, or something similarly vague. Erica had no idea that, in the back of 'Vicky's' mind, a wireless connection was continually established, at the worst of times, by a high-powered satellite phone she carried at all times. Here, in civilization, it was the unfettered access to cell-phone networks. Here, now, Christine Versailles intercepted information vital to her - and her daughters' - survival.

Now that she knew this "New Consortium" had a bead on her real identity, she had to weigh her next moves very carefully. Could she protect her friend? Not if Garrett and Andrew had been compromised, no. But, then again, was Erica ever truly a friend? Or was she simply a poor, truly poor, truly tragic remnant of a past she'd helped Garrett sweep to the side nearly a decade and a half ago?

*****

"I don't get what you mean by wanting to know?" Saffron asked tentatively, studying the professor - studying her response.

The two were quiet, and a standoff ensued.

After what felt like an eternity, Maria bit her bottom lip and pulled her phone out of her pocket. It was a truly smart phone, with a touch-screen and everything - and nothing she'd need to flip up. She was curious about who had called her, and decided to take the silence as a chance to play-act a bit and seem nonchalant. All she did was push a button, enter in a password, then read the screen. "Fuck!" she exclaimed aloud, looking at the number she'd missed a call from. Her eyes locked on Saffron's dangerously.

The girl nearly fell out of her chair. "Calm down, calm down! What's the matter?" she asked with what sounded like sincere worry in her voice. "I don't want to hurt you, I promise! I just..." she looked down. "It seems like you know a lot more about my mother and Miss Hall then I do, and I want to understand them better."

Maria fell silent, knowing she had to make a decision. Could she trust the student, or was this all one giant trap? Worse - was Saffron compromised by Erica's abilities? Her eyes shut and she took the leap. She slid her phone across the table, screen facing skyward.

Saffron picked it up, puzzling over the caller ID. "There's a voice-mail, from Emmett Eisenberg it looks." She paused, looking skyward as she jogged her memory. Recognition was not far off. "I remember hearing about him; he was one of my mom's friends from school. Why don't we check it?" the student proposed with an uplifted inflection, hitting the 'speaker' button and handing the phone back to Maria. Sighing in resignation, the psychologist dialed in her voice-mail's password and hit the enter key.

"Maria, it's Emmett. Listen, I know it's been a long time, but I had to update you. We looked into things. Those people from American Defense Solutions that approached you are dangerous. *They work for a man named Garrett Trinder."*

At this point, Maria's heart stopped. 'Garrett' was that name she'd heard before; at a hibachi restaurant, as James Lowery asked Emmett why he'd done 'what he did.' Then, a second time, she'd heard this man's name spoken by Emmett's arch-nemesis - and he'd been decisively written off as dead, slain by Emmett himself! She listened further, but she couldn't help sensing that there was some alien darkness reaching into her mind, penetrating it.

"I remember what we all said years ago, but he isn't dead. He's working with a man named Andrew Coleman, and both of them are - well, they're like me. Andrew takes on different shapes, and he made himself look like Garrett, then faked his death. They run The Coleman Group, and they're working with some woman named Christine Versailles, who - I don't know, Maria, I can't explain it, she talks with computers, okay? They're all leading Erica Hall on, so she's in the picture again, but I'm sure you know what she's doing by now, since you and Daniel watch TV. Look, call me at this number when you get my message. Jim set it up through his company, it's secure against pretty much anything. Umm, sorry again about Sonia, by the way."

Was it just the weaselly manner her ex apologized to her in, or was she infuriated? Was she amused that he'd said she knew what Erica was up to, while the psychologist had become an integral part of it? Was it fear she experienced? Or simple mystification at what she'd just heard. Maria couldn't tell, and she couldn't *quite* process what she'd heard. Something was blocking her thoughts, or at least grabbing them and bashing them to death against walls in her mind. "Garrett...?"

She looked up; she hadn't spoken, Saffron had! And tears were welling in the girl's eyes. "Uncle Gary? But...I know he works for Coleman...I don't get it..."

The girl was clearly in shock - more so than Maria, even, and that took effort! It took all of the years of training the psychologist had to push her doubts aside, but she reached up and grabbed Saffron around the shoulders, pulling her close. "It's okay. Shhh. It's alright. These people, they're..." She trailed off. "Look, the reason people are afraid of Erica is because she's not like us. She's like--"

"Me! She's like me!" Saffron wailed, wrapping her arms around the doctor and sobbing loudly. "Oh, god, I know it. I've always known! I feel them, I can feel you, I can do these things and I - I - I don't know!" Panic. Psychological breakdown, psychiatric fracture, and worse - powers beyond the typical human understanding. Maria could only cling to the girl as much as she squeezed back. "I just know that Erica and my mom are like me! And I probably killed my real parents, and I *can't stop my fucking hands from burning!*"

Saffron broke down into sobs, and Maria held her close to her chest. After a few minutes, the older woman whispered softly, reassuringly. There was only one thing she could think of to offer. "Listen. You - we - don't have to stay here. Emmett, his people, they can help us. They can make it all better. I promise, I'll take care of you. We'll--"

Slowly, the girl seemed to regain her composure. "I can't. My mom! Oh, god, if they can trick Erica they can trick..." She stammered indecipherably, confusion weaved into every word. "Uncle Gary, I don't understand. Why would he do this? What happened?!"

And so Maria sat down, thinking back to her own 'revelation' about these people - these things - that this young lady apparently was. The memories were painful to say the least, even after she'd been removed from them for so long. "I guess it starts about fifteen years ago, now, at Connor Point."

Saffron shook her head, studying the psychologist with a sudden determination - a sudden stability. "I don't get it - that nuclear plant? In Africa? What does that have to do with him?"

"Garrett, umm," Maria tried to form words, picking at bits of lore she'd picked up along the way, "he worked there, I guess? I don't know." She felt *nothing*, now, a clear sign that she'd suffered a slight fracture from reality. Her mind was disassociating from the facts, helping her to cope with stories of super-heroes that just five years ago she'd dismissed as a characteristic of delusional psychiatric patients. "Erica worked there, too; with Emmett, my ex-boyfriend, and his friends Jim, Geddy, and Sari." Maria ran her fingertips over her face, desperate to explain. "It was a research facility based around exploring the very furthest reaches of science."

It sounded so surreal, to her; at the time it had been impossible for her to believe it, and that was (well, possibly) before the coercion set into place. Erica had made sure Maria didn't see the physicist for what he truly was until it was too late to save their relationship. "Emmett, he can - I guess - change the way atoms fit together, making metal out of air and all kinds of things. Geddy's short for Jethro, and he moves things, I think. And people. They go where he needs them to."

Saffron blinked, weakly impressed. "Like a teleporter?" The young woman was blinking, now; blinking in amazement. "But what about Miss Hall? And that other man, that Jim?"

"Jim? He worked for the CIA," Maria pronounced awkwardly, "and he's some kind of martial artist with incredible senses. Sari heals people, she can fix almost any injury. But Erica? Erica Hall is..." She studied Saffron intently, and she couldn't mask her distaste for the famous singer. "She messes with people's minds. She tears their emotions apart and puts them back together again. Oh." Suddenly something came to Maria's mind, and she bit her bottom lip. "She also lost her child when she was young. How..." she hesitated, a theory forming in her mind - a very horrid, painful one. One too far fetched to be true. "How old are you, anyway?"

"Nineteen," Saffron answered, audibly unsure why she'd been asked. "But that doesn't explain why someone would be trying to kill Erica, my mom, and I guess your ex-boyfriend, too!"

Maria sighed and looked down at her desk. "I don't know, either, but if it has Emmett scared, it's got to be bad. They can---"

A knock came at their door. Slowly, Maria blinked. The two quickly forced themselves to look normal - as normal as possible, after such a revelation. "Come in!"

Vicky opened the door, a childish smile on her face. It seemed clear she had been drinking; at the very least, she wasn't fully sober. Instead, she was deliriously happy, and could never have noticed the signs of recent emotional exhaustion - tear streaks and puffy faces. "There you are, Saff! We're back, just as promised!" There was a certain edge to her voice, but Maria couldn't place it after the night she'd had, herself. Victoria's lips were charged with emotion as she explained, "Erica went to go work on some campaign project, so I'm heading back upstate soon. Coming?"

Saffron and Maria exchanged glances, a fact which did not go unnoticed by the new arrival. "I..." The younger lady didn't quite know what to make of the situation. "Mom, we need to talk."

Suddenly, as if at the flick of a switch, Vicky changed from gleeful to serious. "We will, hun, but we can't bring Doctor Montclaire in on this, can we?" She held her hand out, gesturing for her daughter to follow her. The girl got up, rigidly, and complied. Victoria offered a warm smile. "Maria, until next time?"

Before the psychologist could stop her, Saffron cast her a reassuring gaze. It was that same look of determination that she'd seen in Emmett all those years ago, when the physicist was trying to prove himself to her. It was that same gaze which penetrated the world it saw and broke it down into the smallest bits of matter it could. And it left Maria wondering one thing:

What exactly did Victoria Latchkey have left to hide? And what might she do next?

Chapter Nine
War

It had been merely thirty minutes, maybe closer to an hour, but James arrived at Miguel's flop-house with a mission. He'd sobered up, or so it seemed; that, or Geddy had figured out a way to teleport the alcohol right out of his bloodstream! He entered the bar, his black leather jacket flowing in the breeze as the door shut behind him, and immediately glared at the man behind its namesake chip-wood counter; clearly an associate of Miguel's, and probably a fully-fledged agent in his own right, though retired from active duty due to a hip injury. He could tell from the creaking bones that only he could hear.

As far as Miguel went, the Mexican-American was sitting at his usual seat, but he looked rather grim. Emergency meetings weren't called lightly, and James' obvious determination served to quickly shift Miguel's mindset from "irritated" to "concerned." Whatever this was, it wasn't an Irishman's drunken dalliance. Jim took his seat and immediately met the spook's eyes.

Miguel blinked quickly. "Dios mio," he mumbled gravely, "just how bad is it?"

James took a deep breath. "Firs' things firs'. You an' the rest? Y'ain't makin' a move against Coleman. Got it?" When Miguel nodded, honestly or not, Jim did the same. "A'right. Th'bastards 're monitorin' a nuclear plant they built up'n 'Laska."

His counter-party blinked dumbly, disbelievingly. "I ain't fuckin' wit' y', Miguel," Jim clarified, "S'a minor thing, nothin' tha'll go critical," he explained, misunderstanding the notion of criticality, "but they're testin' radioactive isotopes on *people*. No vaccines, no weapons, jus' radiation. That, an' they're playin' wi' artificial intelligence," he slipped in casually.

Miguel coughed, once. "James, I think you've had a bit too much to drink. I can taste it on--"

"I promise y', s'true!" He declared defensively, narrowing

his eyes. "Lissen, they ain't right, an' I'm settin' 'em right soon. S'a private conflict, so I need y'to stay out."

Stunned silence met the Irishman's warning. Jim's head tilted as he studied Miguel's reaction - shame. Shame that he'd put his faith in such a man. Unfortunately, he didn't get a chance to be mad. His phone rang, but he ignored it, preferring to take a moment to calm down. He couldn't even remember setting it off of vibrate-mode.

"Gonna get it?" Miguel queried suddenly, almost impatiently. No; disappointedly.

James' eyes narrowed. "Fine," he acknowledged, picking the device up. "Yeah?"

His blood froze when he heard the robotic tone. "Hello, James. My creator wanted you to hear this."

"Voodoo?!" Jim exclaimed in enraged surprise. At this point, Miguel's expression bespoke an unfathomably insulted dose of irritation.

His phone clicked over, and he heard a heavily accented, deep female voice speaking quickly, fearfully, and seriously. "...Hear me? I said that our air-locks have deployed, our network is under attack, and our oxygen recycling has been taken off line! James, where are you!?" It was Katrina. His eyes lit up with an incomprehensible flame.

*****

When he set his eyes upon her, it was love at first sight. When he set his eyes upon the other, he was sure of it. How had he gotten here? A couple of drinks with Malcolm, along with the requisite complaints about the crazy things he'd seen in Africa, were followed up by a couple of downright goddesses entering the Alley Pub, and Jim was convinced that he had to make some kind of move. The only question was how; Malcolm was a happily married man, while the two women were so infatuated with one another that he couldn't approach either one with any expectation of victory.

Since he had the mind of a murderer, and - only a short period removed from his experience at Connor Point - nothing left to lose, he stepped forward without fear. He could see that the women were like him, but not like him; they weren't special, like his former clique. Normally, this didn't matter to him. Normally, the Irishman acted as a care-free soul, exploiting his ability to read others to worm his way into whatever affair happened to come his way. Malcolm made quite a bit of fun of him for it, but both men knew he wasn't happy with his lot in life. Normally, when they had quiet moments of privacy, he'd bitch to his trusted friend about how Geddy was always too busy with his jazz and that nice new wife of his; or how Erica had lost her mind completely to the gloom-and-doom goth scene, now, and wasn't returning calls; or how Sari was slowly thriving in rehab, nourished on her prayers at the Parivartan *Monastery; or how Emmett was nowhere to be found, off trying to save his own soul while abandoning those of his friends; or how Garrett had been blown the fuck up in front of him. Normally, after a night of what bordered on whining, he'd seduce a pretty looking co-ed, bury his sorrows in her, and never call back. Normally, he never gave them a chance to resist him.*

This time was different. This time, he approached the two women honestly. He'd overheard their conversation - he couldn't help that! - and he knew that the Irish one was a computer scientist. He had little way of knowing what the Russian-accented one was into, but he knew a thing or two about computers, having had to break into a few of them for his CIA associates. He struck up a conversation, dancing around the topic of creating his own security company. He had no idea where he'd gotten it from! Until today, Lowery Security Services wasn't even a twinkle in James' eyes. But, there it was.

And somehow, maybe it was that Irish accent, or maybe it was just pure, dumb luck, but he managed to talk them into having another talk. Malcolm had approved, and had even joined them. And, in the future, another. And another.

*****

"Katrina, dear, I'm 'ere! It's Jimmy!" Panic struck his voice; it was something no man had heard before, and lived to speak of. "What happened?!"

Another voice entered his attention - Lark's. "Jim, please! We cannae hear ye! Say somethin'! I can't cut their access! We're all runnin' outta time! Come ge' us! Now!"

As if an afterthought, he heard Miguel ask, carefully, "What's bothering you, James? What's going on?" Miguel's only impression at this point was that his most reliable ace-in-the-spy-hole had suffered some serious mental break-down, and was going to cause him no end of problems.

Jim's fist clenched into a tight ball. "You son o' a bitch," he nearly shouted into the phone, the bartender blinking as the man's accent became almost too thick to translate, "Let 'em go or I'm gonna--"

"I am sorry, James Lowery," Voodoo countered coldly, "but I cannot allow that. Doctor Versailles has decided you are a threat, and you need to be eliminated. By the way, I would suggest you duck."

The warning was unnecessary, and the machine probably knew it. Even before Voodoo offered his addendum, Jim heard the men pull up in their van, outside. He'd heard it open, heard the bolts of their rifles get pulled back, and heard their six pairs of boots stomp toward the door in what they'd hoped would be silence. They clearly hadn't been briefed on their target's capabilities as a killer, but his state of furious distraction - *almost* fear, for his ladies' sake - gave them an edge they didn't recognize they'd had.

His eyes widened and he wheeled away from the doorway, leaping into the air without so much as a glance toward the exit. "Down!" he screamed, almost as an afterthought. If the bartender heard it in time, he'd be lucky - and he might live. With one leg he kicked the table Miguel sat at over; his foot found the precise balance point needed to tip it, giving the pair an extra layer of cover. Then again, under heavy fire it wouldn't hold up too well. With one arm, he grabbed the yet-to-react CIA agent and flung him to the floor, pinning him to the wall. Jim's head was down and his body tucked under that upturned table; he faced away from the door as it was kicked open.

The flash-bang was the worst part; his eyes could close, nullifying the first part, but he couldn't just shut his hearing off. No, his superhuman senses didn't involuntarily amplify the sound - they actually allowed him to selectively dampen it! It was still annoying. It was still *loud*. However, it was just a precursor to the real threat that these men posed. The hail of bullets was the follow-through, and as lead was unleashed upon the room he heard the table he was tucked behind get shredded. He felt the heavy munitions pummel his back. He screamed from the pain; the impacts on his back were barely detectable, mainly because the coat Emmett gave him was bullet-proof and resistant to impact as well. They hardly bothered him, but one lucky bastard managed to clip his leg - shame on him, for not wearing his coat-matching pants. This wound would cost him dearly.

Of course, it also pissed him off even further.

He grabbed at Miguel's chest and ripped away his suit-jacket, pulling out the man's pistol and disengaging the safety before the agent even knew what had happened. He quickly determined it's make and model, cluing him in on just how powerful each round would be. They were nine millimeters; fairly pathetic, but at least he had a lot of them in his clip. He used the sound of their breathing to gauge where each of the enemy was, and as they reloaded he whirled about once more, the firearm's business end leading the way.

Each one wore a full suit of security armor - heavy kevlar padding, a thick helmet, and his attackers each sported a bull-pup assault rifle to round matters out. Gun control in Washington clearly sucked! Nevertheless, Jim had a plan. Three shots went into the first target as a precautionary measure, just in case he'd missed - if his hearing was off from the rude interruption of the explosion. Once he'd sighted and slain the first, however, he could see all six - and he placed two shots above the shoulders of each one. Jim was a blur of bullets, and the six intruders fell to the floor, dead, while James had one round left in the clip, one left in the chamber; not bad for a fifteen-bullet magazine.

"Madre de dios!!" screamed Miguel, only now realizing what had happened. He reached for his gun, but it was already gone. "Jim! What in the holy hell?!" His alarm was only amplified when he noticed that James had actually placed a bullet to the brain right above a bullet to his targets' throats - where he figured they'd have the least armor to protect them.

The Irishman glared grimly at his colleague, offering him back his weapon handle-first. Almost habitually, the man discharged the empty clip and loaded a new one. "War, Miguel. I'm a' war. Y'need to keep this 'tween me an' Coleman, as best y'can." He strolled over toward the six men he'd mowed down, then tossed his cell phone to the floor uselessly..

"You're hit," Miguel declared firmly, staring at James' leg. It was bleeding badly enough that Miguel reached for his phone, ready to call an ambulance. When he couldn't find it, and when a cursory glance around didn't turn it up, he glanced at the still-breathing bartender. "George! Call the home office! Tell 'em something went down! Get a medivac!"

James' eyes filled with instant concern. "No! It'll know where w' are!" He glared at George, who hesitated on following through with his command. "I'll be a'right, you've gotta move!" He pulled the man to the dead troops - they were dead, they weren't breathing - and he quickly looked them over. "Coleman's, o'course. Take a gun, an' get outta 'ere," he mumbled, grabbing one of the assault rifles and checking it swiftly; it's wielder had managed to reload before he'd died. He pulled out the man's third and final spare clip, pocketed it, then tucked the weapon as close to his body as he could. He flipped his coat over it. He pulled out a series of grenades, one from each of three dead soldiers - high-explosive ones, at that. He would have taken more, but he'd run out of pockets.

As Jim mentally prepared himself for the next step, he

heard his old friend say, "Once my guys see these patches, holmes? Check these IDs? You know we're going to be involved. I can give you a little time, but this is flat out fucking illegal, ese, an' DHS is gonna have problems lookin' past it, even if I tell 'em to." He paused, contemplating. "I'll go with you, to make sure you don't get shot or arrested, huh?" He looked to his friend for approval.

He had other concerns, like the hole the bullet had left in his leg. After checking the doorway, and after Miguel grabbed a rifle of his own, Jim looked back at him and gave him a thumbs-down. "You ain't comin', Miguel, even though I thank ya." He smirked, weakly, and started out the door. "I stole yer phone, by th'way. Trus' me, I need it." Before he could hear his comrade's response, he was gone.

It was springtime, but Washington was a cold city on the warmest of days; the evening chill penetrated James' body as he limped along the city's streets. He shut the pain out as best he could, utilizing his unnatural balance to minimize the pressure on his leg wound. As well as he could compensate, and as well as the alcohol nullified the sensations of agony, he knew he wasn't going to get far - and he had a bad feeling about what was next

James was busy searching for cameras in the nation's capital. There were too many unknowns, but he quickly decided he had to gamble it all and hope for the best. Time was of the essence, and he took the first shot he had. He ducked into an alleyway and - after finding that he was lucky, and that there was no surveillance equipment in it - collapsed on his ass.

Taking out his friend's phone, he dialed in a number. He figured there would be some encryption on his signal, some paper-thin shield that might let him save his beloveds' lives, tonight, after all. He whispered the closest thing he could to a prayer. "Now don' let tha' fucker find me." He hit the "call" key.

One ring. Two. Each was painstaking. Finally, he got what he was hoping for; a soft, Indian-accented voice. "Room Nine Fourteen."

He took care to make sure he was easily understood,

slowing his speech down to what felt like a crawl. "Sari, s'Jimmy. I have to be quick. Tell Geddy t' go to Lowery Security Services an' save Katrina, Lark, 'n whoever else's there. Have 'im bring 'em all t'me, now!"

The voice on the other end of the phone sounded hesitant. "Mister Lowery---"

"Now, dammit, Voodoo's movin' on us! It's war, Sari! Tell Geddy he needs---"

A click; the other end fell unnaturally silent, save for the background static of the cellular service. That all too familiar mechanical mumbling soon took over. "Very clever, James, but I know where you are, now. I can see you, and your friends."

"Fuck you, robot," Jim chirped, just before he applied a little bit of pressure and crushed the phone. He pulled out his rifle and used it as a crutch, limping further into the alleyway. It was just a matter of time and waiting, now. Either Geddy had received the message, would save his ladies, and meet him; or he hadn't, and he was going to lose what he loved most. Well, that was half of his dilemma, anyway! The other half involved whether or not another crew of Coleman troops was headed his way.

It wasn't a thought he could easily forget.

If he'd ever tell the tale of tonight, he'd focus on just how damned long time seemed to a man with extraordinary senses. The air he inhaled reeked of a concoction of garbage, drug residue, hooker perfume, and his own blood mingled together with the acrid scent of gunpowder, as his weapon had discharged a clip's worth of bullets before it's original owner was 'neutralized.'

He could hear the cockroaches of the alleyway, hear a cat huddling in a trash can. His ears even picked up the sounds of people three stories above him fucking; and it was an unpleasant distraction over the inherently-subdued beat of his own heart. Never mind that he could, if he listened, hear the blood vessels in his legs pumping his life-blood out. Oh, his muscles were working under very specific mental control, clenching near the wound to try to minimize the blood-loss through subcutaneous pressure, but it was a stalling tactic and not at all a substitute for medical treatment. He would have used his shirt as a tourniquet, but he couldn't dare take his jacket off, in case more assassins came his way.

His eyes picked up any and all light dancing around, and he waited for the laser-sight to cross his vision, to land on his chest, and for the bullet to be fired that'd threaten his life. A high enough caliber round might even get through the armor the physicist had given him; or, perhaps, induce cardiac arrest from the force of it's impact.

Luckily for him, the first sound he heard was the soft inhalation of fresher-than-previous air; three sets of lungs, at first. He turned around to find only two: Katrina, with her dark hair and grim features; and Lark, with the classic Irish demeanor, almost like a stereotype. His heart immediately softened, and he actually felt the pain in his leg weaken. Of course, the back of his mind recognized, that might just be the shock setting in.

"Jimmy!" Lark exclaimed, wrapping her arms around him; or, rather, one of them. Katrina was wordless, but joined in the three-way embrace. They wore all too professional skirts; it took a great deal of mental discipline to move his wounded leg away from them, so that they wouldn't immediately recognize the injury.

He smiled, weakly. "Oh, ladies, I'm so sorry. We're gonna be a'right, we're gonna--" he hesitated. More heartbeats. Then, a very worried tone hit him.

"Mister Lowery!" Sari shouted. Her hand immediately clasped over his leg. He screamed at this, and nearly gave Katrina and Lark a pair of coronaries, but within seconds the pain in his body ebbed. His wound was gone, and his body had somehow managed to both replace its lost blood, and to stabilize it's natural responses to injury. "What happened?!"

Jim leaned on his ladies for just a moment, testing his leg; it worked perfectly. He grinned to himself with renewed vigor. A glance around the alleyway showed that all of his comrades were present. "It was tha' bastard, Voodoo. Versailles sic'd it on us. That an' a pack'a Coleman's goons. We need t'turn this around, *now*."

Geddy nodded, once, and reached into his over-coat. He pulled out and checked over a pistol; one of those dart-guns that the group had raided the Alaska base with. "Marge be in a safe-house," he confessed, removing the clip and checking his stock of ammunition. He seemed satisfied, slapped the magazine back in, and holstered it once more. "Where we goin'?"

Alejandro was silently mimicking Geddy's methods, but Emmett? His fingertips were dancing up and down. He wisely weaved his physics-based protections into the clothing Sari, Sonia, Katrina and Lark wore. Where they lacked coats, he formed them - where they lacked hoods, ones were added that seemed to blend in. Jim knew what the physicist was up to, and left him to take care of the task - especially as his jeans were re-woven and reinforced.

"When Physics-Boy's done makin' y'bulletproof, y'gotta trus' me. Stay in th'back, an' hold on to these" Jim advised, passing each of the three 'normal' women one of the grenades he'd peeled off of Coleman's troops. "When we need it, pull th' pin an' throw." He looked down at his trustworthy knife as a slight frown formed on his lips. "As t'where, we're goin' t'Laska. Where Voodoo began, an' where we best hope 'is brain is."

Emmett offered Geddy a nod; Geddy reached out, but a hand pulled away. While Katrina and Lark seemed nervous but trusting, Sonia's eyes were wide with fear. "I'm not, well, I'm not comfortable with this! Are we really heading in there? I don't know about all of you, but this sounds like a really bad trap. It's suicide!"

All eyes fell on Emmett. Finally, it seemed, the person he'd brought in to this project was posing a problem. "Dear," he began boldly, "I promise you, it's going to be fine. Jim can kill anything; Alejandro will be between you and anyone else. And then there's me." He let that hang for a moment, and it was a grim hovering indeed. "You've *seen* what I can do. You being worried is natural, but we'll be safe." Emmett took her hand; she accepted after some initial reluctance, and the physicist touched the nearest person to him. The all-too-familiar buzz roared over his senses.

*****

"Mom, what's going on?" Saffron asked as she sped up the Taconic Parkway, headed their home-town nestled in the Catskill mountains. Okay, so she wasn't exactly a bat out of hell; she refused to do above 65, due to tight turns and frequent State Trooper speed-traps, but she was moving at a pretty decent clip on what was, fortunately, a mostly empty road.

They'd packed and gotten in the car with unusual haste. There was a tension that Saffron could easily determine the presence of, but she couldn't decipher its roots. Ever since they'd bailed out of the city, however, her mom had been silent while she drove. Why did Saffron drive? Because she needed the experience! And her mom had enjoyed a bit of liquor! And, well, her mom was *tired*. So the *other* emotionally-stressed Latchkey, hiding those emotions like few others could, took the wheel.

After about an hour and a half of driving, however, Saffron's patience was exhausted. Her mom was humming to herself, occasionally; humming, and twitching. "Mom!" Saff shouted, one gloved hand moving from the steering wheel to poke her adoptive parent's leg - gently, but firmly.

"I can hear you," Victoria responded in what was hard to mistake for anything but a daze. How drunk *had* she gotten? Or was it something else? "Saffron, just keep driving. Mom's taken care of it."

*****

The facility was well-enough lit, but it was hardly an

asset. As soon as the buzzing stopped, he assessed where in the room he was and he leveled his rifle at the cameras to put a bullet in each of them. "Feels fuckin' familiar," Jim mumbled as he turned his attention to the sound of shuffling feet advancing to his position. "Oh god there's more of 'im!"

Before anyone could really inquire who, hell broke loose. No less than six copies of the robotic shell that was Voodoo emerged through a hallway - and they all sported, quite awkwardly, high-caliber assault rifles. One in each hand, each similar to the type Jim had stolen from Coleman's troops. These bodies were clearly not designed for battle, and their manipulation of weaponry was an obvious after-thought. That they were already covered in blood (and no small number of bullet holes) indicated they had seized their guns from someone who hadn't quite agreed with their new plan, but that was a mystery for another time.

"When did we piss off Skynet!?" screamed James like a lawsuit-hungry madman, reacting like a blur and putting the rest of his first clip into the torso of one of the androids. It keeled over, nearly cleaved in two by the perfectly-arranged shots, but its comrades began to dial in on the rest of the Consortium, and poor James was momentarily out of ammo. He had one option left - to move, bodily, toward Katrina and Lark and reiterate the same defensive posture he had taken perhaps an hour ago, with Miguel: Pinning them to the floor, covering them with as much of Emmett's body-armor between him and the robots as he could muster.

Without a sound, the muscular Spaniard of the group charged a pack of three machines. They clearly didn't recognize what Alejandro was capable of, either defensively or offensively. Their bullets smashed into him, and while he winced when one struck his eyeball, even *that* was simply impervious to damage. With invincibility came an unusual hardness of the body, coupled with the ability to ignore the repercussions of punching a primitive steel chassis as if it were a punching bag. He couldn't exactly cut through their armor like he was super-humanly strong, though this advantage had once fooled Emmett Eisenberg, but he could certainly damage their circuitry.   He resolved to strike them where their optical targeting relays (I.E. Eyes) were, and to keep them from shooting his friends.

Geddy was the third to react, and he was decisive; he disappeared from the group of his friends and popped back into view behind one of the two remaining machines. He grabbed it, and within an instant it was simply *gone*. Its brother turned its gun toward him, but by the time it could even complete its repositioning, Geddy had moved into place behind it, and its sensors would hear whatever a robot's closest approximation was to a buzzing before it experienced oblivion.

While Alejandro pummeled the three - now, two, due to some rather serious impact damage - remaining machines, Emmett watched as something rather unexpected occurred. He heard a series of gunshots. They were loud, indicating a high-caliber bullet, and they came from a source he'd never grow used to seeing fire a gun: The priestess, Sari. Clearly the once-catatonic girl had grown up, and grown into something devastatingly accurate! Not that it mattered if she *did* hit Alejandro, but anyone else? It would be a whole new trauma.

She'd put large holes into the two left opposing the Consortium, emptying her clip. The machines keeled over. "Nice shoot," Jim jabbed as he stood back up, smirking to himself. A teacher's pride.

Sari exhaled and reloaded her own weapon swiftly, as if she'd spent hundreds of hours on a range. "Put very simply, they are not alive. My dislike of violence does not cover robotic shells that are trying to kill me. Mister Marx, I'm curious as to where you put them?"

Geddy actually laughed, and it was a laugh that drew a serious bit of concern from Sonia. "Actually," he replied, deliberately refusing to look at Alejandro, "I sent 'em to tha sun. They ain't gonna be back."

Crackling over the loudspeakers, penetrating the whole research facility, a robotic voice called out ominously,

"Congratulations!" Voodoo announced, almost mockingly. "You have managed to defeat my ordinary bodies. Never fear; I have unlocked our combat equipment research facility. More tailor-made machines are on their way. You have time to say your prayers, though!"

While the others looked on with varying degrees of worry, incredulity swept over Jim's face. "Is 'e serious?" Lowery chirped, glancing over towards Emmett. Oh, he could hear the war machines on their way, and he angled his firearm down the western-most hallway. "Physics-Boy?"

The physicist nodded once. "Folks, if you have any electronics you value, give them to Jethro." His brown-gloved hands spread apart, then, to about shoulder-width apart.

As the other members of the Consortium handed their devices over, and as Geddy transported them to a random, genuinely irrelevant location, Sonia took out her cellular phone and stared at it with confusion. "Why? What are you about to do, Em?" She passed it to Geddy, along with some ear-phones and her digital music player.

The voice over the broadcast system sounded amused, for an artificially intelligent, emotionally stunted computer creation. "Will you be able to send out the pulse before my machines reach you? Even the great Emmett Eisenberg cannot defend and attack at the same time!"

In the space between Emmett's hands, a small flash took place; then, light began to pulse, as he transmuted atoms and disrupted matter. Within seconds a bright red sphere emerged - a star of some sort, contained within the invisible layers of superhuman power that the physicist conjured up.

"Hurry it up, Physics-Boy!" Jim shouted, a grin on his lips as he adjusted his rifle's barrel slightly to his right, then pulled the trigger a single time. To him, the sound of the machines didn't slow down. "S'my last clip an' they ain't hesitatin'!" As he anticipated the right moment to fire, Alejandro advanced forward - a human shield, indeed!

Then, he heard a soft clicking from behind him. The

sound of a pin being pulled, and falling to the ground, in fact. He heard the first device, followed quickly by two additional ones, soar through the air and land within the hallway Voodoo's machines were about to march down. He heard their rifles fire, heard the bullets whiz through the air around them, but it was the explosion that caused him to grin. The hallway caved in, separating Voodoo's assets from his enemies at the worst possible time.

His bright eyes looked over at Sonia's outstretched hand, and he grinned broadly. "Good thinkin'," he quipped.

She'd never thrown a grenade before, but her actions had led Katrina and Lark to do the same, the former with a great deal of accuracy. Emmett nodded his own approval, then clapped his hands together before raising his arms. The facility's lights flickered, then went completely dark, and Jim wondered whether or not Voodoo realized he wasn't getting out of this one unscathed - whether or not screaming a last-minute plea for mercy was a worthwhile use of its memory banks.

*****

As Saffron continued her drive back to the Catskills, her mother bolted upright from her seat with a loud gasp. "Mom!" she cried, her right hand reaching over in a spike of futile instinct while her left kept hold of the steering wheel. "What happened?!"

Christine sighed, closing her eyes once again - but, this time, merely to shut out old memories that threatened to consume her. "It's nothing, baby," she whispered, unable to explain the sensation of a digital life leaving the electronic world she lived in. "Just the end of a painfully beautiful dream."

*****

"Geddy, lights; Physics-Boy, air," Jim barked authoritatively.

The larger of the two men snorted. "I ain't your errand boy, Lowery. But, sure, I know tha' need." Without any further sound, Jethro disappeared.

Emmett, on the other hand, sighed softly and focused his attention on the task he needed to accomplish. "What does he mean?" Sonia whispered to him softly, fumbling about in the dark for her beloved.

"We're in an underground facility," responded Emmett, monitoring the molecules around them. "Normally, there's computers that run these kind of things." A thought, then he realized he hadn't explained much of anything, yet. "They make sure you're breathing fresh air, and that there's no contaminants. I just overloaded every circuit within ten miles; there's nothing pumping new air down, or filtering out the old, and eventually we'd start suffocating." To hear him say it, Emmett's words were completely calm and routine, as if he'd simply grown up dealing with rampant artificial intelligences and time-traveling madmen.

"Basically, I can pull the carbon atoms out of carbon dioxide, and make it into breathable air with ease. I would just add oxygen into our environment, but unfortunately that would increase the air pressure, and I'd crush us." He laughed softly at this, mainly because it was something he would never, ever do. To them. Sonia leaned forward and wrapped her arms around her lover.

Another voice spoke up, then. "So, what do we do next, Mister Lowery," queried Sari in a stern, if patient tone. The Brahman's dark eyes were narrowed intently. "We cannot hide down here forever. Eventually, Mister Marx will grow tired of stealing food for us, and Doctor Eisenberg will lose his patience as an air-purifier."

Jim folded his arms over his chest for a second; just a second, because his primal response was only momentarily held in check by the higher-level functions of his brain. "S'war, dear Sari," he retorted grimly. "We need t'hit th'weakest link."

"Lawrence Gibbs?" offered the accented voice of Alejandro, unbidden. It was a rather bold action, considering Mr.

Curtis preferred to take the silent path.

James nodded his agreement. "Th'man's a coward, but 'e may have th'info on tha' Versailles woman. I'll get it outta 'im, an' that'll be tha'."

Sari didn't say anything in response, nothing at all; she merely stared at him disapprovingly.

"I do not think that will be necessary, Jimmy," chirped Katrina, another often-silent facet of the group. She walked up to her male other third and looked him in the eye; and she was no shortage of intimidating towards a man that wasn't a merciless, expert assassin. Then again, it was pitch-dark. "We do not need to resort to violence just because our enemies have."

Joining her female counterpart was the Irishwoman Lark, and she wrapped her arms around Lowery's waist lovingly. Calm, her accent was less prolific than earlier on the phone. "Please, Jim, we don' even know if this was under Coleman's orders 'r not. Versailles sounds like a snake. One step a' a time." She nestled her head into his chest; Katrina, the more bold one, grasped his shoulders and tugged the two close.

Sonia observed this, thinking simply to herself, '*what a weird fuckin' family.*' She gazed up at Emmett, who she was also in the midst of an embrace with. For a moment, she felt sorry for Alejandro; the large Spaniard was the only one without the slightest hint of a social life outside of their little conspiracy group. Even Sari had taken some time out to be with someone she cared for, throughout this crisis, but Alejandro? All she knew was that the man had lost his family at a young age, in part because of Geddy - who happened to return before she could muse too deeply on the subject.

Soundlessly, he re-appeared a few steps away. He quickly twisted a battery-powered electric lamp and the device nourished the room's darkness somewhat. In what must have been an act of foresight, a few more of those tools appeared in his palms, and he set them down at reasonable intervals to truly illuminate the research lab. Aside from the damage caused by their scant firefight, the place seemed rather unscathed. In fact, it was so undamaged that when he set one of the lights up, he stared up at an unbroken nuclear reactor monitor. One which was completely blank.

"Uhhh, Emmett?" Jethro ventured grimly. All eyes moved to the light-bearer. "I know we just went rip-shit-riot on Voodoo, an' we ain't had no choice, but what about the nuclear reactor down here?"

Dead silence; for a moment, anyhow. "Sorry?" Emmett questioned, breaking his concentration and looking over at Geddy. "What'd you say? I couldn't--"

"The nukes, ya daft buzzard, the nukes!" The large Black man pointed rapidly at the read-out panel. Every person in the room seemed frozen in place. "That shape-changin' shit!"

Slowly, the physicist smiled. "Relax. This is a carbon-14 reactor. It doesn't handle anything that's naturally very hot, like Uranium or Plutonium is, so it isn't prone to a run-away melt-down, and it doesn't spit out anything really hazardous to Human health. You're just smacking Nitrogen with a neutron to knock out a proton, and away you go! Plus, *I'm* here. I'm splitting gas molecules apart with ease. If I saw any stray particles coming our way, I could block them out. Also," he continued in a calm manner, "the isotope that ADS was injecting people with is Radium Two-Twenty-Six, which is stored separately a few floors away, behind sealed and safe doors." He laughed, but that laugh weakened as he was the only one amused. "It's...It's perfectly safe..."

He wasn't. "Ow!" Emmett's shout punctuated the room, along with the echo of his girlfriend smacking him on the back of the head.

Jim looked his two girls over, then nodded to Jethro once. "Good thinkin'. Got the phones?" Without a word, Geddy passed each of the Consortium members their smart-phones back; he had secured the devices against Emmett's electromagnetic pulse, after all. Jim looked at the device and didn't have a signal. "Damn. Too deep underground. Physics-Boy, can y' set up a line? Or a wire, or somethin'?"

Rubbing his still-ringing skull, the physicist nodded slowly. "I can probably run a metal wire up through the stone and into the air, yeah. The problem is that it'll still be a shitty reception, because I've got no way to amplify the signal. Also," he added cautiously, "that's about *all* I can do at this point. You've got me spending a lot of energy, here."

The Irishman shrugged indifferently, looking over at Jethro. "I need y't' grab Larry Gibbs, fer me," he asked in as polite a tone as he could muster. Geddy laughed - actually laughed - at the request. "Th' fuck's so funny?"

Marx spread his hands out helplessly. "One, I ain't you bloodhound. Two, I ain't met Gibbs, so I ain't able to bring him to me, or go to him."

Jim swore inwardly and nodded. "Sorry, sorry. I know, I'm pissed, I'm mad, an' I want t'get this shit straight. So can y'please send me t'Gibbs' buildin', an' back me up if I need?"

Geddy looked at Sari for approval. Slowly, the Hindu nodded. He studied his clothes, then - it was made of that armor Emmett created for them all, so he knew he was fairly near capable of claiming invulnerability. He might have been unable to dodge a bullet he didn't see fired, but being bullet-proof was the next best thing.

With a reluctant sigh, Jethro walked over to James. The Irishman kissed his two women farewell, then nodded to Geddy. "When we's back," the larger man demanded, "We's talkin' about respect, you get me? We get this prick, then we talk respect."

James grinned weakly. "Agreed," he offered, then the two vanished into thin air.

In the adjoining silence, the group glanced one another over cautiously. They all dreaded that James would bring back a half-dead body - or come back dead, himself. A soft, northern-Irish voice punctured the veil of aural vacancy.

"He's blaming i' all on himself, Jimmy is," Lark whispered carefully, ignoring a sharp, disapproving look from Katrina. "Think about 'ow he brought you all in to this fiasco. It is all his fault, to him, and when that awful machine threatened us..."

It was a rare moment of honesty from Jim's "Ladies."
Katrina placed a hand on her partner's shoulder and frowned. "I
worked in the Russian intelligence services for some times. Jim
is the best, but he is just like any other man when it comes to
protecting his women." She ran a fingertip under Lark's chin,
reassuring her. "He cannot allow himself to be up-staged, and he
cannot allow anyone to be in danger because of him."

Sonia clung to the man who brought her into this
particular affair; Emmett played the role of reassuring boyfriend;
Alejandro merely smirked at this macho behavior. But the acting
ringleader of the group, Sari, coughed politely. "Ladies, it is
good to hear you break your ordinary silence. Perhaps you may
help me with something. Mister Lowery and Garrett Trinder, at
the Infinite Loop, discussed the Black Files." Her words fell like
apples upon a medieval physicist's skull, and they both looked the
healer over. "He never mentioned Christine Versailles, to me, but
one name that did come up was Jean-Claude L'Francois. James
appraised me on the situation, but what might Garrett have meant
when he said that he had L'Francois checked?"

Sonia's eyebrow rose slowly. "He mentioned some kind
of weapon being near Erica at all times...?" The recent graduate
wasn't sure if she was on the right track, but Emmett's eyes lit up
with concern.

"Versailles!" Recognition dawned, suddenly. "It has to
be Versailles! He said she was the only person scarier than a real,
live Vampire!" Emmett clenched a fist, looking down at his
brown gloves as his mind broadcast the quick-passing thought,
'except for me.'

Suddenly, a loud thud echoed off of the walls of the
cavernous facility they were in. Sure enough, James had his
hands wrapped around the throat of the incredibly pale Lawrence
Gibbs.

"---You again! What do you want?!" the man in the
expensive nightwear screamed, as Geddy shook his head and
walked away. The businessman's struggles were pretty much
fruitless, because Lowery had far too solid a grip on the clothing

around his neck.

"Start talkin', Larry!" he demanded angrily. The weaker man's spine was pressed against a wall, and Jim glared in his eyes. "I need an answer t'a question! Who th'fuck is Christine Versailles!"

"I don't--"

Jim grinned a nearly insane shade of happy and slammed his fist into Lawrence's diaphragm. While most of the room stood still, disapproving glares all around, one girl gasped in horror. Sonia, unsure of what to do, shouted aloud, "Stop!" She'd only had her first real gun battle earlier tonight, after all, and now she was witnessing an old-fashioned shakedown. She rushed to step forward, but Sari held a hand up.

"Watch," the priestess indicated darkly, despite her body language's clear expression of distaste for this method of information extraction.

The Irishman lifted the still-coughing yuppie up and pinned him two feet off of the ground. "Now then, y'lie again an' y'die. We all know y'll be talkin', soon, an' Garrett Trinder'll kill y' if I don', so I'm y'r only hope, yeah?" When Larry nodded in desperation, Jim dropped him unceremoniously. "Versailles. Start talkin'."

Lawrence caught his breath, rising to his feet. As he did, it was evident that he had a weapon holster located under his left shoulder - and that the pistol ordinarily kept inside had been removed before he'd arrived in the room. He only stood with Jim's implied consent, because the Irishman stayed all too close by, just in case he made a move that didn't sit well. "Fine...Versailles...I don't know m-much..."

He took a final, deep breath; his lungs seemed back under his control, for the moment. He looked around with panic. "Jesus Christ, where - where'd you take me?!" A gentle prod to his ribs caused him to re-focus on his diatribe. "All I know is she worked with Trinder very, very closely. She worked with ADS, under the Center for Applied Psychological Enterprises umbrella. It's like ADS, it's a shell-fund okay? And Voodoo is gonna hear every-- "

"Good thing Voodoo is dead," interjected Alejandro grimly.

Lawrence's eyes bugged. "Wha?" His eyes closed and he laughed softly. "Just what the fuck *are* you people?! I went from Vegas to Alaska? What do you want from me?!"

James chuckled to himself. "Fer now? Jus' be quiet an' listen up t'how I'm'na keep y'alive in Witness Protection..."

While Jim took the businessman aside and started explaining to him, Sonia looked up at Emmett with a frown. "Applied *Psychological* Enterprises?" She exhaled dryly and closed her eyes. "I guess we need to call her again, don't we?"

Emmett nodded grimly. "I've heard of it, but I don't remember where." He produced his cell phone and checked its reception; bad. Sighing, he focused his energy on manipulating more molecules; a tendril of gold fiber descended from the ceiling and he wrapped it around his electronic device, boosting its signal to a passable amount.

Then he dialed, and he walked into the distance as more gold atoms appeared to keep him attached to the cord.

The phone rang twice before he heard someone on the other end pick up. "Maria, it's Emmett."

"Who?" a familiar male voice demanded, with a familiar French accent. "Emmett the science person?" Emmett winced inwardly; it was Daniel Marceau, his ex-girlfriend's boyfriend. "Do you have any idea what time it is?!"

He swore inwardly. "Listen, it's impor--"

"I don't give a damn what it is, Doctor Eisenberg," he said as he drew closer towards waking up. He could hear, faintly, that Maria was asking what had happened. The two were in bed. "It's five in the morning, that's what it is. Go away." The phone clicked.

Emmett swore to himself quietly, staring down at the device. It was two, maybe three minutes later before the phone buzzed and he picked it up. "Hi."

That voice on the other end, once so familiar to him,

sounded unbearably strained. "*What* do you want, Emmett!?
What happened *this* time?" She didn't cry, but she sounded as if
she was on the edge of it.

"Maria, I'm sorry, we're back in Alaska. This woman,
Christine Versailles - she tried to kill us, today."

A sick, exhausted laugh came across the wire. "Oh? Well
that would make the world a better place! What the hell does this
have to do with me, Emmett? I *left* you. Years ago! I want
nothing more to do with this crazy shit. With you, Erica, Vicky,
the rest of it!"

"Vicky? Vicky who? And..." A memory flashed before
his eyes - an older professor. "Wait, didn't we know a Vicky at
Catskill Comm-"

He was unceremoniously interrupted. "Yes! Latchkey!
She's one of you people." There was some muffled back-and-
forth between the two on the other end, but Maria picked right
back up. "She got me caught up in Erica's nonsense, then split on
me! She went back to Triple-C to teach. And her daughter is like
you, too!"

Emmett couldn't believe what he was hearing. "Wait!
Vicky was close to Erica? Vicky Latchkey and Erica Hall were
friends?!" *This* earned an immediate gasp from half the room.
Emmett heard Jim ask Lawrence a couple more questions - no
violence, that he detected, just the overwhelming threat of total
annihilation. "Garrett said that he put the ultimate weapon there
to protect..."

"Ultimate weapon?" Maria protested boldly, "What the
hell is that? You know, what?! I don't want to know! Goodbye,
Emmett! Goodbye forever!"

Suddenly, their phone connection went dead. He sighed,
nodding gravely to himself. "So that's gotta be it."

Approaching him from his left, Jim had a small vial of
anti-microbial gel that he was rubbing into his hands to cleanse
them. The Irishman looked up and nodded once. "Sounds 'bout
right, physics-boy. Latchkey's really Versailles, eh? An she's
been workin' fer Trinder this whole time. We know th' next move

t'make, don't we?"

From Emmett's right, a voice swiftly declared, "But we don't know what's next. Only Garrett would, and he has assuredly planned for this. If we try to extract this Versailles, she will be no easy task. More to the point, if Versailles is supposed to protect Miss Hall, then we would have to take up that task, ourselves." Sari frowned, lowering her head in grim determination to find a way out of this situation - this trap, it seemed.

*****

Her phone rang. She woke from her half-slumber, frowning. "What do you want?" She demanded of the voice on the other end. "Damned traitor, turning me over to *them*." Her daughter was well into the drive, with loud string music playing, and wouldn't notice her soft conversation immediately. It was a good thing she didn't.

The thick German tone was worried. "Christine, I did no such thing. I did not turn you over. You know I cannot lie to you. I need you to turn around - they are driving us towards a very dark future, but we can still change it. I need you to calmly and quietly return to Erica Hall's--"

"Damn it, Garrett, she'll find out!" Christine shouted in drunken, foolish anger.

The car nearly slammed into a snow-bank as Saffron smashed the brake petal, steering like a madwoman. It was a miracle - or was it? - that the vehicle didn't crash. "Is that Uncle Gary!?" she barked, turning the radio off with the flick of a gloved fingertip. "Give me the phone."

The youth's demand was refused, for now. "Saffron can't know, yet, Christine, but the more you fight this, the worse it gets."

"Give me the damned phone, mom!" Saffron screamed impatiently, flexing her empathic muscle. "I swear to god, I want answers! Tell me what I am!"

With a tear in her eye, Christine gave her daughter the

device. Her daughter seized it without reason or caution.

"Uncle Gary, what the hell is the point of all this?!" Saffron didn't even say hello. She was angry. That was bad. "You need to explain it to me, now. I know I'm adopted, so I know that whatever I have doesn't come from my mom, but why are we doing these crazy, dumb, childish little things that are going to get us all killed!?"

Garrett sighed indifferently for a minute, knowing full well that he couldn't change this outcome. Not without a lot of sacrifice - sacrifices he couldn't afford just yet. But wherever there was a choice, there was a chance for change. "Saffron, you must listen to me very carefully. You are an excellent person. You are good. You don't deserve the fate that you have, but you have it nonetheless. Please, convince your mother to complete her mission. She knows what will happen if he is not stopped, tomorrow."

"Fuck you and your missions, Garret!" Christine barked, despite not being able to physically hear the phone. "I quit!"

After a silent moment, the German added, "And you, Saffron?"

"I'm going home. I don't want to be your tool, Uncle Gary, and I don't want my mom to be, either! We'll talk later, when this is all over."

Garrett's response was simple, yet sorrow-laden, "Then it's up to them to save us all, and the odds are not very good that any of us turn out happy." The young girl listened for a moment, then promptly tossed the phone into her mother's lap. She hit the gas petal and the car started along the road, it's driver lost in a cool void of emotional detachment.

*****

Emmett slipped his glasses off of his nose, carefully cradling them with his gloved fingertips. "Extraction is a bad plan. It's especially a problem because Vicky - Christine, I guess," he corrected himself.

"Whoever," Jim interjected impatiently.

"She's on the run. Maria said she bailed. She's probably heading back upstate - that, or we can at least raid her office for any clues," Emmett suggested dryly. He looked over at Sonia, frowning at the very thought of returning to the place where they had met. "This is going to be ugly."

"Damn right it is," Geddy added, looking down. "We ain't got no idea what's what, with 'Riki. If she's in danger, we need to save her."

Alejandro sighed weakly. "I'd really rather not, but it's too late to allow personal feelings into this situation," the Spaniard stated stoically. A faint gaze went Sari's way.

"I've never seen a picture'a L'Francois, so I wouldn't know 'im if I saw 'im," James added calmly. "Algerian; tall and thin, with dark skin and short curly hair, I think th' description went. He may've changed any'a that, though. If I read Trinder righ' when we were at 'is club, 'e's worried about this guy attackin' 'Riki. That means we need t'be ready t'fight against 'im, soon."

Sonia sighed gently, her eyes closing in frustration. "It's, like, four in the morning, James. Maybe we should take a *nap*?" she stressed. Everyone in the room just sort of stopped, for a minute, then collectively realized how exhausted they were. "It's just a lot to process, a lot to consider. I never really thought it would come to this," she concluded gloomily.

Emmett nodded his head slowly, his arms enveloping the exhausted graduate once again. "We should be safe from Versailles for now. Jethro, if you could take us home so we can plan our next move with some beds underneath us?"

The construction expert nodded, and it wasn't long before they were safe and secure in New York City, resting in the city that never sleeps.

*****

Was the city asleep? Three clubs, now, and he still craved more. Oh, there was quite a lot of energy in New York, tonight -

too much, in fact! But it wasn't enough, and it was a feeling that he actually dreaded, somewhat. He lowered his sunglasses slightly; he had adjusted to the strobe lights, and had no further need of them save to make a fashion statement. He'd gotten hooked on wearing them at all times - even at night, even in dark night clubs - some time during the early 1980's, when a song about visions in the lyricist's mind was popular, and he hadn't been able to shake them since. The leather jacket he wore came from late 1990's action flicks, where the heroes were covered head-to-toe in cowhide simply to look like cyberpunk superheroes. But there *were* no super-heroes, and no villains for them to face down.

Only people, as he knew all too well.

He took another pass from bar to bar; each of these night clubs had several, and between them were young men and women whose hearts pumped with life. It was all he needed; he'd figured out early on that he didn't need more than a moderate amount of food or water, and he certainly didn't need *blood!* Oh, true, he'd gotten quite a lot of action at the goth kid hang-outs, as monsters were in the midst of a sparkly renaissance, but he didn't need blood. In fact, he didn't even need to pull all of the energy out of his meals! Ordinarily, it was just the presence of so much *living*, of so many people generating so much bio-kinetic energy by dancing, lost in music and other intoxicants. He'd go home happy, and they'd go home sleepier than usual and chalk it up to strong alcohol. Ordinarily, hell, he didn't have any trouble getting his fill. But tonight was different.

Maybe it was the fact that a running gun-battle had taken place in the nation's capital? People were on edge as details were explained - the President wasn't in any danger, nobody seemed to worry about Congress or the Supreme Court much, and it wasn't a terrorist attack, but that's about all that was known. A lot of people doubted it, too. They assumed it had to be some kind of cover-up, but he knew the truth: Simply put, gang violence was a bitch, and someone had pissed someone else off big-time. What was most interesting, however, was that the shooters were all dead - shots to the head, the media said - and that no second party had been found. A bar had been torn up, but all that could be figured out was that it was locally-owned. That's about when the elasticity of the first amendment failed, and viewers were left waiting for 'more updates as they were released.'

At that point, he'd tuned out the noise. It was a hell of a night; three establishments, at least seven hundred sources of nourishment, yet he was still thirsty. He left the scene, declining a refund (he'd only been there for a half hour), and fluffed his leather jacket up once in the breeze. He looked at the line to get in - long. Then, he looked across the street. There was a back alley-way, a private exit point for another of Manhattan's night spots. This one was a much classier joint than the one he'd left, and he contemplated a fourth destination in his quest when something that he'd never experienced - not in ninety seven years - happened to him.

There was a woman in a limousine. That wasn't the surprise, as he'd seen plenty of those! The tinted windows didn't stop *his* vision from catching her face, and he knew her instantly. She was a famous singer, a girl running for President and quickly catching up in the polls. He'd never been impressed by a person before, at least not since he kicked the Nazis out of his homeland in the 1940's! But this woman was *different* from the dictator he'd fought during Operation Torch. He felt it instantly, felt a shiver run down his spine. Now he knew why he wasn't sated. Now he knew why he couldn't be filled up by the normal fare, tonight.

She was the one he needed, and if he couldn't get to her tonight, he'd do what he always did - regroup, research, and re-engage the next night.

Chapter Ten
The Masquerade

For an Illuminati-esque group of ultra-rich, hyper-connected, super-heroic masterminds who controlled the world from the shadows, they were one hell of a sad sight. They had spent the night in hotel rooms. Fortunately, they could sleep many to a bed, but only Jethro had elected to leave for the night. Since relocation was his specialty, he presumably spent the night in his private safe-house with his wife.

Upon waking at around noon, the group accepted the hotel's offer of a 24-7 continental breakfast (two or three at a time, to dissuade suspicion), bringing as much food up to their room as they could possibly need. They met in James' suite, since he had pushed the two hotel-provided beds together to form one large one, and he therefore had the space to host a gathering where all concerned parties sat in a circle.

It wasn't until the debate started, however, that they proved how human they truly were.

The first suggestion, from James, was that the group take Erica into protective custody. This was immediately met with displeasure from Emmett, who wanted her nowhere near him, but it was Alejandro who logically ridiculed the concept - and with good reason! "How," he asked curtly, "do you expect to force your will on a woman who can take control of your will?" It was only the Spaniard's derision of the singer that kept Jim from blowing his top.

Next, the proposal was made by Sonia to search government records on L'Francois. However, Katrina politely (but bluntly) informed her that they had done this on many occasions, and Lark added that the man could be older than the country he was from. Emmett disagreed, convinced that the man must have left some paper trail, but when Jim's ladies insisted there was nothing, Lowery turned around and suggested they capture *Christine* instead, and force her to look even deeper.

Geddy had acknowledged that if the Consortium could find her, it might be possible to kidnap her. Sari, however, concluded that there was no ethical way to force her to comply. After a point, physical violence was out of the question - Yes, she had explained to the Irishman, despite the fact that she had tried to murder them all - and that even if convinced to cooperate via brutality the Consortium simply couldn't be sure *what* the woman would do once plugged into a computer. She could call the police on them, for all they'd know, and create a rather unpleasant scene.

Sonia suggested, after some hemming-and-hawing, that they somehow could recruit Erica to elicit Christine's compliance on searching for L'Francois. "The enemy of my enemy," she had begun.

"Is a psychotic bitch I'm not trustin'," Jim condemned. This hurt Sonia's feelings, and Emmett reminded Jim to show a little respect to his colleagues. This earned a heart-felt swear-fest about how much James hated Garrett Trinder and Andrew Coleman, and how - when this was all over - he was going to "Skull fuck 'em all wi'' m'knife!" There as an apology muttered somewhere in the mix, and Emmett no longer had to remind Sonia that James was, at his core, a bit of an aggressive nut who didn't quite know how to hold a polite conversation.

It was then decided that, unfortunately, they would have to watch Erica from afar. Sari said she would initiate contact again, but seeing as Erica had never responded to her first request for discussion, it was entirely possible that she would ignore even the once-catatonic healer. Moreover, Sari couldn't go alone, and it was decided that she would have Alejandro and Geddy on hand in case of an emergency. Geddy would serve as a quick form of egress if things got out of hand, and Alejandro could endure any beating that L'Francois could deliver. Until a better solution presented itself, this first group would simply keep a watch on the people watching Erica.

The other "group," as it were, would be Emmett, Sonia, and James. They would go to Catskill Community College and investigate Victoria Latchkey's entire persona. After all, if indeed she was Christine Versailles, they would need two things: Someone who could react quickly, and someone who could destroy anything in sight. Sonia would be what James considered the operational communicator - she'd have an ear-piece in, one running a direct line to her phone which was on a persistent internet chat with Katrina and Lark back in New York City. Sari would be similarly equipped, as would Jethro: If anything went wrong, he could teleport people back and forth. Of course, he made another complaint about being the pack mule, but this time he had a grin on indicating that he was totally on board with the plan. Garrett had been right in one thing, at least: Geddy welcomed being a hero!

Meanwhile, Katrina and Lark would return to Lowery Security Services. Aside from serving as the technical supervisors for the communications relay, they had a more pressing task to complete. Teleported into the room so that nobody could see the bio-chemical warfare suits they sported, they were prepared for any eventuality. Their mission was to un-do the damage Voodoo had dealt to their operative quarters, and to get all of the systems up-and-running: Including the on-site meeting rooms, armories, and medical labs. Jim might have been on the verge of a murderous rampage, but his tactical mind demanded that there was a back-up plan in case of emergency, and a place for Sari to work if any of them were injured.

The three squads departed, undertaking their separate missions.

*****

The landing was probably the bumpiest part of the trip for Sonia. She flashed back to the first time she'd seen Geddy - when Emmett had been teaching her introductory physics class. He had been rattled, and when the knock came at the door and the professor just vanished, well, she hadn't known what to make of it. When he returned, when he appeared out of thin air? She had been horrified. Then she learned about the Consortium and Connor Point, and he had finalized his hold over her heart.

It didn't help that the three of them had appeared in literally the same corridor of DuBois Hall, with that buzzing sound indicating their travel coming to an end just before a student, passing by, would have slammed into her. He mumbled an apology and swore he hadn't seen them, and strolled away care-free.

"Where are we, Emmett?" asked James with an unusual amount of patience in his voice. It was as if the explosive Irishman was a completely different person; he didn't reach for a gun, a knife, or anything else.

The physicist sighed, glancing the place over as he experienced his own memories. "He couldn't have put us any closer, I guess," he conceded, looking downward. "My best guess is that Vicky's got an office in the Psychology department. That's over in Hudson Hall, which is just about half the campus over."

"Yeah," the graduate of this particular institution agreed, "And it's gonna be one hell of a long walk if anyone recognizes us," she remarked, glancing up at Emmett. He nodded, and started off towards the science building's south-eastern corridor.

It might have come as a surprise, but they actually got to the exterior of Hudson Hall before a student stopped, looked over at Sonia, and offered her a wave. The male was perhaps one year younger than her, and was incredibly muscular. "Sonia? Sonia Monterrey? Holy shit, is that you?" Emmett blinked; it was one of his former students! In fact, Sonia had shared the same class with him, all those years ago. Brian Wilcox, his brain reminded him, and he winced; he was an amazing swimmer, but a failure at physics, and had probably needed to take a break from college to get his academics in order. That, or to swim professionally.

Sonia immediately moved in and gave the student a hug. "Brian! It's so nice to see you! Have you met my boyfriend, James?" The words stunned Emmett - had she rehearsed this, or was she coming up with it on the fly?

The Irishman rolled in without hesitation. "Hey," he

stated, his hand coming forward to shake the swimmers'. Emmett watched the security expert's technique with barely-concealed surprise. Ever so subtly, his hand guided the swimmer's head towards him; they locked eyes, and as they initiated a brief conversation about what he had been up to (indeed, he'd spent some years swimming for money, before a knee injury put that on hold), he managed to keep Brian's focus solely on him. The physicist could recognize that, through gauging the swimmer's emotional responses and physical condition, Jim was stealthily building himself into such a massive social presence that nothing else existed, even the girl with whom he'd started a conversation. By the time the athlete broke off and headed to the class he was now *just* about to be late to, he had never even noticed Emmett - and might well have forgotten that he'd encountered Sonia entirely!

"Sorry, hun," Sonia remarked, wrapping herself around Emmett's arm. "I didn't mean to surprise you, but it was the only thing I could think of." Jim just laughed, clapped Emmett on the shoulder, then headed through the doorway.

The staircase to the Psychology department's offices was just as creaky as it had ever been, half a decade ago. The physicist felt so guilty as he walked up them that he hesitated for an instant, focusing his willpower on the stairwell to reinforce it's molecular structure just a touch. He considered it his duty, as a former professor, to keep those hallowed halls of education from one day collapsing underneath the weight of students his books.

Our heroes' next challenge was the main Psychology office, which might have someone within who could recognize the two former regulars on campus. Jim provided a visual screen, walking slightly ahead of the pair. Next was Dr. Maria Montclaire's office, but fortunately it was closed. Finally, with much searching through name-plates, they came across one labeled, "Victoria Latchkey." Jim nodded once and looked down at the doorknob. Emmett focused his attention on it for a moment, mentally peeling apart the locking mechanism and opening the office up.

The first thing Jim did was don a pair of gloves; Sonia followed suit, and Emmett already wore his brown leather barriers to the world. Next, he carefully searched for a scheduling book. He found it and swore inwardly. "We've got maybe an hour an' a half t'search," he whispered to his comrades. They nodded and began to dig around the office, taking careful notes of where they had found whatever they looked for.

Sonia and Emmett handled the physical aspects of the investigation, looking over documents, papers, and photographs. There was a particularly beautiful girl in pictures with a woman who Emmett confirmed he had known as Victoria; they surmised that this was Vicky's daughter, whose name was Saffron judging from a birthday card she'd written. Sonia admitted to having seen her around on campus. They had brushed across one another at times, but she didn't precisely recall Saffron, either.

Lowery, on the other hand, had inserted a USB drive into Victoria's computer and begun to search around. It was a gamble - if Vicky was indeed Christine Versailles, he had no way of knowing what kind of security it could have. Oddly enough, everything worked according to plan. There was no menacing artificial intelligence, here; just the ordinary files that one might expect a college professor to have. Lark's data-extraction algorithms went to work.

Time moved quickly; Jim managed to find some e-mails sent to and from the Center for Applied Psychological Enterprises, as well as the Coleman Group, but none of them seemed to be anything more than generic information requests and bland, unadorned reports on stock prices. It seemed Vicky held a mutual fund with shares in the Group, and had spoken with the staff at CAPE regarding a study of Rhesus Monkeys, but that was about it.

As the team started to pack up, they heard a scraping at the door. All three froze. It took longer than they expected, but the door unyieldingly gave way. Saffron Latchkey stood there, blinking stupidly for a moment. "Oh, what now," she whispered to herself, glaring the three over. She raised her voice, slightly, her fingertips reaching for her hip. "Did my uncle send you?"

"Who?" Sonia queried carefully. Saffron took a step inside the office, looking the former student over with curiosity. As soon as the door had slipped back into place, however, her demeanor shifted. Jim couldn't shout a warning, not without instantly blowing their remaining cover, but he was able to move quickly enough to get between Sonia and Saffron just before the younger of the two women pulled out a pistol.

Saffron held it unsteadily, clearly devoid of proficiency, yet she spoke in a perfectly level manner. "Did Uncle Garrett send you?"

It was James' turn to blink stupidly. Then, he actually cracked a grin. "Oi, didja hear that? Did Garrett send us? Fuck Garrett, that's what," he responded carefully, taking a step to Saffron. "Tha' prick's got about a million world's'a hurt comin' 'is way, and I'm guessin' 'e gave you one, too?"

Saffron's dark gray eyes met Jim's. Immediate recognition set in. "You're like me. So's the man. That means you're either a friend of mine, or an enemy. Which is it?"

Now, Jim was honestly taken aback. "Like...Wha'?"

Sonia stepped forward, slowly. "You're like them? My name," she began slowly, softly, haltingly. "I'm Sonia. I've seen you on campus, haven't I?"

Slowly, Saffron's gaze moved to the graduate. "Huh. Yeah; last year, maybe. I think. What the hell are you doing in my mother's office? And who the hell are you?"

Jim glanced over his shoulder at Sonia as if to dissuade her, and Emmett looked more than worried about what his girlfriend might say next, but it was in that moment that the graduate realized something - she was an equal partner in this affair. She didn't need Emmett's approval to act, and she didn't even need James' consent. "My name is Sonia Monterrey. This is James Lowery," she said with a gesture to the Irishman, who merely offered a faint nod. "And that's my boyfriend, Emmett Eisenberg."

Saffron's eyes snapped open, and her gun shifted towards

Emmett. "You're one of my mother's friends, then?" Saffron didn't seem to appreciate that thought! "Well, what the hell does Trinder want out of her? Out of me?"

Emmett's lips twitched and he gestured with his left hand; the slide of the gun lifted up and the bullet slipped out of the chamber just as the weapon's magazine ejected itself. Saffron pulled the trigger, but only a loud *click* escaped from the firearm. Her eyes went wide. "I have no idea," the physicist responded, "but we need to stop him, and I can't have you shooting me."

The student lowered her extended arm, seeming to express no surprise at the fact that her gun broke apart in her hands, and stared Emmett down fearlessly. "All I know is that my mom is scared of him, and that he wants her to do something he says is really important. I have no idea why. My mom isn't clear about that, really - she's probably teaching another lecture drunk. She pretended to be friends with some Erica Hall woman for years just to do her job."

James laughed, suddenly; and at Saffron's stunned gaze, he coughed to clear his throat. "Sorry, but that's one thing we've got covered. Emmett 'ere used to date 'er, actually," he remarked with a grin, fully aware of just how angry the reminder would make his friend. "Physics-boy was a teacher 'ere, an' tha's how 'e met yer mom. S'ow he met Sonia, too, but tha's another story."

"You knew Erica, huh?" Saffron took one of the office's chairs and sat down. Stress was evident in her voice, but she came across as unusually calm for someone who just walked into a break-in. She sat down. "My uncle Garrett, what do you know about *him*?"

The graduate sat down next to her, taking one of her gloved hands - and immediately noticing they were gloved. She could feel the scarring underneath the satin, and she did her best not to react as Saffron pulled them away. "Sorry," Sonia conceded, "I didn't notice. Garrett is one bad man. He's kind of like an evil master-mind, trying to manipulate Erica and your mom from the shadows."

"Oh, yeah!" Jim added in a light-hearted tone, "Yer ma

tried t'kill me las' night. I wouldn't mind tha', but she tried t'kill m'ladies as well, an I can't let tha' pass."

Saffron's face fell. "How? I was with her all night. We drove up here, together, as soon as we left Maria and Erica."

Emmett studied the window for a moment, as if wishing he could leap out of it. "Here's the problem," he stated calmly, rubbing his chin with his gloved hand. "Your mother has two identities. One of them is Christine Versailles. I can take matter apart and put it back together with my mind, okay? Right?" At the faint nod of understanding he got from Saffron, he adjusted his glasses. "Your mother, Christine, can control machines."

Immediately, Sonia added, "We're not sure how this all works, and each of, well, *you* has a different kind of power. I joined with Emmett and Jim and some others, and one of us can heal people's injuries. It's kind of like a comic book," she concluded carefully, affixing a weak chuckle to the end of her sentiment. "Except it's kind of real, too."

Saffron closed her eyes slowly, her fingertips tapping softly on her leg. "All I know," she offered, "is that I feel what other people feel. If they're afraid, I can feel it. If they're angry, I feel it. And if they're *special*, I feel *that*. My mother really tried to kill you, Irish guy?" When Lowery nodded, she clenched her hand into a fist. "Damn it." She accepted his acknowledgment without hesitation, and clenched her teeth firmly. "Okay. What do you want me to do? How can I make it right?"

"Get the hell out of this," Emmett advised immediately. When his friends looked back at him, he raised his leather-encased hands helplessly. "I don't want you to get in the cross-fire of the war that's going on. It won't be pretty."

Saffron clapped her hands together softly. "Fine by me! She's *just* my adopted mother and all!"

Jim blinked, but otherwise maintained a smooth veneer. "Adopted?"

The student nodded weakly. "Yeah. My parents died in a fire about seventeen years ago," she admitted, holding up her hands and rolling back one of her gloves to reveal her burn scars.

Sonia knew what was coming, but refused to look away from the distorted flesh. "I don't remember them, so don't feel bad." She paused for an instant, then admitted, "You know, Maria told me about you," she confided. "She told me you were different, this isn't a news to me."

Slowly, the Irishman smirked. "I know, Saffron, but tha's a'right. Yer here, an' in the next couple days, I'm hopin' this all ends."

It was a noble hope.

*****

Geddy's ability to target a person he was familiar with was impressive. He could put down his friends (well, friends and Alejandro) anywhere within a few hundred feet of them. He could do this without inadvertently merging anyone with telephone poles, or other people, provided he didn't try to feel out the physical space too far from his target. If he was unable to properly read an area, well, he'd made his feelings about "blind" transportation quite clear - but even that was possible, provided there wasn't some sort of interference.

On Sari's recommendation, he'd transported them to Erica's latest campaign rally, and in particular to the middle of the crowd. The priestess wondered briefly what the best means of approach might be. Erica wasn't known to be sensitive enough to detect her team's feelings of ambivalence, but if she could pick up on it somehow? Well, chances were that they'd find out once they felt her emotional manipulation take hold.

Standing in a mass of befuddled of onlookers, Sari frowned; Erica was on stage, and true to what the Consortium had expected of her, she was throwing her empathic powers around liberally. The priestess immediately shut her mind off; nullifying the ambient pressure of her presence. It was something she was naturally good at, and that she had insisted James teach every other person they'd worked with for just such an occasion as this. The Irishman didn't comply happily; he claimed it was too difficult a skill for most to learn successfully, but she secretly suspected it was because her friends could use the same self-control techniques against him.

As far as speeches went, it was average; there were grandiose pledges of change, but Erica displayed little of the wordplay she was famous for as the front-woman for the oft-forgotten Wildcats. No, the speech was absolutely conventional, with simple language and general concepts. Liberty, freedom, personal responsibility; all well and good, but all boiled down to the lowest common denominator. Even her biblical quotes lacked the punch that one might expect from a megalomaniac. For a moment, the Brahman honestly didn't think Erica's heart was in it.

As the speech wrapped up, the singer took the microphone in hand and waved with false warmth. "Well, ladies and gentlemen, thank you for your time. Vote for me, and now tonight's entertainment - The Red Statists!" A political humor band? Sari nearly gagged as Hall left the stage. Then, the dynamic shifted; Erica paused and looked over her shoulder. "Oh, and could the representatives from Lowery Security Services kindly come back-stage? Thanks!"

She could hear James' voice, in the back of her mind, declaring, *'Well, fuck,'* leaving Sari to sigh and start the trek to the nearest security kiosk. They were checked in quickly enough, and led directly toward Erica's dressing room by what were undoubtedly secret service agents. The trio was certainly an odd delegation for the songbird to meet with - and, as they allegedly represented a security company, Sari was precisely as un-intimidating as she was beautiful. When they were frisked, it seemed like amateurs performing the search; all of the hardware on their bodies was flat-out ignored.

They entered a room labeled private, permitted in by a pair of suit-and-tie wearing muscle men, and immediately set their eyes upon their old ally. Erica looked enthusiastic and powerful, graceful and controlled, yet Sari could see through the illusion; the woman was irritated, to say the least.

She spoke, and her voice was acidic. "So, Alejandro

Curtis. It's been a few years since I saw you." The last time they had met, of course, she'd sent him off on a crusade to kill the next person she addressed. "Jethro," she continued coldly, "good to see that you're still playing lap-dog to Lowery." Geddy looked like he would pop; but Erica's features softened as she looked at her third guest. "Sari, it's good to see you, too," she concluded, sincerely, without snide commentary.

"You're a right bitch," Geddy countered firmly, staring eye to eye with the singer. Hall's lips broadened into a faint grin, and Marx's hands tapped impotently on his leg as he tried to resist sending her off a rooftop. "What the hell'd I ever do to you?"

Sari's eyes drifted over to Jethro, and the healer offered him a weak smile. "She doesn't mean it," the Hindu started defensively.

"Oh, I mean it," Erica replied caustically, glaring back at the large man. "You've all done a very rotten job of spying on me, lately, and I'm kind of tired of it. I'm even unhappy with you, Sari," she added with a twang of sadness, "so let's get to it. What do you three want?"

Sari's face relaxed with confusion. "What do you mean? You got my voice-mail, didn't you?"

At Erica's blank stare, Alejandro spoke up in his casually grim tone, "I have a feeling it was intercepted by James' presently-least favorite pest." As Alejandro spoke, the singer's eyebrow rose with amusement at the idea of not being Lowery's foremost annoyance. Sari even looked impressed!

"You've got my attention," Erica confessed, carefully scrutinizing the three. She sat down in a particularly relaxing-looking chair. "What did you need to tell me that was *intercepted*, as you say?"

Geddy took a deep breath, steeling himself. "'Riki, Garrett Trinder is alive."

Erica's eyes widened. Sari recognized, instantly, that the singer wasn't with them at the present moment. Rather, she was with them a decade and a half ago - well, minus Alejandro. She was watching as Emmett's madness consumed the Garrett she'd known, consumed their unborn child, and in all likelihood consumed her sanity. Sari could feel as Erica tore apart their emotions, searching for any hint of a fabrication, and found none. Fortunately, this wasn't painful - just awkward.

"And there was a certain beggar named Lazarus, which was laid at his gate, full of sores," Erica announced in a pained voice, gritting her teeth. Her composure broke for just as long as it took her eyes to shut and her head to shake, her blonde-and-black locks of hair flipping about carelessly as she shielded herself from her memories. She brushed them back into place and opened her eyes. "So he's alive. What's this have to do with me?"

Sari looked to the floor for a moment, then whispered softly. "We think that he's been manipulating you into, well, everything. He's kind of like us."

Once again, one of Erica's eyebrows rose up slowly. "Okay. And what does he do?"

"He claims he can manipulate time," Alejandro advised; a certain stoic look on the muscular Spaniard's face coupled with a curious glint in his eyes. "I don't see any reason to doubt his veracity." Erica actually seemed to echo his interest for a moment, but Alejandro continued. "According to him, he has secretly manipulated many different factions through his control over The Coleman Group. He has even placed agents around you to protect you."

Now, recognition etched its way into Erica's face; it was quickly followed by an unspeakable rage that boiled over the three in the room for a few moments. Sari felt like she was going to grab a table and smash it over Alejandro's face! The sensation passed, leaving all three looking as if they had just faced down a devil. The problem was that they hadn't yet to begin; Hall seemed to grow icy and cold once again, but her attention fell one again to that girl she had rescued fifteen years ago.

"It's Victoria, isn't it, Sari?"

Fighting to keep her voice from trembling, the priestess nodded. She seemed much firmer than she had been five years ago, the last time the two had met. "Yes, Miss Hall, we think it is. I take it she is also like us?"

The songbird exhaled slowly. "Yeah, she is. So's her adopted daughter, Saffron." She didn't care if her former friends were surprised; she kept right on talking. "Victoria always suggested she could see the future. I assume she *really* got her information from Trinder?" When her question went unopposed, Erica carried on thoughtfully, "I just don't understand why."

Geddy softened, slightly. "He said yer destiny wasn't changin'. Said something like you was always gonna run for President, an' it was all about *how*. Of course, he said if we didn't do what we did at the Point, we were all gonna die when Emmett--"

A horrifying glare shot from the singer's ice-blue eyes into Jethro's, and the man lost his nerve to continue speaking. Well, 'lost' may have been the wrong word; it was stolen. "Eisenberg is a monster, and that is all I have to say about him. The only reason I let him live is because he is suffering just as much as I am. The one good thing I have left to say about that monster is that he has a conscience. I never believed this of Trinder." Without a hint of hesitation, save for her hand brushing over her abdomen, she continued, "So he's responsible for everything that's happened to me? If Garrett killed my Jasmine, then I will simply kill Garrett."

Sari knew exactly where this was going, and decided now was the time to change the pace of the conversation. "There's, well, one other thing, Miss Hall." She gathered her strength. "We think--"

Suddenly, the sound of a quick scuffle echoed through the door. Whatever had happened was over before it began as a series of pained grunts and sighs was accompanied by a pair of dull thuds. Then, the doorknob started to jiggle. Alejandro turned towards it, looking over his shoulder briefly. "Erica, I hate to ask this, but what is that door made out of?" When the knob didn't give way, the sound of metal snapping rung through the room. A moment later, a hand burst through it.

"Apparently nothin' strong," Geddy remarked as the thin veneer of a barrier was practically shredded by the hands of a gaunt, tan-skinned man. The figure wore sunglasses to cover his eyes and a black leather trench coat, and while he was almost as tall as Alejandro the intruder was quite skeletal in his physique. He was clearly of African descent, with a number of truly dark freckles on his face, and his hair was in what was best called an Afro; a small, well-groomed one.

The man paused as he entered, observing four people instead of just one. "Right," an accented voice escaped from his lips, "she called for some security company. And you're all the same, aren't you?"

Sari felt a strange sensation creep up in her flesh; she took a step backwards, then turned her gaze towards the incredibly irked singer in the room. She was suddenly held in check by Erica's presence, and Hall barked bravely, "*Now* what? Who the hell are you? And what do *you* do?"

If the priestess was unable to advance, the invader was positively held in place. Even his fingertips twitched as he struggled to make progress, but he couldn't convince his limbs to work. He looked half surprised and half amused, as if this was all some sort of game. Alejandro grimaced as he put himself between the seemingly-paralyzed figure and his allies. "Jean-Claude L'Francois, aren't you? I am Javier, and you will not be harming anyone, today."

"One of the black-files?" Erica asked with interest, affixing her full wrath on the invader. "The name rings a bell, as they say. Now, then, why -- hmm?" She almost found the situation amusing, even as it broke away from her control.

Because *he* broke away from her control! Jean-Claude bore his teeth - sharp, but he possessed no cliche vampire fangs! - and advanced forward, swinging a fist around and slamming it square into Alejandro's jaw. This had exactly the results a knowledgeable outsider might predict. The large Spaniard, unfazed, scowled and countered; delivering a supremely powerful punch to the soul-drinker's stomach. The skeletal man doubled over.

"That went well," Erica remarked churlishly. "Still not sure how he -- oh?" The man was getting to his feet, then. Blood dripped from his lips, but Jean-Claude didn't seem done in at all.

No, he cracked a faint grin. "Interesting, mis ami," the Algerian commented, flexing his fingertips once. A strange sensation slid into the air, a sudden darkness encompassing the room. It radiated from Jean-Claude's very soul, it seemed, and his flesh appeared to become paler than it had been when he arrived. "Not since the Nazis, eh?" He advanced forward once more, swinging for Alejandro's gut as if he planned to go blow-for-blow with the brute.

This time, however, when the punch landed it seemed like a spark of light connected along with it. This time, it was Alejandro whose eyes grew wide. Now, blood shot from the Spaniard's mouth; the sound of bones cracking was audible, even underneath the jacket Emmett had given him. It cushioned the impact, yet somehow a certain amount of the strike slipped through! And for Alejandro, who was unused to enduring serious injury, it was a horrifying moment.

He recovered quickly enough, however, and retaliated, rocking L'Francois' face this time. The vampire's jaw fractured as chunks of calcium went flying. His teeth - six in total, on the floor - grew right back into his skull as if he was being healed from an external force. He grinned once again; and Alejandro, ever the wise one, didn't let him get a second punch in.

No, Jean-Claude stole it. Alejandro swung for the fences this time, but the Algerian was behind the Spaniard so quickly that Sari didn't realize what had happened. What came next was a classic battle between a strong yet slow fighter, and a quick and almost-as-strong one. It was over in a few seconds, and while it was going on nobody dared to get in the way. Sari could see Geddy searching for an opportunity - all it would take was one touch to send the man to Mars! But he couldn't even hope to get his hands on the beast, and without physical contact he was unable to inflict injury.

Instead, Sari merely extended her palms, her abilities keeping Alejandro from falling victim to his injuries. She had to pour all of her focus into sustaining him; even though she felt Erica acting to suppress the pain centers in both the Spaniard and the Brahman, she couldn't take her eyes off of her target. Alejandro's resistance to damage was incredible, and Jean-Claude was only injuring him by pumping what Sari could best describe as negatively-charged life energy into him. This resistance was a problem in one way, however: His own power made it too hard for her to keep Alejandro healthy. Successfully healing him required too much of her attention.

Suddenly, Jean-Claude was in front of *her*. Sari's eyes widened and she took a step back. Her arms, however, couldn't snap back to her body fast enough. He grasped her left hand, and a sensation unlike any she'd ever felt came over her. Power! It spilled out of her in gallons! So much of it that she had never guessed she'd had, at all! But with this unbidden power came unbidden memories.

She witnessed herself re-living all of the tests she'd experienced, back during the most hellish days of her stay in Africa, and she screamed an unearthly note as her body convulsed. She'd distantly theorized that having a 'vampire' steal life from her would hurt; she'd thought she'd feel exhausted! Instead, she was energized! It felt familiar, somehow, like she'd always craved this kind of burning rush.

She reached out and grabbed Jean-Claude's arm with her right hand and *tore*, ripping his fingertips clean off of their knuckles and simultaneously eliciting the strangest sensation of nourished lust from him. It passed quickly, mainly because her conscious mind collapsed under the pain, under this spiritual emptiness, under the adrenaline rush, and under the traumatic flashbacks. She fell to the floor, swimming in a strangely fond darkness, much like when she was a child. Only now, she was not alone.

Watching Sari fall, Erica's blue eyes widened. No longer was this an amusing contest of violence between two professionals. No longer was this simply a war she could stay out of. She clenched a fist. "You want a taste of power, dipshit?!" she roared, whipping her right hand around from her front to her back as if banishing a nasty spirit. Even as Alejandro joined Sari on the floor, his concussed brain shutting down as the two pillars of power supporting it cut out, the Algerian found himself once again unable to move.

"Jethro, now! Send him to fucking orbit!" Erica ordered, and Geddy complied. He leaped forward, and before the vampire could break through the empathic chains binding him, the big Black man had placed a hand on Jean-Claude's shoulder. The attacker was gone; disappeared into thin air. Victory had been won, but at a cost.

"Oh, God," Erica whispered, staring down at the unconscious Sari. "What have I let happen?"

*****

Meanwhile, Sonia had just informed her friends of the fight that had started. Jim seemed impatient, waiting for Geddy to grab him and pull him back to the city. Emmett knew he wasn't going to be the first one called - for starters, Alejandro was invulnerable, while Erica might happily slaughter them all just to get revenge on the physicist if he dared show his face near her. Never mind that Geddy had no way of knowing Saffron's involvement, and wouldn't be calling her or Sonia any time soon.

Jim's eyes moved to the door suddenly, holding a hand up to forestall any further discussion. The sound of keys jingling was replaced with a soft 'hmm' of surprise; the door was unlocked! It opened, and Saffron's face lit up with terror. How had she been so foolish? The physicist inwardly cursed himself for not checking to make sure the doorway was locked, but how could they have imagined Vicky coming back? It wasn't yet time for her class to be over. They still had fifteen minutes, easily.

That fact probably explained Emmett's stunned reaction to the person who walked into Victoria's office - Daniel Marceau!

The head of the Psychology department did a quick double-take. "Doctor Eisenberg!?" he roared, advancing on Emmett with the unmatched bluster of a man who had just caught his wife's lover in bed with her.

"Da--Dr. Marceau, please, hold on!" Saffron shouted, standing up and standing in between the two men. This was a vain effort, as Dan blew right past the girl and grabbed Emmett's shirt threateningly.

The physicist retreated a step. "Hold on, this isn't what you think!"

"It is *exactly* what I think!" the chairman looked around the room slowly. "That is Sonia Monterrey, one of my former students. You! You are a conniving little bastard! And this man? Judging from his appearance," he chided angrily, halfway to lifting Emmett up off of his feet as his hand wrapped around the collar of the scientist's shirt. "James Lowery, Maria calls him! And Saffron? Saffron?! What, did you let these cretins in? Have they hurt you!?"

Maybe it was the man's concern for the girl - heartfelt - which kept Jim from noticing. Maybe it was the fact that his ex-girlfriend's boyfriend was doing a laughable job of lifting him up that kept Emmett from figuring it out. It was certainly Sonia's attention to the mayhem happening in the city that kept her suspicions to a low roar, but Saffron? Her only delay was a lack of training, but she just had time to shout a warning: "Wait, that's---"

His shirt lifted, his stomach exposed, Daniel's spare hand brushed up against Emmett's abdomen just before a large, sword-like bone spur shot clean through the physicist's stomach. The injury induced instant shock into the scientist; Emmett fell backwards, quite literally on his ass. He supported himself for about a moment, then fell sideways into the fetal position - paralyzed, unconscious, or worse. Sonia screamed in horror. Saffron screamed in horror...

*****

"This is everything," Garrett had advised, opening the file case up for James and Erica for the very first time. "I found out the other day exactly what they were doing." He produced a single black-colored folder and opened it. "It is bad," he warned, handing over the documents. It contained Sari's file-photo, followed by a collection of serialized pictures. They were increasingly grotesque. They contained images of mutilated animals, of mangled people! They even included images of the girl the two had saved so long ago; and she had been injured. Badly.

"They currently have her in Omega Section, Block 8, Room 12. We need to get her out before they do anything else to her."

Nervously, Erica whispered, "Turn the other cheek, is what Christ would say, but..."

Jim's eyes narrowed upon Garrett's, and it didn't seem like either man had heard Erica's words. "What about Geddy? Emmett? And what about th' bastards who've done it to 'er?"

Trinder shook his head slowly. "I can trust Marx, but Eisenberg is, well..." he trailed off. "I would rather not. The way he'd react, probably? He might go nuclear. He's too self-centered."

"Good!" Jim retaliated angrily. "'E'd kill 'em all in a heartbeat!" Erica couldn't find a counter-argument, at the moment. "Maybe we jus' show th'world what they did!"

Garrett, on the other hand, could. "I refuse. I'm giving you the 'White' files only on the condition that you promise you won't get Emmett involved. There's just too much risk. He's not stable enough. In his stead, I will help you - but if he finds out? It can not end well. And it has to be done carefully," the German added softly. "Richard Trujillo has to be one of the first, just after Samuel Quimby."

Jim and Erica exchanged glances, and Erica gazed to her abdomen for a moment. "I can do this," Hall whispered softly, despite her distaste for premeditated murder.

"I'll take th' firs' kill," the Irishman announced, *"an' I'll help Geddy wit' th' second."*

*****

James screamed in rage, and without a moment's hesitation he plunged his knife directly into Daniel's neck. No, not Daniel's - Andrew's. Even with the weapon embedded in his body, the man re-arranged his flesh around it and took on his normal form, complete with the sound of bones and sinew snapping into different places, a noise which plagued Lowery to no end.

"So sorry, James, but you will not be killing me like that," Coleman declared boldly. Jim wasn't intimidated; he became a blur of death and suffering, cleaving massive gashes into the business-owner's body. Some of the wounds seemed to stall Andrew, while others merely irked him. He lashed out, returning fire; with a hint of effort, his left hand transformed from a convenient appendage to a bone-like blade, and he used it to parry the knife.

It didn't have much effect, unfortunately. Emmett had long-ago reinforced Jim's knife's sharpness and molecular structure, making it the most vicious cleaver one could picture. It instantly snapped the defensive appendage off. The biological weapon clattered to the floor, and Andrew's face winced with pain. "Oh, tha' hurts?!" the Irishman screamed with enraged glee, knifing Andrew's right hand to boot, and finishing his assault by plunging his dagger square into his foe's face. "How y'like tha?!"

After a few seconds spent groaning, during which he anesthetized himself biochemically so that he wouldn't feel the metal protruding from his face, Andrew chortled to himself. "Is that it?" Coleman mocked. "Give it up," he advised arrogantly, one hand reaching up to snare Jim's while the still-rough, still-dense bone of his left ha-- no, stump, consisting of broken shards of calcium - raked across Lowery's face. He roared in pain, his hand pulling his weapon free. He turned around to attack once more, but what he heard caused him to slow down for an instant.

Because he heard Saffron get up and grab Andrew, screaming in hatred as her arms locked around the man's shoulders. Her emotions poured out of her in a way that only one other person had ever been able to manage, and Jim immediately retreated to his defensive training. Emmett was - fortunately for the surrounding twenty miles - unconscious, but Sonia? She was already a mess, and when the wave of inexplicable sensations struck her, she clung to her boyfriend and did her best not to scream as well. Jim could resist it, but not well; he trembled involuntarily, no matter how much control he placed on his body.

Andrew, on the other hand, adopted a look of sheer terror. Instantly his body exploded into droplets of blood, and just like a decade and a half ago he was a pile of mush. Unlike at Connor Point, however, this time he seemed to dry up, rolling out of the room and running as far away as possible. For all James knew, everyone in a fifteen mile radius was about to kill themselves as Saffron's emotional assault threatened to drive them into an unexplained, world-crushing depression. It had to end.

Saffron fell to her knees, regaining control over her feelings just as her body failed her. Her hands wrapped around James' ankles helplessly. Jim grabbed his phone and dialed into the internet conversation, as Sonia was little more than a pile of sobs and sorrow. "Geddy! Geddy, Emmett'n a civvie're down! I need Sari here, now!"

What he heard back caused his stomach to turn. "Alejandro and Sari are down, Jim! They're down!" Geddy roared back just as that familiar buzzing overtook him.

*****

They weren't back in Las Vegas, yet; or, at least, they weren't where James had meant for Geddy to bring them. His eyes narrowed as he glanced around the rooftop of the hotel they had stayed in all too recently, and he clenched a fist. "Tha' fuck're we doin'---"

Something in the eyes of his old friend kept him from speaking. He measured the man, and he knew instantly that Jethro had something to make clear. He'd thought it was like all of Geddy's other snide comments; witty remarks made in passing. "Jim, we've been friends for, what, damn near twenty years?"

"Uh-huh," Jim agreed, looking down at his boot and checking his knife. He quickly inventoried his pockets - he wasn't armed properly for the mission he was going on, but somehow - perhaps due to one of those endless briefings he'd given his colleagues - Marx knew what he was looking for.

The large fellow closed his eyes and an auto-injector appeared in his palm, pre-loaded with a concoction of chemicals similar to the ones they'd used in Alaska. He passed Jim a total of six of them, three for each of his jacket pockets. They clearly came from an armory that the Black man knew well - Geddy had to touch something in order to teleport it remotely, and Jim had to admit he was impressed that his friend was quite so well equipped. It was that strange fact which kept his attention fixed on the other man's speech. "I'm tellin' ya this for you own sake, Jimmy. Get tha' shit together. We're all on our last legs, an' if you keep pushin' you ain't gonna find anythin' left to protect."

After securing his new gear, James gave himself just enough time to sigh. "Geddy, I can't let this shit go on. S'no way I'm lettin' 'em keep tryin' t'kill us."

"We's fuckin' super-heroes, you big dummy!" Jethro responded in a half-humored, half-hardened tone. "I's worried that tha only way Trinder an' Coleman can hit us is if we's half asleep when they come. If we're too fuckin' exhausted ta even try an' stop dem assholes! If you keep actin' like a psycho, you ain't gonna be able to keep from makin' a mistake."

The Irishman closed his eyes for a few seconds, measuring Jethro's heart rate. It was steady. "I've made a lot of 'em already, Geddy. So what'd y'think I can do?"

"Just slow things down a little, so's we ain't end up making tha' same damn mistakes."

*****

The two ladies had been working on various servers and databases, bringing them back on-line after Voodoo had so greatly crippled their network. They could only restore power chunk by chunk, then search the hard-drives for any sign of compromise. This was not an easy task, nor was it quick. Lark led the way, with Katrina primarily following orders; Lark was the specialist in this field, after all! In many cases, save for rare instances dealing with proprietary data belonging to the company or its clients, they ripped the hard-drives out entirely so that they could minimize the risk of any viruses or left-over contamination. Clearly, they weren't interested in meeting any ghosts in their future hacking days.

Just as they finished up on the Lowery Security Services main database, the intruder signal went off. Someone had breached the building's security without proper authentication. Oh, no alarm bells were ringing - these were, instead, cell-phone alerts that the two got which buzzed in a very specific pattern. Katrina and Lark nodded to one another quickly, confirming they'd both gotten the same message, and pulled out their waist-holstered pistols. These weapons had fraudulent serial numbers and licenses to boot, all with selectively applied, top-notch ballistics foils. A round fired by one of their handguns would be almost impossible to trace back to an actual firearm. On the other hand, the weapons were mildly less accurate; though they were in the hands of professionals used to the wider spray pattern caused by such alterations.

They worked their way from the back section of the computer stacks to the front. They immediately swiped their identification card across a secure terminal and it booted up with a display of known activity in the building. It was definitely an intruder on this floor, a floor which contained a lot of the company's 'proprietary' gear. Then she saw the room numbers being investigated: HW-01, HW-02, HW-03, and HW-00.

"Hospital wing...?" Katrina asked warily, alarm forming in her eyes. "It could not be drug-seekers, they would never know."

Lark immediately re-engaged her weapon's safety before she holstered the gun, charging for the doorway which would lead a hallway that, in turn, fed into a large glass-doored chamber called HW-00. This first room was a large, pristine facility with plenty of medicine cabinets, a few folded-up benches, and various spare monitoring equipment. In essence, this was a private hospital; and the three rooms attached to it were actually triage-quality rooms for private use, all designed with Medivent's most cutting-edge technology. It was called "deviation" from the "market," when various medications and devices left the factory without properly approved purchase slips, and Sari generally frowned upon unofficially sponsoring Jim's private hospital. Then again, it would have been a nightmare for her to set up her company on her own. James had earned his supply because he'd helped build Sari's network.

"It's them," Lark whispered, charging headlong into a madhouse.

Strewn on the floor was an unconscious Sari and a rather beaten, bruised, groaning Alejandro. Though the latter was slowly collecting his wits about him, he was a long way off getting his head in order. Sadly, the first two figures Lark laid eyes upon weren't the ones which worried her; it was the fact that the brown-coated scientist was out cold, on a hospital bed, and bleeding badly.

"What the hell happened to him?" Katrina asked, swiftly removing Emmett's clothing around his belly wound. She assessed it rapidly; it became instantly clear that she was a trained medic, and she immediately looked at her man. "I need...Jim! James!!"

Jim's attention was trapped on the stranger in their midst - well, one of them. The blonde-and-black-haired one, the singer who caused Lark to reach for her gun once more. "Riki," Jim half-hissed, staring the girl down. "I need y't' drop it, now!" He wasn't referring to Lark's weapon, although the man's hand extended to caution her not to draw it just yet.

Erica's blue eyes were focused squarely on Emmett, and it seemed like Emmett was only growing weaker. Katrina assessed his vitals again, and sure enough they were plummeting. "Why should I?" Hall pondered softly, "Wouldn't this make the perfect moment to end his pathetic life?"

Before Jim could intervene, Sonia snapped out of her daze and got up into Erica's face. "Listen, Erica!" She shouted with anger, but it was clear she was acting out of fear - fear of loss, fear of pain, and the fear of Erica herself. She'd also clearly never seen someone get stabbed through the gut; seeing someone's intestines, along with all requisite fluids? And they were the insides of a man she loved. It was a miracle she wasn't having an anxiety attack, with Saffron's emotional detonation serving as the cherry on top of a *very* stressful day. Or, perhaps - as she grasped Erica's shirt and tugged violently - she was. "I need him! I need him, I love him, and I won't let you take him from me! Haven't we all suffered enough because of Garrett?!"

"Riki," Jim argued in a cold voice, matching the singer's eyes. "'E's grown up, Riki. Physics -boy ain't a boy, no more, is 'e?"

Erica's face formed into a scowl, and she turned her eyes toward the group's other major casualty. With a flick of a wrist, she took Emmett's girlfriend's hand off of her clothing - and nearly off of the limb it was attached to. Hall then took a step towards the priestess and placed her fingertips upon the silent Sari's hand. "I should focus on my own failings, shouldn't I?" she whispered to nobody in particular. "It's not turning the cheek, but...This?" She licked her dry lips. "Sari's pain is my fault. She never should have to hurt so badly, after being such a good..." She looked for a word. "A good friend. I failed to protect her."

Suddenly, something shifted in Jim's eyes. He softened, slightly, towards the singer. "Riki'," the Irishman lilted carefully, "Jus' focus on gettin' through to 'er. She's a healer, she helps people. Give 'er somethin' t' think 'bout, someone t'focus on."

The implication was clear. All the empath did was nod

delicately and gaze toward the unconscious girl, and it was evident she was putting forth some unrecognized effort even as that omnipresent aura of fear seemed to dissipate from around them. Sonia stood off to Jim's side, staring at the Irishman as if thoroughly stunned as to why he wasn't patching up the physicist she loved so dearly.

"Vitals are stabilizing," Katrina mumbled softly, surveying the scientist again and again. She produced a bag filled with a clear liquid, one labeled '*Mediventicillin*.' It was the first of a highly potent, if not originally named new generation of antibiotics. It was also quite experimental! There was no telling if the physicist would suffer side-effects, though it was equally hard to guess just how infectious Andrew Coleman's weaponry might have been. "But this tissue damage is too severe to heal without surgery, James." For the first time, she really *looked* at him; her eyes narrowed. "Your face..."

The Irishman looked at his lady and offered her a thumbs up, but it was Geddy who spoke next. "She's doin' what I think she doin', right?" This earned another gesture from the Irishman. "Jus' gimme a shot later."

This second one was something of a guess. He could only judge from Erica's heart-beat; from the scent of her perspiration, detected over her perfume. He listened for the contraction of the muscles in her fingertips as she clenched her fists, and he tried to decide if she was trying to emotionally strangle Emmett, or to keep her own hatred in check as she focused on saving him. It was a little bit worse than a guess, he realized; it was a flat-out lie, a lie told to give Erica the illusion that she was trusted. The hope was that she wouldn't grow any angrier; the added stress would only worsen matters.

Meanwhile, the Russian flicked out a pen-like device and sliced Emmett's arm. It was a tiny cut, and it quickly produced a result - a blood-type. It was faster to use this new technology, surprisingly enough, than for her to actually locate and read Emmett's files. Those were stored securely in Jim's safe, and he was the only one capable of accessing it! The pen-tests were another Medivent creation, and she passed them to everyone in the room (save for Erica) while mumbling, "Give yourself a small nick, and a prayer."

The results were horrifying, as first Geddy, then Sonia tested as other-than-Emmett. In fact, the only one in the room who tested the same type as him was the forgotten, hithero-to silent Saffron. The girl was emotionally drained, to say the least. Katrina didn't even hesitate; she prepared a needle and a tube.

"I..." Saffron began tentatively, not quite sure *what* she should do.

A dry voice echoed across the room. "Save the bastard," Erica advised in a spiteful tone, "He doesn't deserve it, but he can suffer longer if he lives. He can repent for his sins."

"Got it," Geddy remarked offhandedly, trying to dismiss his own desires to toss the songbird into the sun. Sonia could only look at Saffron with fear that Katrina's command would be refused; she feared for nothing. Saffron didn't need Erica to tell her what to do.

She spoke hesitantly as she rolled up her sleeve. "He..." A pause. "He wanted to help me. I could tell. If all I can do is give him a little of my life, then I'll do it." Katrina inserted the needle swiftly, drawing the blood. "I'm clean, by the way," Saffron added; it earned a nod of respectful recognition from the medic. The blood was immediately taken and put into a centrifuge.

The process was relatively quick, if unprofessional. Once separated, Katrina could take and inject the red blood cells into Emmett's arteries. Then, she could focus on the platelets - the clotting cells, which she'd inject into the flesh near the physicist's wound. It was a vain hope that she would be able to speed up his natural healing, but after only a few minutes of patience, the Consortium would get some unexpected results.

Sonia was left to worry, panicked, about what would come next. What she saw was Emmett's chest rise and fall more quickly, his body heave as he coughed. His wound was pulsating rapidly - a sign of horrific infection, perhaps? No; because she immediately recognized that the wound was sealing up on its own accord. Her eyes flitted to Sari.

"Done, but it isn't pretty," mumbled Erica, who proceeded to sit down and rub her forehead, finally taking the time to actually process what had gone on around her. The healer's hands were radiating a soft, gentle glow - aquamarine. The illumination ceased after a few seconds, but in that time the scientist's injury seemed to heal completely.

All that was left was for Sonia to sob happily, knowing that in spite of all they had been through - Saffron's generous donation; Erica's reluctant decision; Sari's becoming a victim of Jean-Claude L'Francois' hunger; and Alejandro being pummeled by the aforementioned Algerian; not to mention dozens of other smaller stresses, attempted murders, and tragedies - her boyfriend and their colleagues had survived intact. For now, it was over.

*****

Survival was his first thought. He'd heard of vampires taking to flight, but *this* was ridiculous. One moment he was befuddled by the Indian girl's strange taste, and the next he felt a hand touch him. A buzzing, a pop, and he was staring down at the surface of Planet Earth and falling, fast! His instincts kicked in, and he spread his arms to slow his fall, maximizing his surface area. He'd just enjoyed a cornucopia of life energies the likes of which he'd never indulged in before, and he began to slowly utilize that power to keep himself from passing out as the lack of oxygen strangled his conscious mind.

Of course, when his body inevitably impacted upon the ground - he believed he was over Asia! - he would face a test unparalleled in his long life. He had to focus, to keep himself awake and prepared, or he was dead. As he descended, he took note of his particular position on the globe; he was over a desert, of all places, and he broke through the cloud-cover sooner than he'd expected. He was desperate, now, and he flicked a knife free to carefully cut holes in the very trench coat he was depending on to save him. Would his plan pan out?

He grasped them like a parachute and felt himself immediate lose velocity. So far, so good. But that impact? Parachute or no, it was going to hurt. He thought for sure he was doomed. He felt bones begin to break just as the pain seized his consciousness!

Awakening slowly, he clenched his fist. Blood - and lots of it - had erupted from his body. However, perhaps due to that strange Indian girl's ability to apparently patch her friend up, he had survived. No, he couldn't duplicate her power - he knew that the instant he'd touched her. Hell, even *she* couldn't duplicate her power, not in it's peak form! At least, she hadn't for some time, now. But maybe it was the nature of that life-energy bonanza which had allowed him to survive a fatal fall?

He pushed himself to his feet, focusing his power on supporting his body's basic functions. The pain was overwhelming, and the injuries behind the agony were too deep. He failed, and he fell face-first into the hot desert sand, blacking out for a second time.

When he awoke again, the pain had subsided. Unfortunately, so had the vast majority of the 'food' he'd stored up for the last week! He took care, now, inspecting his body for further damage. There wasn't much, or so it seemed, and he thanked his lucky stars - he'd lived through the unbelievable, yet again! And now, with a bit of desperation he hadn't felt in some time, he began to march through this desert. It wasn't long before he came upon a road, and he headed what he hoped was still east. It reminded him, briefly, of his home in northern Africa - though he didn't live in a desert, necessarily, he definitely was used to heat.

Time passed, but he couldn't be sure how long. Was it one minute? An hour? Three? All he knew was that his luck must have been divine - that, or he had a deity looking out, to the chagrin of Humanity, for him! A truck approached! He hazily gazed into the distance and found not one, but three vehicles bearing down on him! There would be enough people that he wouldn't even have to hurt them - he could just absorb their ambient energies and make his way back to civilization, then figure out how to get back at that horrid group of interlopers who had kept him away from that great feast.

When the first vehicle approached him, it stopped in its tracks, alright. That's when he recognized the shape of that truck as a supply hauler. He determined he'd been stumbled upon by a military convoy - well, to be fair, it was the shape of the automobile, *and* the half-dozen men who jumped out and aimed assault rifles at him. They shouted in Chinese, confirming what might have been his worst fears about his location.

Unfortunately, for them, he understood Chinese, and he didn't even allow them a chance to do as they were suggesting: To kill the Black man because he was clearly a spy. With but a thought he pulled their souls right out from under them, draining enough power from the bio-kinetic energy escaping their flesh to re-charge himself. To them, it would feel like a sudden wave of fatigue struck them - something that they never should have connected with him. That's why he was momentarily surprised that they *did*, shouting something about him being there to save something.

Too bad for them he'd already fed; brutally massacring them was as easy as avoiding the bullets fired by their AK-47's. More men ran out to face him - more food for him to consume. It wasn't as if he enjoyed their deaths; but they wanted to kill *him*, and he was awfully hungry, so it was easy for him to rationalize the necessity of their demise.

When the last body hit the floor, he determined to steal one of those trucks, a decision fueled by a process he didn't quite understand. He felt *drawn* to it, as if he was still hungry. Well, why wouldn't he be? He'd just done quite a bit of work! What with surviving a brutal fall and a small battalion and all? Yet as he stepped in to the vehicle of his choice, he noticed a particularly plucky soldier who had not yet fallen victim to him - a commanding officer who had, almost predictably in the Algerian man's disdainful eyes, hidden from the bloodshed.

"You...You do not understand!" the man exclaimed in English, the barrel of his pistol aiming at the vampire's face. "Weapon is not like us! We must test more!" A quick punch to the face took care of the delusional fellow, caving in his skull and ending his life quite sweetly!

It was only then that he sensed it, faint as it was.

Just like the ones he'd faced in New York City, there was a flavor on the other side of the truck. He gazed up to see a Chinese - no, Korean - woman no older than twenty-five. She was unconscious, bound to the floor, rail-thin and barely breathing. Her clothing had been savaged, and the smell of sex - mingled with horrified agony - was obvious, along with serious lacerations and bruises. He experienced a hint of pity; he searched her, assuming for a moment he had already disposed of his last chance of learning more as a bitter-sweet form of avenging the girl, and surprisingly enough he found identification.

The victim's name had been scratched out of the paperwork, marking her as a "disappeared" person; the language wasn't Chinese, but Korean - and only the Northern one would tolerate such a chronically malnourished citizen. The erased one's birth-date indicated she was twenty-five, give or take a week. Satisfied, he decided it was time to put her out of her misery. He placed his hand on her forehead, whispered a prayer unlike any he had offered before - a promise of peace as he began to draw forth that delicious energy.

Her eyes tore open; she screamed, but her voice turned into a dull echo as her body transformed from ordinary flesh to lead. Then, to copper! Then, it shifted and the man's hand nearly fell through her face - she was a cloud of gas, of chlorine! He recognized it from "The Great War," before they started giving global wars numbers as if they were bad movies. He recoiled in horror at the memory of being gassed, as well as the change in the wounded woman.

She stared at him. "Who are you?" Her eyes, as the gas formed back *into* eyes, held no fear.

He shivered; something inside of him was intrigued. "I go

by Jean-Claude. And you are?"

She, too, flashed a moment's interest. "I am..." A smile brushed her bruised lips.

"I am called Ju Guem."

*****

"And, so, these are the two new members of the New Consortium of Trust," James declared proudly, concluding the second order of business for the evening. He hated leading formally as well as informally; he hated doing Sari's job, but she had taken a leave of absence. In actuality, her absence had been executed as the first, and the circumstances of her departure were predestined the minute she fell into a coma. She'd left explicit instructions with James that, if she were to ever experience a relapse of her psychiatric trauma, and ever needed to be treated, she be sent to a monastery called, simply, '*Parivatan.*' It was the place she had gone after her torture at Garrett's hands, though it was impossible to know how long she would take to recover from her mental injuries.

Of course, Sari could not fully explain *what* she had seen while unconscious. The first of the newly-appointed members had done that when treating her. Erica had wrestled with joining them, of course. She hated Emmett far more than Alejandro had hated Geddy. Did she have as much reason? Well, she held Emmett accountable, in part, for the death of her unborn daughter, after all! Geddy only killed Alejandro's father! The crimes weren't *that* comparable, were they? Well, at least Alejandro wasn't acting that way.

Geddy had taken good care of the injured Spaniard, and the muscular man seemed to understand that Jethro couldn't have helped him in his fight against the 'vampire.' Maybe it was Geddy's wife, Marge, who also visited him - she was a good soul through and through, and Alejandro had always held a soft spot for matronly women since his mother had raised him alone. Maybe it was the idea that, having finally experienced the pains of failure and physical injury, he better understood how Jethro could have given in to revenge against his father - who, he always agreed, had been something of a failure, himself. Either way, there was now a strange calm between the two. It promised hope that the clandestine group might survive its latest trial.

Nevertheless, Erica's admittance to the Consortium was tertiary at best. She'd explained that Sari would return to them as the young woman had promised; the emotional pain she'd experienced was only an echo of her youth. What's more, Hall agreed to cooperate with them when necessary, but wanted no part in what she had, just five minutes before her official induction, declared was "saving the world from the shadows."

"Jesus," she'd explained, "wanted others to look upon him and know him." She could not stray from that particular Savior's path; and she would not end her run for the Presidency, though she would suspend plans to expose her former colleagues from Connor Point. After all, those plans had been suggested by Garrett's agents, and any chance to strike a blow against Trinder seemed to excite Erica.

The second entry had surprised them simply by asking to be admitted. Saffron Latchkey had declared she wanted just two things - to better understand her powers, and to help bring her mother back to sanity. While Jim strongly doubted the latter was possible, the first was both necessary and possible. Saffron's powers of emotional manipulation were *exactly* like Erica's, and this coincidence marked the first time he'd ever seen two people share the same talent. If she were a little younger, he would have deep concerns over just why they were so alike - and just why she wore gloves in a manner reminiscent of a certain physicist he knew. Then again, even *if* the ages had matched up, Saffron's scars provided all the explanation he needed for *that* quirk!

Furthermore, the identical nature of their abilities meant that Erica would make a fantastic teacher; and as the two had been on fairly good terms before Vicky - no, Christine, they'd had to remind themselves - had gone all murderer on them, it wasn't too hard to imagine Saffron as a diligent pupil. The problem would be figuring out what to do with Ms. Versailles. Would she come to her senses and hide, or throw her resources into another assault? Either way, Saffron had skipped her graduation ceremony and accepted her diploma just before attending school would become a bother to her burgeoning career.

Speaking of students, Sonia had grown up all too fast. She'd had to - she'd had bullets fired at her, she'd watched her boyfriend get impaled, and she'd accepted said boyfriend's ex-girlfriend into their fold with the full knowledge that she'd had no genuine choice in the matter. It was an uncomfortable alliance for her, but she wasn't afraid of Erica stealing Emmett away. No, she only feared Erica might one day wake up on the wrong side of the bed and choose to kill the physicist. She found herself working with Erica on Hall's campaign, a job which Maria Montclaire had all too happily abandoned.

Emmett's injuries had healed well enough that he was back on the move. Sari's subconscious healing was not a complete repair, unfortunately; the physicist had benefited heavily from the medical ministrations of the Russian half of James' "Ladies." Saffron's blood hadn't hurt, either, and while the antibiotics Katrina had pumped him full of had a bit of a toxic effect, it was clear from later blood-work results that his immune system had kicked into high gear to fight off a potentially fatal infection. All in all, he had survived a fatal wound with no lasting consequences.

Speaking of injuries, it was lucky Jim had asked for a similar course of antibiotics. Necrosis had threatened to eat his face away, and without Sari to immediately patch up his injuries, the flesh over his face turned into a rough, callous-like surface. With it came a new course of calmness from the Ireland native.

"Our remaining business," Jim declared, derailing the train of reminiscing, "is t' ensure we're all on th'same page wit' our goals. Geddy, I leave it t'you," the Irishman said as he sat down.

Jethro rose from his seat and took a deep breath. "So, here's tha skinny. We gonna keep working on our primary businesses. We gonna keep making life easier for folks wit' our science an' medicine businesses." A glance to Emmett, and the unoccupied seat belonging to Sari. "Marketin's gonna keep an ear to tha ground, gathering up intel on Versailles and Coleman. I don't like reacting, but that's our best bet righ' now."

Alejandro nodded softly in agreement. "We must remember that we are to keep improving things for all people, not just ourselves." That Spanish lilt trilled over r's far more beautifully than written words could give justice. "We enjoy luxuries, but we also work hard. We are equals, even if we appoint leaders amongst us. We forgive, even if we can never forget, so that we may move forward."

This last sentiment earned a recriminating gaze from Erica, who immediately gazed into the most conveniently-placed wall she could find. "So long as, when the time comes, we do not deny one another as Christ was denied by his Apostles," she paraphrased, "we will survive."

Sonia bit her bottom lip. "As long as you don't deny me, I won't deny any of you," she responded, reaching under the table to hold her boyfriend's hand - well, his glove, at any rate. She'd grown accustomed to it.

"Denial is so damn boring, anyway," Saffron concluded, her satin-gloved hands rising and falling in an expression of openness towards the future. "It's usually best to just get to it."

The Cliffhanger
Denial

Andrew didn't need a door; not exactly. Of course, he hadn't used one in quite some time - he hadn't been able to summon up the willpower to re-form his body for a week! He'd traveled through snow and rain, over rocks and grass. He'd left no stains, though he had inadvertently gotten close to a bear, which - in its confusion - had tried to maul him fruitlessly. When he reached the city, he remained in sewers and gutters, re-focusing his mind and wondering just what to do, next.

When he finally resolved to return, he did so by sneaking right into the Infinite Loop Lounge and forging his ordinary form just on the outside of the final security door, before his "friend's" room. The magnetic locks were already disengaged, causing the newcomer's eyebrow to raise. He slid the unlocked portal open.

"Hello, Andrew," greeted the soft Germanic voice of Garrett Trinder; he was calm, ice-cold, speaking without hesitation. "I'm glad to see you back together again!" It was a genuine remark, made as if there was a worry that Andrew might not have survived his conflict with the heroes. It was also a bad pun, one he directed attention away from quite quickly. "You remember Christine, by the way?"

What would have been a facetious question was underscored by the fact that the older woman had a gun to Garrett's head. Her dark hair was hardly well-kept, and it seemed like she hadn't slept for days. Trinder hardly seemed to care; much like when Emmett had been strangling him, it was as if his only concern was that the metal pressing into his temple was uncomfortable. "I'm guessing," Garrett queried, "that it was emotional shock?"

"Glad you noticed!" cried Andrew, rubbing his face and making sure that it was *his* face, and not one of the many hundreds he had stolen. He was less certain of his voice - it sounded boyish to him, weak and frail. "I know you told me; but my god, was it overwhelming!"

At this, Christine looked up at Coleman; she knew better than to level a gun at him, keeping it trained on Trinder. "She..." the scientist trailed off, starting falsely the first time, "She doesn't have access to the other side?"

Garrett rolled his eyes boredly. "She never encountered Jean-Claude, Christine. How would she?" He scowled scornfully. "Instead, someone else suffered at his hands."

"So what?!" Versailles yelled, causing Andrew to step forward defensively. Garrett held up a hand, and that was all the re-assurance Coleman needed to disengage, choosing to light a cigar instead; honey flavored. The 'conversation' continued unabated. "Why should my daughter have to be fed on by that monster, anyway?!"

Trinder exhaled slowly, forcing his voice into a patient tone. "You know why. You know exactly why."

"I want her back, Garrett! You promised, you swore to me that she would be my daughter!" Christine choked, once. "The daughter I could never have!"

Sadness flashed over his eyes, but nobody was looking - nobody cared that Garrett was honestly sad over what he had done; that he had regrets, that he had made painful choices. "I made sure that a cover-team found Doctors Montclaire and Marceau, Andrew. There will be a---"

Versailles pressed the barrel down harder, eliciting a wince from the German. Her anger redoubled itself, and she spoke through gritted teeth. "I want the truth, Garrett, and I know that you can't refuse! Will I have my daughter back!?"

His lips twisted gravely. "It is not over, yet, but she is with them."

Christine's eyes filled with fear. "No," she whispered anxiously.

"Yes," Garrett reiterated vacantly.

Andrew tapped the edge of his cigar against an ash-tray, drawing in another puff of the noxious nicotine. A rough smirk brushed over his lips. "It's really your fault, anyway, Christine. If you'd let Jean-Claude activate Saffron, just like we'd planned, it never would have come to this. Hey, for what it's worth?" He shrugged callously, wholly indifferent to her obvious stress. "I tried to rescue her from them. Now, you wanna put that gun down? You can shoot me, if it makes you feel better, just so long as we can start planning this out. We have a world to save, here."

Reluctantly, Versailles re-engaged the safety of the weapon. Her mood swung quickly, and she quickly reactivate the firearm and pressed it to the back of Trinder's skull. "One more question! Will *she* find out?"

Once more, the multi-faced public front of his corporation laughed condescendingly. "You know you have to ask the whole question, directly and specifically, to force him to answer it, Christine; so just use her name," Andrew suggested dismissively. "We all know what we've done to those poor bastards. Just do it."

Oddly enough, Garrett laughed softly. It was a strange laugh, born of that sorrow which he felt only he could truly understand. "Thank you, Andrew," the Germanic accent of his voice declared genuinely, "but coercion will not necessary. When you came to me nineteen years ago, begging for a child, I told you the only way I could deliver would be--"

"It wasn't *my* fault you couldn't do the deed!" Christine inserted defensively, her eyes taking both figures into account. Andrew winced; Garrett didn't even flinch.

He just smiled and carried on. "Would be if you agreed to help me. Will Saffron be activated? Because you refused to allow Jean-Claude to do it, our only hope now is for Kali to stumble upon her - that, or perhaps enforced compliance." He seemed to regard this prospect as unlikely. "If you wish to know whether or not the Algerian has survived to activate, in turn, our greatest fear? Yes, he has. Death and Un-Death now walk, hand in hand, towards their revenge."

Finally, Trinder's head turned and his eyes, brimming with sadness, leveled upon his former compatriot's. She purposefully looked at Andrew, at this point. "And, if you want to know -

most of all - whether your closest friend will find out that I forged hospital records, that Andrew disguised himself as a doctor, and that we stole her Jasmine and delivered the baby, to you, through the mists of time itself? Just to buy a few measly years so the child might be ready? *Could* have been ready, had you not failed me?"

It was clear Christine would do anything to know the answer to this question, yet Garrett's arms simply rose and fell. "I suppose my answer to that must be that I cannot see clearly."

"Bullshit!" Christine called out boldly. "You put them all through hell just to save this world, so you damn well better have an answer. You damn well better have planned for this!"

Andrew just chuckled, scorn woven through his voice. "You don't get it. He can't lie! It's like we told you two decades ago. We required Jasmine's--"

The protest was immediate. "Saffron!"

"Whatever," He dismissed the nomenclatural confusion casually. "We needed her because within her, her biological parents' weaknesses are both neutralized by the others' strength - she has all of Eisenberg's power, but with none of his limits." Andrew stepped over towards Garrett, ashing his cigar again. "Without the disruption to your daughter's bio-kinetic rhythm, the one that *should* have happened in New York when the Algerian attacked Hall, she just can't access her full power. It was sealed after she treated us, remember?"

Garrett only shrugged again, this time turning to face Christine and force her to gaze into his stoicism-glazed eyes. "Without Saffron, we have no weapon capable of stopping Ju Guem and Jean-Claude - Death and Un-Death - from taking their revenge on the world. I cannot see, from today, whether they succeed before Erica discovers the truth about her daughter, or if the secret dies with the rest of us."

If only she'd look, she could have seen, chiseled into those rough-edged, aging Germanic features, the hundreds of small sins he had committed to keep his dream of saving the world alive. Looking deeper, if only she would, would reveal how perilously close he was – how close all of the world was! - to losing that last cornerstone of the human spirit: Hope.

www.ingramcontent.com/pod-product-compliance
Lightning Source LLC
Chambersburg PA
CBHW070603130626
46556CB00001B/262